Murder at Bramhurst Chapel

The Canterbury Mysteries Book 1

Izzie Harper

ASIN for the ebook: B0FF53P5HN

ISBN for the paperback: 978-1-7392189-9-7

This book is dedicated to the seasonal workers of Kent,
whose stories deserve remembering.
With quiet thanks.

Chapter 1
MONDAY

Ellie Blix poured coffee into a mug, the steam curling into the chill of the chapel's nave. The camping stove hissed faintly behind her, its blue flame flickering beneath the battered kettle. She wore jogging bottoms and a thick jumper. Her feet were tucked into trainers.

She rolled up the duvet, still warm from sleep, and stuffed it into a black bin liner. The double blow-up mattress sagged slightly as she leaned it against the wall, beneath the faded plaque that read "Bramhurst Chapel 1242". Her back twinged as she straightened. She rubbed it absently, muttering, 'Builders at 8am on the dot. Unheard of.' There was definitely no time to use the camping shower that Dave had set up.

Outside, Rebus was snuffling around in the chapel garden, tail stiff with interest. Ellie peered through the arched window and spotted him nosing at the brambles near the old boundary wall. A visiting cat, perhaps. Or rabbits. The garden had once had a large orchard, and the ghosts of apple trees lingered in the air: damp bark, leaf mould, and the faint sweetness of windfall fruit.

Ellie cradled the coffee mug between her palms, letting its warmth seep into her fingers as she stood beneath the old oak, facing the chapel. The tree's branches arched protectively overhead, still clutching a few amber leaves that fluttered in the breeze. The morning air was brisk, scented with a whiff of wood smoke drifting from a distant chimney.

She took a slow breath, letting it settle her.

Before her, the chapel stood quiet and dignified, its stone walls mottled with age and ivy. The arched doorway, slightly askew, gave it a lopsided charm, and the stained-glass windows caught the low sun, shimmering faintly. Moss softened the edges of the steps, and a robin hopped along the sill as if inspecting the place on her behalf.

The chapel wasn't grand. It was half-derelict. But it had a kind of serenity to it. Ellie could already picture the place finished. Renovated and converted into a home. It would take work, of course. A lot of it. But standing there, coffee in hand, she felt something she hadn't in months: the quiet stirrings of possibility.

This was going to be home.

Inside, the chapel was a patchwork of old and new. Stone walls. A vaulted ceiling that echoed every footstep. The scent of dust and damp timber mingled with the aroma of coffee. Her breath fogged faintly as she moved, and the only warmth came from the stove.

This was her new life. Week two of the renovation. Gone were the soft routines and comfort of her old home: the kettle always full, the bed always made, the dog always curled beside her. But here, in this half-ruined chapel with its crooked charm, she felt content. She was excited for the future: a future with Dave. They were back together, and that counted for more than comfort. Much more.

The builders arrived with their usual clatter of vans, shouts and the crunch of boots on gravel. Today, it was plastering and someone to check the floor.

Ellie opened the chapel door and was met with expectant faces and a chorus of 'Morning,' followed swiftly by, 'Any chance of tea?'

She grinned. 'Already on.'

As they set to work, chatting about what they'd done the evening before, and bringing in bags of sand and cement,

Ellie returned to the stove and tipped oats into a saucepan. The porridge bubbled slowly, and she stirred it with a wooden spoon, watching the builders through the open doorway.

She ate straight from the pan, perched on a crate that doubled as a seat. The spoon clinked against the metal, and Rebus padded in, damp and triumphant, with burrs stuck to his cheek and soil round his mouth.

Ellie scratched behind his ears and looked around at the chaos. The mattress, the bin liners, the half-sanded pews.

Half an hour later, Ellie was in the old nave, reflecting on her decisions. She'd imagined many things about converting a thirteenth-century chapel into a home. She'd pictured herself wandering through sun-dappled rooms, making thoughtful decisions about period features and sympathetic renovations. She'd envisioned cosy evenings with Dave, excitedly planning their future in such a wonderful, sacred space.

What she hadn't imagined was standing here at 8.30am, after another night's poor sleep, listening to Gary-the-Plasterer explain why yesterday's render had fallen off the wall in wet chunks during the night.

'It's the damp, see,' Gary said, scratching his considerable belly through a Manchester United shirt that had seen better days. 'This old place, it's like a sponge. Soaks up moisture from the ground, breathes it through the walls. You can't just slap modern materials on centuries-old masonry and expect them to stick.'

Ellie shivered. The October morning had a nip, and without heating, the chapel was chilly.

'Would've been helpful to have mentioned that before you started,' she muttered under her breath, careful to turn away so he wouldn't hear. It had taken ages to find a plasterer who turned up. She didn't want to offend him. 'So, what do we do?'

'Well, you need to sort your damp first. With stone walls, that's a specialist job. You'll need a few dehumidifiers. Let everything dry out properly before we can start again.'

'Any idea how long that'll take?' She groaned inwardly at the thought of having to research any more tradesmen.

Gary shrugged. 'Could be months. Depends on the weather, doesn't it?'

Ellie closed her eyes and counted to ten. When she opened them, Gary was still there, still scratching his belly, still looking at her with the patient expression of a man who'd delivered bad news to desperate homeowners many times before.

'You're best-off living with bare walls. Get some heat and ventilation into the place. Let nature take its course.'

'Right,' she said. 'Well. Thank you for letting me know.'

'No problem, love. We'll sweep up the mess and be off. Be back next week sometime to start stripping off the old plaster.'

'My mate, Simon, does a bit of damp proofing,' Kevin ventured. 'He might be able to help you out?'

Ellie thanked him, not hugely inspired by the mention of 'a bit of damp proofing'. She'd ask around for a specialist company.

While the two men fetched shovels from their pickups, she surveyed the damage. The sun had just risen, and the chapel's gothic windows cast long shadows across the stone floor, highlighting every crack, every stain, every sign of the monumental task ahead. It was a beautiful building but, for the first time, Ellie wondered if they'd made a mistake. Taken on too big a task.

Her phone buzzed.

Dave.

Sorry, Ells. Was called out to a suspicious death in Whitstable.

So that's where he'd gone. His side of the mattress had been empty when she woke up.

How's it going with the plasterer?

Ellie stared at the message, then at the walls where chunks of concrete render lay on the ground.

She hastily typed back: *Brilliantly.* Then deleted it. It wasn't Dave's fault he'd been called out. Or that he always seemed to miss the important meetings.

She was still mulling things over when she heard voices from the far end of the chapel. Male voices, getting louder.

'Good grief,' said the older one. 'Look at this.'

'That's wild,' said the younger. 'What's that doing there?'

Ellie hurried towards the sound, her footsteps echoing in the vaulted space. She found Andy-the-Builder and his young apprentice, Wayne, crouched near the altar end of the chapel, staring at a section of floor where several flagstones had been lifted.

'What's wrong?' she asked, though she suspected she didn't want to know. And definitely wasn't in the mood for more bad news.

Andy looked up, his weathered face grave. 'We've got a problem, Mrs Blix. A big one.'

He gestured to the hole they'd created. Where Ellie had expected to see solid earth or concrete, there was empty space. Dark, empty space that seemed to go down further than her phone's torch could illuminate.

'The floor's not stable so we took up a couple of flagstones to investigate and...' Wayne said, his voice hushed with excitement. 'There's some sort of space down there. A crypt, perhaps.'

'A crypt?' Ellie's voice came out higher than she'd intended, wondering if her morning could get any worse.

They'd seen the paperwork at the auction. No mention of anything like that. Didn't crypts often have tombs and remains in them? She wished they'd got a survey done – but at the time they'd decided it was a risk not worth taking, in case they didn't win the auction.

'Well, it makes sense, doesn't it?' Andy said, standing up and brushing dust from his knees. 'This was a proper chapel once, belonged to the manor house. Rich families, they liked to bury their dead close to home. Probably been down there for centuries.'

Ellie peered into the darkness at the suggestion of secret spaces that had been sealed away from the world above. The beam of Andy's torch revealed glimpses of stone walls. Ellie half-expected to see –

No.

She was letting her thoughts get carried away.

'The thing is,' Andy explained, 'we can't continue our work with this underneath. It seems to have been sealed up, so you'll need to get someone to check why the floor's unstable.'

Ellie's heart sank.

Another delay.

'It could collapse at any moment, see.'

She groaned.

'You might want to check whether there are any bod–'

The older one nudged him and he changed tack.

'... check what's down there.'

'Hmm.'

'This is going to delay things, I'm afraid. Place like this. You've got to get it done proper, like.'

After the news about the walls and the damp, this was the last thing she needed.

'And you won't be able to stay here while it's unsafe. One person too many walking about up here, and you could find yourself taking an unexpected trip to meet whoever's been lying down there all these years.'

Ellie shivered. She sank onto a nearby crate.

The campervan.

They'd bought a second-hand campervan just last month, thinking it would be useful for weekend trips once the chapel was finished. It was currently parked behind the building, looking small and cramped and utterly unsuitable for two adults and a boisterous, mud-loving dog to live in indefinitely.

'Right,' she managed, because someone had to say something. 'The campervan it is, then.'

Andy nodded sympathetically. 'Could be worse, Mrs Blix. If it is a crypt, they were places of love. Anyone down there will have been at peace, near their family. And at least it's not raining.' He forced a small laugh, presumably trying to lessen the blow.

That was when Rebus appeared.

Ellie's golden cockerpoo trotted through the chapel door with the confident air of a dog who'd found something interesting. Something he was rather proud of. Something he wanted to share with the humans who were, inexplicably, standing around talking instead of paying attention to him.

'What's he got there?' Wayne asked.

Ellie looked at her dog more closely. Rebus' tail was wagging with the particular enthusiasm that meant he'd discovered treasure. In his mouth was something brown and weathered, with a matted cord hanging from it. Something that looked like–

'It's a boot,' she said. 'An old work boot.' The cord was a remaining lace.

Rebus dropped his prize at her feet with a satisfied woof and a wag of his tail. The boot was made of worn, faded leather. But it was the size that made Ellie's stomach do a small flip.

'That's a woman's boot,' Andy said, bending down for a closer look. 'Old, too.' He moved his head, assessing it from different angles. 'Similar size to the missus' shoes. Four or five, I'd guess.'

'Where did you find this, Rebus?' Ellie asked her dog, who was now sitting back on his haunches, with even more soil round his mouth and the pleased expression of a job well done.

Rebus glanced towards the door, then back at her, then towards the door again. The message was clear: there was more where that came from.

'Reckon he wants us to follow him,' Wayne said.

They trooped outside, Rebus leading the way. He headed straight for the overgrown flowerbed behind the chapel, where brambles and ivy had claimed much of the garden.

Rebus stopped beside a patch of disturbed earth near an old stone wall. He looked at Ellie expectantly, whining.

'There,' Wayne said, pointing. 'There's something else.'

Ellie saw it too. Something pale, something that didn't belong in a garden. Something that made her mouth go dry.

'Andy,' she said quietly. 'I think we should call the police.'

'Why? It's just an old boot and some–' Andy stopped talking. He'd seen it now too.

It was a bone. Greyish-white. And long – fifteen to twenty inches?

'What on earth?' She slid her phone from her jeans pocket and opened Google. Typed in 'thigh bone'.

'Is that a…?' asked Andy.

Ellie looked from the bone to her phone screen. 'Yes. Femur.' They'd need a…? 'Who's it that deals with old bones? Anthropologist? Archaeologist?'

'Something like that.' He shrugged. 'Definitely got '-ist' on the end.'

She cast about for other pieces. The path. Beneath the elder bush. The buddleia. And, behind an overgrown hydrangea, she saw curved bone. Off-white, mottled with ochre and brown. And a row of small teeth. Even to Ellie's untrained eye, and half-buried in the damp earth, it was clearly a skull.

'Blimey,' Andy whispered, his voice quiet with shock.

Rebus sat down next to his second discovery, panting happily. His work here was done.

Ellie knelt, staring first at the femur, then at the patterned boot with its low heel. And the skull. She realised with a clarity that cut through her shock that this wasn't just about delayed renovations anymore. These bones belonged to someone. A young woman, probably. This was about whoever had been wearing that boot, and why they'd ended up buried in the garden of a private chapel.

She glanced around her. Was this an unmarked grave that Rebus had disturbed? And, if so, were there any others?

She dialled Dave's number. His voicemail clicked in. She left a brief message and dialled 999.

As she was thinking, the first drops of rain began pattering against her skin and on the gothic windows of the building they'd bought.

How had the bones got there? Had the woman been forgotten – or put there deliberately?

Then, before she had time to stop him, Rebus made a dive towards the femur, grabbed it up and charged off with it.

Chapter 2

Ellie wasn't sure: if you discovered human bones in your garden, was it simply a scene of interest that required investigation? Or was it a potential crime scene? There was nothing to suggest a crime had been committed – was there?

If only Dave was here. She wasn't sure of the correct terminology when the bones in question were clearly very old indeed. And how had they got there?

The first responders arrived with efficiency.

'Right then,' said one of the police constables, a young man who looked barely old enough to drive, let alone investigate deaths. 'PC Williams. You're Mrs Blix? You found the remains?'

'My dog did, actually.' Ellie gestured to Rebus, who was watching proceedings from what he clearly considered a safe distance. The arrival of multiple vehicles had switched his focus from treasure hunting to visitors.

'And you touched nothing after the discovery?'

'Well, I had to wrestle the thigh bone off Rebus.'

He frowned and Ellie explained that Rebus, who was now safely on the lead, was the dog. 'He dropped it at first but likes to...' She broke off, sparing the young constable information about the dog's games of chase and "make me drop it". 'But we haven't touched anything else.'

PC Williams typed notes into his phone. The rain had stopped, but the sky remained grey and threatening. 'We'll need to secure the area. That means you won't be allowed in for some time, I'm afraid. Is there somewhere you can... er... go?' He blushed.

Ellie looked around her property, which was rapidly filling with vehicles, and realised there wasn't really anywhere left. The chapel was now off-limits, obviously. The campervan seemed more appealing by the minute.

'I'll put the kettle on,' she muttered to herself.

She wanted to speak to Dave. Get his input on the skeleton and chapel floor situations.

As she stood, watching the scene unfold, Ellie found it rather surreal, seeing the garden of their new home transform into a cross between something from a television crime drama and an archaeological dig. Blue and white tape fluttered in the breeze, marking boundaries she was no longer allowed to cross. A white tent was being erected over the spot where Rebus had made his grisly discoveries.

'Ellie?'

She turned to find a woman in her forties approaching.

DS Carmichael, Dave's sergeant.

'Dave asked me to tell you he'll be on his way from Whitstable as soon as he can; he shouldn't be too long.'

'Oh good.' Ellie felt a wave of relief. He would know what to do, how to handle this. 'Can I ask: what happens now? With the bones, I mean, and the chapel...?' She gestured helplessly at the building.

'We'll need to establish a few things first,' DS Carmichael said. 'The chapel basement won't be anything to do with the police unless there's something in there that shouldn't be. We will, of course, get that checked out.'

Ellie was taking in the information. 'We bought the place through auction and were told there wasn't a crypt. No graveyard either.'

'Hmm. I'll pass that onto the archaeological team. We'll start with the remains in the garden. Age. If possible – identity. Whether there's any evidence of foul play. How long they've been there. Having had a quick inspection of the femur, it seems fairly certain we're looking at a historical death. The skull will help with identification.'

'And the sub-floor? Crypt, or whatever it is?'

'We'll come onto that. It may or may not be related. However, we can't have you living above an unstable floor, obviously, and we also can't ignore what's undoubtedly an important historical site.'

Ellie's heart sank.

'Until we know what's in the crypt, we can't know what we're dealing with.'

'Is there only one set of remains in the flowerbed?'

'Impossible to say at this stage. We have an archaeologist on the way and an anthropologist. The area around the flowerbed will be searched. All the bones will be excavated and then analysed and tested, along with soil, clothes, and the boot your dog found.'

'I see.'

'Along with anything else we might find.'

Ellie didn't like the sound of that. What on earth had happened here? They'd been told there'd never been a graveyard at the chapel. Surely, if there had been, there would've been gravestones? And the remains would've been put in proper plots, not a flowerbed?

DS Carmichael heaved in a breath. 'It's going to be a big job.'

Ellie and Dave had spent the last two weeks sleeping in a corner of the chapel. The prospect of living in the campervan made Ellie feel slightly panicky. She loved Dave dearly, but they'd only just got back together. Throwing them into a space the size of a garden shed with a large dog wasn't going to be the reconciliation they'd both imagined. It would either cement their relationship or destroy it entirely.

'Ells?' It was a woman's voice. 'What's going on?'

She turned to see her mother-in-law picking her way across the church yard, carefully navigating the police tape with the determined expression of a woman who had no intention of being kept away from anything interesting or important.

'Sylvia.' Ellie gave her a hug. She'd never been so pleased to see her.

At sixty-eight, Sylvia Blix had recently married the vicar of St Mary's in Ellie's old village, transforming herself into a vicar's wife with typical Sylvia enthusiasm. She was wearing what Ellie had come to think of as her 'pastoral visiting outfit'. Sensible shoes, neat skirt, and a cardigan.

'I heard there were police cars,' Sylvia said. 'Daphne from the village shop rang me in quite a state. She runs the Neighbourhood Watch. Said there were flashing lights and goodness knows what else at the old chapel. Are you all right, dear?'

'Reeby found bones in the garden,' Ellie said simply. *'Human bones.'*

'Good heavens.' Sylvia's eyes widened. 'Are they recent?'

'Old, we think. With a small woman's boot.' Ellie paused.

'A woman's?' Sylvia frowned. 'How–' She broke off, as though not knowing what to say.

'Exactly,' said Ellie. 'Shocking? Disturbing? I can't decide.'

'Well – both. Where's Dave?'

Ellie explained. 'And the remains aren't all of it. We've also just discovered there's a space of some sort under the chapel. Something we didn't know about from the auction paperwork.' She groaned through gritted teeth.

'A *space*? D'you mean, a crypt?'

Ellie shrugged. 'We don't know what it is.' She hadn't even mentioned the damp yet.

DS Carmichael had been listening to this exchange with interest, and spoke to Sylvia. 'You and the vicar know everyone, Mrs Jackson...'

'Not really. Leonard, perhaps, because of his job. Before he took over at St Mary's, he was the vicar at Harbledown.'

This was a neighbouring village on the Blean side of Canterbury.

'I do, however, know Bramhurst quite well through my first husband, Dave's father. We lived here for a while.'

'Any idea about the history of this place?' asked DS Carmichael. 'The chapel, and the manor house it used to belong to?'

Sylvia considered this. 'I know it was sold when the last of the family died. Must've been around the time we moved.'

'Oh?'

'Yes. The Hollinghursts, they were called. Old Kent family. Wealthy. Been here for centuries.'

DS Carmichael was making notes.

'This was a private family chapel, part of the estate, I believe. There was a farm too. Presumably they were all split up and sold separately.'

'The Hollinghursts?' DS Carmichael repeated. 'Where do I know that name from? Any of them still around?'

'I don't think so. The line died out, which is why the estate was sold.' Sylvia paused. 'Though there might be distant relatives. You'd need to check with someone who knows the local history more recently.'

DS Carmichael made another note.

'Actually,' Sylvia continued, her face brightening, 'there's a local historian here in Bramhurst. Runs the antique shop. Gideon Marsh. Old friend of my late husband's. Gave a fascinating talk to our U3A group just last month about the medieval history of the Canterbury villages. Their connection with the cathedral. He'd know far more than I do about the Hollinghursts and the chapel.'

Ellie felt a familiar stirring of curiosity... and concern for the person whose remains they'd found.

'Where does Mr Marsh live?' DS Carmichael asked.

'Wisteria Cottage. On the high street. Terraced house with the mauve door, next to the old forge.'

DS Carmichael tapped the details into her phone. 'We'll want to speak with him, certainly. Local knowledge is always helpful in cases like this. Especially when they're historical and records might not be available.'

Cases like this? Ellie realised that despite the age of the bones, it seemed as though this was being treated as a potentially suspicious death.

The sound of a car engine made them all look towards the lane. Dave's familiar Audi was pulling up behind the police vehicles, and Ellie felt her shoulders relax for the first time all morning.

'About flippin time,' she murmured, watching her husband climb out of the car and survey the scene with a practised eye.

Even from a distance, she could see the moment he shifted from Dave-the-Husband into DCI Dave Blix. He'd been promoted to chief inspector recently and was relishing his new role.

His posture straightened, his expression became more focused, and when he started walking towards them, it was with the purposeful stride of someone taking charge.

A mixture of pride and something else swept over Ellie. Dave was good at his job. Respected and well-liked. But she had a feeling the investigation would take precedence over the chapel... and their relationship.

'Right then,' he said as he approached, nodding to DS Carmichael and giving Ellie a quick, reassuring squeeze of the shoulder. 'Given there's never been a graveyard on this plot, what I want to know is, why are there human remains in one of our flower beds?'

Chapter 3

A little while later, Ellie and Sylvia were squeezed into the campervan's tiny diner with Rebus, watching through the window as Dave and his sergeant organised what looked like a small army of specialists.

A scene of crime officer in a white suit moved methodically across the garden, taking photographs. A woman and man were pulling on hard hats and high visibility jackets, gesticulating as they talked. A man in a suit waited at the chapel's entrance.

'Well,' Sylvia said, lifting another warm *pain au chocolat* from the paper bag she'd brought with her, 'this certainly isn't how you imagined renovations on your dream home.'

'That's one way of putting it.' Ellie shifted uncomfortably. The campervan's seating had clearly been designed for people smaller than her five-foot-eight frame.

'I keep thinking about the poor person in the flowerbed. And how they might've got there.'

'Tell me about the boot that Rebus found?' said Sylvia.

'It was covered in mud but I'm pretty sure it was a woman's. Hang on.' Ellie swiped her phone into life and opened Google. 'I'm tearing through the data allowance on my mobile, not having any broadband here yet.' She held the screen out for Sylvia to look. 'Bit like these.'

It was a composite image of women's work boots over the decades. She stopped at one with her finger: a pair of tan, mid-calf-length, leather boots with slim ankles, laces and hooks. Small heel. One-and-a-half-inches. Light broguing on the toe.

'If the boot belonged to the remains, I agree it must be a young woman,' said Sylvia. 'How awful. I wonder how long she's been lying there.' She hesitated. 'Unknown. Forgotten.' She replaced the *pain au chocolat* on the bag.

'Hmm.'

'I'd say that boot is post-war. Rubber sole, heel shaped slightly, rounder toe. 1950s? Something like that.'

Ellie watched as another white tent was erected near the hydrangea bush. 'Someone's daughter; maybe someone's sister. She deserves better than being called "the remains".'

Sylvia nodded thoughtfully. 'You know, we might be able to help with that.'

'How do you mean?'

'Well, the police will be thorough, of course, but they'll focus on the procedural side. Evidence, forensics, bone and teeth analysis, official channels.' Sylvia's eyes had taken on the recognisable gleam that Ellie remembered. 'But we could find out who she was. Give her back her name. Get a proper grave for her, perhaps.'

Ellie felt a familiar stirring of excitement. 'We're meant to have given up sleuthing. It was Dave's key request when he and I got back together, and when he was made chief inspector...'

'Things change...'

'He won't be happy if we start interfering.'

'He doesn't have to know everything we do in our spare time,' Sylvia said primly. 'And we won't be interfering with his investigation. We'll simply be... researching local history and getting to know your new neighbours.'

It was not the sort of introduction Ellie had been hoping for.

'And I adore Leonard,' Sylvia said with a roll of her eyes, 'but I need something else to do that doesn't involve church committees, coffee mornings, rotas and fundraising...'

Ellie laughed. Both she and Sylvia were adjusting to new phases in their lives.

'And how exactly would we research local history?'

'We could start by talking to Gideon Marsh. The police will consult him, but there's no reason we can't have a friendly chat first.' Sylvia stood up with the decisive air of someone who'd made up her mind. 'Come on. Let's go and find out what he knows.'

Ellie was just about to grab Rebus' lead when her phone rang. Zoe's name appeared on the screen.

'Mum, are you in the campervan?' Zoe's voice was urgent. 'With Gran?'

'Yes, why? What's wrong?' Ellie put her phone on loudspeaker so Sylvia could hear.

'Don't look out the window, but there's some true crime bloke live on TikTok right now. He's filming the chapel and talking about the remains.'

'What on earth is TikTok?' screeched Sylvia.

'It's a social media platform. Bit like Instagram but more focussed on video. I can literally see the campervan on his feed, and I'm pretty sure that's you moving around inside. Are you in a dark jumper?'

Ellie froze, Rebus' lead dangling in her hand. 'Yes. What? He's filming me and broadcasting it?' She wasn't up on all these social media platforms.

'Yes. The "lives" are like the ones on Instagram. He's doing a feature on "the Bramhurst Chapel murders"

– making it sound like something out of a Netflix documentary. He's got about three hundred people watching.'

'Three hundred?'

Ellie had watched a dog trainer live once on Instagram and he'd had about three people watching. Clearly true crime was a bigger draw.

'It's how TikTok works. The lives go crazy. Notifications flash up on your page and you get people joining from all round the world.'

'Where's he filming from?' said Sylvia. 'I can't see anyone.'

'He said something about being in a field on a public footpath. Could he be behind a hedge or something?'

Ellie scanned the scene. 'Can't see anyone. How can he be allowed to film our garden? It's private property. It can't be legal, surely?' She set down her mug with a clatter, yanking the curtains closed. 'He can't just film without permission, can he? And how did he hear about the remains?'

'I'm not sure. He said he's local. You know what village gossip's like. As soon as a helicopter flies overhead, or a firework goes off, someone posts on the village Facebook page.'

'I suppose.'

'He keeps saying stuff about "reporting on a local story" and "public interest" and how the scene is visible from the footpath.'

'Where the heck is he then?' Sylvia barked.

'I've looked on Google maps. Going on the angle, I'd say he's in the field behind the hedge.'

'I'd imagine it's a case of: if you're on public property, not obstructing justice and not trespassing, it's legal,' said Sylvia in a begrudging voice.

'He's zooming in on the archaeological dig now,' said Zoe, 'talking about "where the bodies were found".'

Ellie felt her stomach drop. '*Bodies*, plural? Who said there are more than one?' She glanced at Sylvia. 'This is a disaster. Dave's going to be furious. It's an investigation scene.'

'Now he's asking for information from anyone who knows the chapel, the manor house and the village...'

Sylvia shook her head furiously.

'I only found him by chance,' Zoe explained. 'I'm on Hambrook Marshes. I was uploading a video of the beavers to the centre's TikTok account.'

Zoe worked for a wildlife rescue charity.

'You know how they like us to do social media for PR... Once I'd posted it, the algorithm showed me this "local creator" who was going live. Nearly dropped my phone when I saw it was the chapel… and you in the campervan.'

'How long has he been filming?'

'About ten minutes, I think. Said he grew up here. He's giving a whole commentary about the history of the place. Family called Hollinghurst? The patriarch a judge or something.'

'Well, that's accurate at least,' said Sylvia.

'He's definitely embellishing. Making it sound like something out of *Tess of the D'Urbervilles*.'

Ellie groaned. 'Who is this TikTok person?'

'His handle is "Criminally Curious".'

'Don't like the sound of that. Aren't these TikTok people all chasing clicks?' Ellie said it as though she knew what she was taking about.

'I haven't a clue,' said Sylvia, 'but it's much more exciting than church committees and flower-arranging rotas.' She had that familiar glint in her eye again. 'I'll google.' She swiped her screen and opened her internet browser, tapped at a few keys. 'His name is Rory Henderson. He's got a P.O. Box address. Typical.'

'Often true crime reporters make it easy for people to get information to them but a nightmare to track them down in real life,' Zoe explained.

Ellie rolled her eyes. 'Has he got contact details on TikTok, Zoe, lovey?'

'Hang on, I'll check his profile... got it. There's an email and... oh, he's just said on the live that he's planning to come back tomorrow for more footage, and later too if there are developments.'

'Oh, crikey.'

'He's treating your new home like it's some sort of tourist attraction,' said Zoe.

'Right, that's it. Screenshot his profile and a bit of his live, can you? We might need evidence if we have to take this further.'

'Already on it. Oh blimey, he's now speculating about whether the current owners – that's you – might be in danger from "the Bramhurst Killer". He's really milking this.'

Ellie rubbed her temples, feeling a headache coming on. 'How many people did you say were watching?'

'It's over six hundred now. People are sharing the live. The comments are going mad. People are asking for more details, saying they want to visit. Some woman in South Carolina is sharing her own theory about the murders and–'

'Good grief. It'll be all conspiracy theories and cults. This is exactly what we didn't want. And the last thing we need is social media creators tramping all over the village, interfering with the investigation.'

'Should we report him?' asked Zoe. 'For invasion of privacy or something?'

Ellie sighed. 'I don't know if we can, if he's on public land. But filming into the campervan surely crosses a line? It could compromise the integrity of your dad's investigation if details get out on social media before they're ready to release them.'

'Want me to contact him through TikTok? Tell him to stop?'

'No,' said Ellie. 'Let me handle it properly. Just get me those contact details and keep recording. How long do these live videos stay up?'

'He can save it and post it as a regular video afterwards if he wants, or end the live and it disappears. He's wrapping up now. "I'll be back later for more exclusive content on this breaking story from Bramhurst Chapel, where the bodies are literally buried." Goodness, he's really leaning into the dramatics.'

'Text me everything you've got. And Zoe? Don't engage with his content – no comments, no likes, nothing. We don't want to encourage him.'

'Got it. Mum, are you okay? This must be really unsettling.'

'I'm fine, lovey. Just frustrated. We came here for a fresh start, not to become some sort of true crime circus act.'

'I know. Look, his live has ended now. I'll send the screenshots over.'

'Thanks. I'd better inform your dad of this. Warn him before someone does some damage.'

Ellie rang off and flung open the campervan door, trainers hitting gravel before the hinges had finished creaking. 'Come on,' she called over her shoulder, already halfway towards Thimble Lane.

Sylvia followed, cardigan flapping, and Rebus bounded ahead, nose to the ground, tail high with purpose.

The footpath from the lane, down to the field, was barely visible, swallowed by late summer weeds and the dry rustle of nettles. Ellie pushed through, breath quick, jumper snagging on brambles. The chapel loomed behind them, its slate roof catching the morning light, but she didn't look back.

They reached the stile at the edge of the field. Rebus wriggled under. Ellie climbed over, followed by Sylvia, and then they were in the stubble. Golden stalks crackled underfoot, the remnants of harvest sharp against Ellie's shins. The field stretched wide and empty, bordered by hedgerow and the low hum of distant traffic. A crow lifted from the fencepost with a harsh cry.

She scanned the hedge that ran along the chapel grounds, eyes narrowing. This was where he'd been. Rory Henderson, the TikTok sleuth with the click-bait-y comments.

But now, nothing. No tripod. No phone. Just dry leaves and a path along the field's edge.

Ellie stepped closer to the hedge, peering through the gaps. The chapel garden lay beyond, a hive of activity. She felt Sylvia come up beside her, breath steady, eyes sharp.

'He's gone,' Ellie said, more to herself than anyone.

Rebus nosed at a patch of flattened grass, then sneezed.

Ellie crouched, fingers brushing dead stalks. Someone had stood here recently. The earth was scuffed, the hedge bent slightly inward.

She straightened, brushing dust from her knees. 'I hope he's not going to be a problem,' she said.

Sylvia gave a small hum of agreement. 'He's got reach. And no editor to rein him in.'

Ellie looked out across the field. She didn't like being watched. And she liked even less the idea of someone turning grief and suspicion into "content".

'Come on,' she said. 'Let's get back. Speak to Dave.'

They turned, shoes crunching through the stubble, Rebus trotting ahead with ears pricked. Rory would be back. And next time, she'd be ready for him.

When they found Dave, he was talking to a uniformed officer.

He greeted Ellie and Sylvia.

'We've got a problem,' said Ellie, face tense. 'A TikTokker has just been filming this entire scene and broadcasting it live to the world.'

'What?' Dave's voice went sharp.

'He's just finished.' Ellie filled him in.

A deep frown stretched over Dave's forehead.

'Called it "exclusive content from Bramhurst Chapel, where the bodies are buried".'

Ellie told him they'd been to see if Rory was still in the field, and peered round cautiously as though he might still be lurking. 'He's planning to come back later. Zoe's got all his details – screenshots, recordings, everything.'

'Right. I'll need to speak to the press office about this. We can't have crime scene details being broadcast on social media before we've released them officially.'

'That's what I thought. Look, Sylvia and I are going to walk into the village to get proper WiFi and do some research on this person. See who we're dealing with.'

'Be careful, Ells,' he said, in a worried voice. 'You never know who these people are. And let me know what you find out.'

Chapter 4

Twenty minutes later, Ellie and Sylvia were walking through Bramhurst village with Rebus, and Ellie found herself charmed by how pretty the place was. A collection of timber-framed houses and flint cottages clustered around a triangular green. Ancient oak trees provided shade for wooden benches. An elderly couple walked hand-in-hand. A young mum sat on one of the benches, buggy to one side.

'There's the ford,' Sylvia said, pointing to where the main road dipped down to cross a shallow stream. A sign warned drivers to check the depth before proceeding, though the water looked barely ankle-deep. 'When Ron and I first visited, before we moved here, we took off our shoes and paddled.' She smiled wistfully. 'Felt like kids.'

A red setter was bounding in and out of the water, snatching at it with its mouth and spinning round. A woman appeared transfixed, joyfully laughing at her dog's antics.

Rebus whined, and pulled on his lead, eager to join the other dog in the water.

'Sorry, boy,' Ellie spoke soothingly. 'I don't want you getting wet. We're going to be in and out of shops and houses.'

Ellie and Sylvia chatted as they walked. In a few minutes they reached the high street. Paws & Tails was the pet shop. Hand-painted sign, a sable greyhound curled up on a bed in the window, seemingly oblivious of all the stuffed toys and treats on display around him. Next to this was Needle & Groove, which had boxes of second-hand vinyl outside. A Pink Floyd track wafted out of the open door. Dave was going to love this place. In the window of the next shop, a woman sat at a potter's wheel, hands deep in clay, fair hair in a messy bun, attention focused on what she was making while another woman with purple hair talked to her. Ellie glanced up. Thrown Together. What a brilliant shop name. There was a sign in the window saying: BUY, EXHIBIT, LEARN.

'Ooh, wonder if that means they do classes?' said Ellie. 'I could never get into the ones in Deal. They were always booked up.'

Then there was Bramhurst Bikes.

'Morning,' Sylvia chirruped to the bald man outside, as though they were having a jolly, not going to find out about deaths in the village.

He was leaning over a powder-blue electric bike. A younger man with a ponytail and an Australian accent was helping him. He put his hand out to Rebus and gave him a fuss.

They passed the pub, the Hop Picker's Rest, a thatched building with tiny leaded windows and lamps twinkling within. It looked cosy and inviting. The blackboard outside mentioned home-cooked meals, Sunday roasts and local ales. Through a window, Ellie could see the warm glow of an open fire.

'That's where all the village gossip happens,' Sylvia said knowingly. 'Leonard says the landlord, Terry, has lived here all his life and knows everything about everyone within a twenty-mile radius.'

'Worth noting,' Ellie murmured, remembering how much local knowledge had helped them on previous sleuthing cases. 'I suggest we pop in later then.'

Next, Ellie spotted Bramhurst Books. When Dave had first mentioned the chapel to Ellie, as a potential home, she'd done a recce, and the bookshop was one of the things she'd come back raving about. And it wasn't just a bookshop. They ran events and it had a café with wholefood salads, fresh soups and delicious cakes.

And it was dog friendly.

Ten minutes later, the two women were inside and settled on cosy sofas, away from the till and out of the earshot of a man who was reading the newspaper. Sylvia had a large cappuccino and a slice of Kentish apple cake, and Ellie had a pot of Earl Grey tea and a Belgian chocolate flapjack. Rebus was on the floor, eying up a bit of biscuit which a toddler had dropped at another table.

Rebecca, the owner, was in her forties. She had black hair which she wore loose. A cream jumper and jeans lay under a floral apron.

The bookshop's quiet atmosphere was exactly what Ellie needed to calm her nerves after the morning's developments, and to focus on the things she needed to sort out.

First, it was safety.

She entered the shop's WiFi password into her phone and typed 'Rory Henderson Criminally Curious' into Google and was surprised by what came up.

Henderson had an undergraduate degree in social history from the University of Kent and a postgraduate degree in forensic linguistics from Cardiff University. His LinkedIn profile showed he'd worked as a researcher for several TV production companies before going freelance. He wasn't some amateur true crime enthusiast with a phone and too much time on his hands.

Ellie rang Zoe. 'You're not going to believe this.' She spoke softly so as not to be overheard. 'Our TikTokker has serious academic credentials.'

'Really?'

She relayed the details and elaborated. 'Yup. He's published papers on the use of dialect analysis in historical documents to solve crimes.'

'*Forensic linguistics?*' Zoe sounded intrigued. 'Isn't that about analysing language patterns in legal contexts?'

'Exactly. Which makes me wonder...' Ellie paused. 'He might actually be a useful person to have on side.'

'Or he might use his expertise to exploit the situation for content,' Zoe pointed out. 'Having degrees doesn't make him ethical.'

'True.' Ellie scrolled through more search results. 'He's got a website, a podcast, YouTube channel, Instagram, TikTok, obviously. He's building quite the true crime empire.'

'Is any of it actually good, or is it all sensationalist rubbish?'

Ellie had skimmed an article of his on a historical murder in Rochester. 'It's well researched. He cites sources, interviews experts, presents multiple theories. It's not just speculation and drama.'

'So, he might be genuinely interested in solving cold cases rather than just exploiting them?'

'Possibly. Though filming our home without permission doesn't exactly scream ethical journalism. Hard to know if we can trust him. He's already shown he's willing to film private property for content.'

Ellie stared at Henderson's professional headshot on his website. He looked younger than she'd expected, probably late twenties, with an earnest expression and thick-rimmed glasses that gave him a scholarly appearance.

'I need to talk to him. Find out what his intentions are; maybe set some boundaries. Like not filming through the hedge and *definitely* not filming the campervan.'

'Or tell him to back off completely,' Sylvia muttered.

'Maybe. Though if he's determined to cover this story, it might be better to have some influence over how he does it, rather than making an enemy of him.'

'Just be careful, Mum,' said Zoe. 'People with platforms can be dangerous when they feel threatened. And if he's got hundreds of thousands of followers across all his channels...'

'I know. The last thing we need is him turning his audience against us.' Ellie saved Henderson's contact details to her phone. 'But we can't just let him treat our home like his personal content factory either.'

She ended the call and sat back in the comfortable bookshop sofa, weighing her options. Outside, Bramhurst carried on with its quiet village life, unaware that its small community was about to become the focus of intense online scrutiny.

And one thing was certain: Rory Henderson had just made himself a player in their investigation, whether they liked it or not.

Chapter 5

Wisteria Cottage was easy to spot. Tiny, terraced and with the promised mauve door, squeezed between the old forge and an antique shop. The wisteria that gave the cottage its name was only bare branches at this time of year.

Sylvia knocked confidently.

Rebus whined, just as he always did when they visited a house. There was bound to be something interesting inside, right?

The man who answered was in his sixties, with wild, black hair and ink-stained fingers that suggested that, as well as being a historian, he did a lot of writing, the old-fashioned way – by hand. Gideon wore corduroy trousers and a homemade jumper that had seen better days. His face lit up when he saw visitors.

'Sylvia. What a lovely surprise. Though I rather suspect this isn't a social call, given the excitement up at the old chapel.'

'Nothing gets past you, does it?' Sylvia smiled. 'This is Ellie. My daughter-in-law. She and my son bought the chapel.'

'Ah, the lucky people who discovered they've acquired more than they bargained for.' Gideon's eyes twinkled with curiosity. 'I had a call from Daphne.'

'She's been busy,' said Sylvia. 'She rang me too.'

'Her son is one of those true crime podcasters.'

'You mean Rory? Criminally Curious?'

'That's him.'

'Ah, of course. Henderson. I'd forgotten that's Daphne's surname.'

'Between the two of them,' Gideon explained, 'they know everything that goes on in this village.' He stood back, holding the door open. 'Do come in. I was just about to prepare a lecture for the Women's Institute. I've got my young lad at the shop this morning.'

'OK to bring the dog in?' asked Sylvia.

'No problem.'

The cottage's interior was exactly what Ellie had expected: low-beamed ceilings, book-lined walls, and papers scattered across every available surface. A fire crackled in the small grate, and the whole place smelled of old books, cat food and wood smoke. It was homely and intimate.

'I imagine you're here about the... er... developments at your chapel,' Gideon said, settling them into worn but comfortable armchairs in the lounge.

Rebus made a beeline for the rug by the hearth.

'Daphne told me about the discovery. Human remains, is it true?'

Ellie didn't mention Rory broadcasting from behind the hedge. 'Yes, from the post-war years, we think. The 1950s?' She told him about the work boot. 'The police are investigating with some archaeological input, but we were hoping you might be able to tell us about the family who used to own the chapel.'

'You'll know more than me,' Sylvia added.

'Yes, the Hollinghursts.' Gideon's expression grew thoughtful. 'Now there's a family with history. The patriarch was Sir Roger Hollinghurst – quite famous in his day. High Court judge, known for his harsh sentences and moral rigidity. Very much a person who got stuck in the attitudes of Victorian society.'

'What about his family?' Sylvia asked.

'He had a young wife, Maria. A strange match, by all accounts. She was something of a progressive. Dare I say, a feminist.'

'Oh?' said Sylvia, glancing at Ellie. 'That's unusual. Good for her.'

Gideon nodded. 'And a son, Edmund. Only child, which was unfortunate for the family line.' Gideon paused to lift a book off a dusty shelf. 'Edmund was... well... everything his father wasn't. Gentle where Roger was harsh, romantic where Roger was practical. Something of a disappointment to the old man, I suspect.'

'Did Edmund marry? Have children?' Ellie asked, though something in Gideon's tone suggested the answer might be complicated.

'That's where the story gets interesting.' Gideon's eyes gleamed momentarily and then turned sad. 'There was quite the scandal back in... oh, it must have been 1950 or thereabouts. Edmund fell in love with a young woman who'd come to the village for the harvest.'

Ellie felt her pulse quicken. 'A seasonal worker?'

'Yes. The farm was attached to the manor house, along with the chapel. It was common in this part of the country for workers to travel from London, particularly the East End, to help with the hop-picking and fruit harvests in Kent.'

'I've heard about this,' said Ellie. 'Sure I saw a book on the subject in Bramhurst Books too.'

'Indeed. There are several on the subject, including one by me.' He gestured proudly to a shelf. 'Sometimes it was whole families who came to work, sometimes just the children. Hard labour, but it paid better than the factories, and it got them out of the city for a few weeks.'

'And this young woman...?'

'Her name was Violet Chapman. She came with her brother, Tommy. They were lodging at Bramhurst Farm, which was part of the manor house estate.' Gideon leaned forward conspiratorially. 'According to the stories that have come down through the village, she caught Edmund's eye at church one Sunday. Love at first sight, or so they said.'

'I'm sure it was a frequent occurrence,' said Sylvia. 'What happened?'

'Well, that's where the scandal comes in. Edmund's father was horrified, of course. The idea of his son, heir to the Hollinghurst name and fortune, marrying a working-class girl from London? Unthinkable.' Gideon shook his head.

'Of course.'

'There were terrible rows. All the staff could hear them shouting up at the manor.'

'Did they elope?' Ellie asked, though a cold feeling was settling in her stomach.

'So the story goes. Although some of the details are unclear. One morning, both Edmund and Violet had vanished. Left notes saying they'd gone to Scotland to be married, where the laws were more forgiving.' Gideon paused. 'Of course, Edmund's father was furious. Cut Edmund off completely, refused to have his name mentioned in the house.'

'And did they marry? In Scotland?'

Gideon's expression grew sad. 'That's the tragic part of the story. Nothing was heard of them until the judge received notice a few years later that Edmund had died alone of consumption. It was very common then.'

Ellie and Sylvia shared a look.

'What about Violet?'

He shrugged sadly. 'No-one knew. There was no mention of her. Lots of whispers about her running off with someone else.'

'Always blaming the woman...' said Ellie, rolling her eyes.

'Yes,' Gideon continued. 'And claiming she left poor Edmund heartbroken, no doubt. Others thought the family – possibly old Hollinghurst himself – had done something to separate them.' Gideon lowered his voice.

'And there were those who wondered if Violet Chapman had ever left Bramhurst at all.'

The silence that followed was broken only by the crackling of the fire.

Ellie thought about the small boot, the delicate bones, the skull half-hidden behind the hydrangea. If they belonged to Violet, had they been there long then? 'What happened to Edmund's body?' she asked, thinking about the sub-floor area at the chapel.

'Hollinghurst refused to acknowledge his son in death, just as he'd refused in life. There was no family funeral.'

'That's very sad,' said Ellie. 'Where was Edmund buried then?'

'It's not mentioned anywhere.' Gideon continued. 'Not that I've been able to find, anyway. When Hollinghurst died, the estate passed to distant cousins who sold it immediately to distant relatives.' Gideon looked between them. 'You don't think... the remains you found could be Edmund?'

'We don't know yet,' Ellie said carefully. 'We assumed the remains are female because of the boot. But DS Carmichael said an archaeologist will search for all remains. See what's there. Perhaps he is too.'

'I see.' Gideon was sombre.

Ellie was absorbing Gideon's information.

'Sounds like this young woman could well have been Violet Chapman,' said Sylvia.

'I would say so,' replied Gideon. 'The chapel was their personal, family place. Whoever is buried in your garden must've had some sort of relationship with the Hollinghurst family.'

Chapter 6

It took a bit of cajoling to persuade Rebus to leave the warm fire at Wisteria Cottage, but a treat worked.

'Well, that was illuminating,' Sylvia said as they walked along the street.

'And confusing,' Ellie added, her mind racing. 'So, Edmund died alone of consumption, but where? And what happened to Violet? Did she die with him, or separately, or–' She stopped walking. 'We're getting ahead of ourselves, aren't we?'

'How do you mean?'

'We're assuming the remains *are* Violet Chapman's because it seems likely. But we don't actually know that yet.' Ellie gave Rebus a stroke. 'The timing fits, and the location makes sense, but until we have definitive proof that they're Violet's, we need to be more systematic about this. Treat Violet as one possibility among others.'

Sylvia nodded thoughtfully. 'You're right. Working conditions were harsh then. It may be that other seasonal workers went missing around that time and one of them is in the chapel garden.'

'We need to do some proper research. Find out if any other farm workers died in the 1950s, and establish what actually happened to Edmund and Violet: where they died, where they're buried, if they're buried.'

'That sounds like a job for someone with excellent research and technology skills,' Sylvia said with a meaningful look.

'Are you thinking...?'

'... Zoe,' said Sylvia. 'She already knows a bit about what's happened. And she's been moping around at Dave's flat for weeks. A proper mystery might be exactly what she needs. Take her mind off the breakup with Finn, and him leaving for Norway.'

Ellie pulled out her phone. 'I'll call her now. Ask her to meet us back at the chapel as soon as she can.' She paused. 'Should we tell her about our ... unofficial investigation?'

Sylvia's eyes twinkled. 'Yes. And ask her to start researching workers who died in the Canterbury area from 1948 onwards.' She paused. 'Actually, not just those who are on record as having died. They're more likely to have had proper burials. We need to find out about anyone who vanished.'

The call was brief. Zoe's voice perked up at the mention of a mystery that needed solving. She had an injured goose in the van. She agreed to drive over once she'd dropped it off at the vet.

'Hmm,' said Ellie. 'We have an hour to kill and several burning questions. Fancy a drink?' She glanced towards the Hop Picker's Rest. 'Or a hot drink?'

'It would be rude not to introduce ourselves to the locals,' Sylvia agreed solemnly.

Inside, the pub had low beams blackened with age, horse brasses gleaming in the firelight, and worn wooden tables. A few locals sat at the bar, nursing pints and watching the newcomers with polite curiosity.

'Afternoon, ladies.' The landlord was a stocky man with a pleasant face and welcoming manner. 'You'll be the ones from up at the old chapel, I expect. Terry Hobbs.' He extended a hand.

A younger man was serving at the other end of the bar. Ellie caught his accent. It was the ponytailed chap they'd seen at the bike shop.

'And that's Ryan,' Terry added. 'My barman.'

Ellie smiled and shook Terry's hand. 'Afternoon, gentlemen. Two sparkling mineral waters, please.'

Rebus settled at Ellie's feet.

'Heard you've had some excitement up there at the chapel.'

'News travels fast,' Ellie said, accepting her glass of water.

'Village like this,' said Terry, 'it travels faster than the postman. You never know who's watching or listening.'

Ellie wondered if Bramhurst was any different. It was like that in all villages, wasn't it? Gossip was the downside of people caring about each other...

Terry polished a glass with practised efficiency. 'Terrible business though, finding human remains. You must've had a shock. Though I can't say I'm entirely surprised.'

Sylvia took a sip of her drink and raised an eyebrow. 'Oh?'

'Well, old buildings like that, they've all had their tragedies over the years. The Hollinghurst family had more than their fair share of trouble, that's for sure. You know what these aristocratic families are like...' Terry leaned against the bar confidentially. 'My grandmother used to work up at Bramhurst Manor, back in the day, as a cook. Mabel, her name was. Saw a lot of the farm workers, she did. Had some stories, I can tell you.'

'Oh, wow. What sort of stories?' Ellie asked, trying to keep her voice casual.

'Family arguments, financial scandals, servants disappearing without notice, mysterious illnesses. All manner of strange goings-on.' Terry's voice dropped. 'Gran always said there was something not right about the way old Hollinghurst behaved towards one of the seasonal workers.'

Ellie forced herself to sip her drink calmly. 'How so?'

'Young girl called Violet Chapman. Came for the harvest work. Summer of 1950. Pretty little thing, according to Gran. Got herself mixed up with young Hollinghurst.' Terry shook his head.

They knew about Violet and Edmund from Gideon, but Ellie let him talk in case he had any new or different information.

'Course, that was never going to end well, was it? Different worlds, those two. And the judge, he wasn't happy about it.'

'What did your grandmother think happened to her?'

'Well, the official story was that she ran off with Edmund to get married. You've probably heard this. But Gran reckoned...' he lowered his voice 'she never left the village at all.'

This was the same phrase Gideon had used.

Terry's expression grew serious. 'The judge was determined to get rid of young Violet, so he was.'

The words hung in the air like smoke from the fire.

'Really?' Sylvia asked, her voice low.

'The man was used to getting his own way by all accounts. He wasn't going to have a girl like Violet marrying his son and heir.'

Ellie and Sylvia caught each other's eye.

Terry started unstacking the glass washer. 'Easy enough to make her disappear. Girls from working class families in the East End, they weren't exactly high priority for the authorities. And after the war, so much was changing, rural police officers were stretched.'

He stopped what he was doing for a moment. 'Gran always said the Hollinghursts knew more about what happened to Edmund and Violet than they let on. The judge especially. Powerful man. Money. Charming one minute, nasty temper the next.'

'Did your gran ever say what she thought really happened to Violet?'

'No. Just that whatever it was, the judge hushed it up.' Terry's voice dropped to barely above a whisper.

Ellie cringed.

'Your grandmother,' Sylvia said carefully, 'is she still...?'

Terry had talked about her in the past tense.

'Died a year ago, bless her. But she left journals. Boxes of them. We've had them up in the attic since she passed.

Never looked through them properly, if I'm honest. But they might have more details about those times.'

'Would you mind if we...?' Ellie began.

'Course not. Happy to dig them out for you. Might take me a day or so to find the right ones, mind. Got decades worth up there. She loved her journals, my gran.' He pulled himself up straight. 'In fact, someone else wanted to come and look at them but never arranged a time.'

Ellie frowned. 'Oh? Who?'

'Can't remember now. My missus, Deb, spoke to him. I'll ask her who it was.'

Ellie noted that it had been a male.

They finished their drinks and walked back along Thimble Lane towards the chapel in thoughtful silence.

'There's Zoe,' Sylvia said, as they approached the chapel.

Ellie's daughter was leaning against her battered work van, her dark hair tied back in a practical ponytail. At twenty-five, Zoe had inherited Ellie's curiosity and determination, along with her father's gift for research and deduction. She brightened when she saw them.

'Mum. Gran.' She gave them both quick hugs and bent down to give Rebus a stroke.

Ellie was about to ask how her daughter was.

'This case is fascinating,' said Zoe, standing back up. 'I've been doing some preliminary research.'

'Already?' Ellie asked, relieved to see a smile on Zoe's face. Usually when they saw her, the first thing she mentioned was Finn and how much she missed him.

'I couldn't resist. I had to wait at the vets with the goose. Mystery involving missing persons from 1950. Right up my street.' Zoe pulled out her phone. 'Packed with class issues, power and patriarchy.' Her eyes shone with excitement. 'The seasonal work went on for months. Different fruit, different farms. Apples, pears, cherries, late plums. Hop picking often runs into October.'

She scrolled through her notes.

'And that's just what I've found in an hour. Give me a proper research session, and I bet I'll find more.' She looked between them. 'So, are we officially investigating this? Because if we are, I've got some ideas about where to start.'

Before Ellie could answer, she saw Dave leave the campervan with a uniformed officer. The officer was carrying a laminated sign which he hung over the open door: S.I.O.

Ellie knew what those initials stood for: Senior Investigating Officer.

Great. So, Dave had commandeered their campervan. And as she didn't have family living round the corner anymore, where was she meant to go?

Chapter 7

Dave was walking towards them, his expression carefully neutral. Ellie knew it meant he was about to deliver news she wasn't going to like.

Around them, the chapel grounds had been transformed. Archaeological grids marked out precise squares in the garden, each one numbered and flagged. White tents dotted the landscape like a small camping festival, and the steady scrape of trowels, and tap of hammers, suggested painstaking excavation work.

'Ellie, could I have a word.' It was an instruction, not a question, and Ellie felt her hackles rise. The tone was the one he used for speaking to his staff.

She joined him, leaving Rebus with Sylvia and Zoe by the car.

'Just seen the sign.' She gestured to the campervan.

He shrugged. 'You don't mind, do you?'

'It would've been nice to have been asked,' she said, swallowing her irritation. 'Couldn't you get a temporary building like you usually do?'

'Won't be for long.'

Ellie let it go. There were more important things at stake. 'How's it going?'

'Slowly.' Dave looked tired. 'Listen, I need to ask you something, and I want you to be honest with me.'

'Always.'

'Have you and Mum been asking questions in the village? About the Hollinghursts, about what happened here?'

Heat began to rise in Ellie's cheeks. 'We had a cup of tea with the local historian. Sylvia knows him. And a drink at the pub.'

Dave frowned at her, pursing his lips while he formulated his words.

'We're living here now.' She took a deep breath. 'We're allowed to talk to our neighbours.'

'I know. And normally I wouldn't mind. But this is a potential murder investigation, Ellie. A very old, very complex one.' He rubbed his forehead. 'I can't have you conducting your own inquiry parallel to our official one.'

'I'm not conducting an inquiry. I'm just–'

'Ellie.' He held his hand out in a "stop" gesture, his voice gentle but firm. 'I know you. I know how your mind works. And I know what it looks like when you're on the scent of a mystery.' He glanced towards Sylvia and Zoe, then back at her. 'Promise me you'll leave this to the professionals.'

She looked into her husband's eyes and saw the conflict there. And although it wasn't the same, it mirrored her own. He knew her skills and respected her abilities, but he also had a job to do. She wanted to help but also knew Dave didn't want her to.

'I promise,' she said, crossing her fingers behind her back like a schoolchild, 'I won't interfere with your investigation.'

After all, they weren't planning to interfere with the police work. They were just planning to do their own. It wasn't quite a lie, but Ellie nevertheless winced a little as she uttered it.

Dave nodded, satisfied, and went back to his team.

Ellie rejoined Sylvia and Zoe, who were watching the archaeological work with fascination.

'Well?' Zoe asked.

'We're officially "not investigating",' Ellie said, making quote marks with her fingers. 'Which means we'll have to be very careful about how we proceed.'

'But we *are* proceeding?' Sylvia asked.

Ellie looked at the campervan, now Dave's site office. Then at her home-to-be, which resembled an archaeological dig more than a future residence.

Somewhere under all that careful excavation lay the remains of a person who had died seventy-five years ago. Whether it was Violet Chapman or Edmund Hollinghurst, or someone else entirely, the person deserved to have their story told; to have a marked grave.

'Oh yes,' Ellie said. 'We're *definitely* proceeding. But Dave has worked hard for his promotion. We've got to make sure we don't tread on his toes – or cause problems for him.'

Chapter 8

'Right,' Ellie told Sylvia. 'We need a plan of action.'

They left the chapel plot and joined Thimble Lane, leaving Zoe to start her research in earnest.

'Agreed.' Sylvia pulled out her phone. 'And thinking about what Terry said about his gran's journals, I think we need to follow up with Gideon. If someone else has been asking questions about the Hollinghursts, and Bramhurst Manor, he might know who.'

They were heading back towards the high street. With no campervan to leave Rebus in, they'd brought him along.

'And given that the manor house, farm and chapel were split up when they were sold,' said Ellie, 'I think we should pay the first two a visit. Find out who lives there now and what the setup is.'

'Yes, I'm curious about that too.'

'I've been so busy, I haven't been round to introduce myself yet.' Ellie kept glancing over her shoulder, half-expecting Dave to appear and demand to know where they were going, or Rory to jump out from behind a hedge with his phone and tripod.

'Going back to the journals,' Ellie said, 'ever since Terry said a man has been asking to see them, I've been wondering who it could be.'

But Sylvia was already dialling.

She put the phone on loudspeaker. 'Gideon? It's Sylvia. I hope you don't mind me calling, but I have a rather urgent question.'

'Fire away,' came his reply, through a mouthful of something.

'It's about the Hollinghursts again. Has anyone else been in contact with you recently? Anyone asking about Violet Chapman or the Hollinghursts?'

'Actually, now you mention it, yes. My memory is dreadful these days.' He gave an embarrassed laugh. 'An academic from Kent University. What was her name? Elizabeth... what was it? Murray? No. Elizabeth Merrin. Pleasant woman. In fact, our historical interests overlap. Except that she's done a PhD and I just make a living giving talks and writing books.'

'When did she contact you?'

'Let me see. I'd just done the BBC Radio Kent interview... so, around two months ago. Not sure of the exact date but I can check my diary.'

'That was when Bramhurst Chapel was listed for auction,' said Ellie, elbowing Sylvia, who added, 'Did the auction prompt her to get in touch, did she say?'

'I don't know. She contacted me to ask for my help.'

'On what?'

'She wanted me to ask Terry for his grandmother's journals. This Elizabeth Merrin woman is – or was – on sabbatical in Pembrokeshire and said she couldn't get over to Canterbury to collect them.'

'What did she want them for?'

'Said she was extending her doctoral research into the role of women's labour in the post-war period in Kent and had read about Mabel's journals. Something about prior connections with the county... That's about all I can remember.'

'Wow. Did she know about Violet's disappearance?'

'I'm sorry. I don't know. But I'm sure you'll be able to ask her. I have her contact details somewhere.'

'We'll be able to track her down via the university.'

'Did Gideon get them for her then, or what?' Ellie hissed in Sylvia's ear.

'It's OK,' said Gideon. 'I heard that. No. I thought about it and decided I felt a bit uncomfortable asking on her behalf when I don't know her. And she wasn't sure if she wanted to me send them to her or hang onto them, and I've got enough clutter in my cottage...'

Ellie nodded.

'I had a brief chat with Deb about the journals. She said I could have them, but I left it and explained how I felt to Ms Merrin.'

It made sense.

'Was that the last you heard from her?'

'Actually – yes.'

'Thank you so much, Gideon,' said Sylvia. 'You've been a great help. If you think of anything else, do call me.'

Sylvia rang off. Her phone buzzed with a text. She read it. 'Leonard, wondering if I could take the minutes at a meeting this afternoon.' She rolled her eyes. 'Sometimes I feel like his secretary. Let me call the pub and ask if we can have a look at these journals. I'm intrigued now, aren't you?'

The call to the Hop Picker's Rest was answered on the second ring by a woman with a cheerful Kent accent.

'Hello, is that Mrs Hobbs?' said Sylvia, flicking on the loudspeaker. 'My daughter-in-law and I were in earlier, talking to your husband about the Hollinghursts.'

Ellie heard the woman's voice clearly in the quiet of the village street.

'Yes, Deb here. Terry mentioned you.'

'Terry said someone else had asked about the journals recently.'

Of course, they knew it was Gideon but Ellie wanted to check no-one else was sniffing about.

'Oh, only Gideon. To be honest, I was a bit relieved when he changed his mind about needing them. They've been up in our loft for years, and I knew we'd need to go through them. I'm not keen on going up there as there are mice.' She gave an embarrassed laugh. 'Anyway, I got Terry to bring them all down. Given them a good sort out for you. They're all labelled by year. Terry's gran was very organised, bless her.'

Ellie and Sylvia exchanged excited glances.

'Would it be possible for us to see them?' Sylvia asked.

'They need to go to Dave,' Ellie hissed.

Sylvia waved Ellie quiet. 'Particularly the ones from 1950? And anything from a couple of years either side?'

'Course, love. Terry said you were welcome to look. I'll have them ready for you whenever you want to come round.'

'We could be there in ten minutes...?' She peered at Ellie, who nodded.

This was more urgent than visiting the manor house and farm.

'If that's convenient?'

'Perfect.'

After Sylvia ended the call, they stood for a moment in the middle of Bramhurst's quiet high street, processing what they'd learned.

'We've got to tell the police about the journals. I promised Dave we wouldn't interfere...'

'We're not going to.'

Ellie recognised Sylvia's mutinous expression.

'So,' Ellie said slowly, 'an academic historian wanted to see Mabel's journals. That suggests there's something in there worth reading.'

'We need to contact her,' said Sylvia. 'See if she knows anything that could help us.'

Ellie looked back towards the chapel, where decades-old secrets were being carefully excavated. 'Absolutely. Two months ago, she was researching women's labour in the post-war period. Today, we're standing next to an archaeological dig where the remains of what might be one of those women have just been discovered. That's either an extraordinary coincidence, or Dr Merrin knows more about this case than she's let on.'

Sylvia considered this. 'I agree.'

'But first,' said Ellie, 'we must get our hands on those journals before someone else does. And let Dave know they exist.' She started walking briskly towards the pub.

Sylvia fell into step beside her.

They walked in companionable silence for a few minutes, each lost in thought. It was hard to believe that this pretty, tranquil place was keeping a secret from seventy-five years ago.

A thought occurred to Ellie, and she came to a standstill. 'Hang on. Is there anything suspicious about Dr Merrin being on sabbatical?'

'No. Academics go on sabbatical.'

'What if something has happened to her?'

'Why?' asked Sylvia. 'Because she's in Pembrokeshire?'

'No. Because she wanted the journals badly enough to ask Gideon to get them for her and he hasn't heard from her since.'

'Doesn't mean other people haven't,' said Sylvia. 'Could be perfectly innocent. Let's ring the university switchboard and check.'

Ellie googled the number and dialled.

'Oh, hi. I wanted to email Dr Elizabeth Merrin. Is she still on staff, please?'

The operator confirmed she was.

'She's on sabbatical, isn't she?' Ellie tried to sound informal.

'I'm not able to give out that information, I'm afraid. If you'd like to get in touch with her, all staff have contact pages on the university website.'

Ellie thanked her and rang off. Then texted Zoe and asked her to research Elizabeth Merrin.

As they approached the pub, Sylvia stopped walking. 'What if we're wrong about all this? What if the remains aren't connected to Violet Chapman or seasonal workers? What if it's just... some young woman who died of natural causes and was buried in the garden for perfectly innocent reasons?'

Ellie came to a standstill too. 'Like what?'

'Dunno. Perhaps her family were poor? Or she got ill. Maybe she got consumption too? It was very common then.'

Ellie considered the question seriously. 'If it's a coincidence, then we'll have spent a few days learning some fascinating local history, and meeting some of our neighbours. The police will close the case as a historical curiosity and the person in question will be buried properly.' She paused. 'But I don't think that's what happened.'

'Why not?'

'Because people don't bury loved ones in secret garden graves unless they have something to hide. And they don't hide things unless they've done something wrong.' Ellie looked at her mother-in-law. 'Someone killed that young woman and buried her where they thought no one would ever find her. And I think we owe it to her to try and find out who.'

Ellie was wondering which specialists the police would've recruited. She knew from yoga one of the anthropologists that Dave used in investigations.

They had reached the Hop Picker's Rest. Through the window, Ellie could see three cardboard boxes stacked on one of the tables near the fire. A woman was bustling about with a duster and polish, straightening chairs. Deb, hopefully.

'Right then,' Sylvia said, her hand on the door handle. 'Let's see what Terry's grandmother knew about the missing women of Bramhurst.'

From the direction of the main road, they heard the sound of a car engine.

They both turned to see a silver BMW pulling into the pub car park, moving slowly as if the driver was looking for something.

'Probably just someone who's taken a wrong turn,' Sylvia said, but her voice lacked conviction.

The BMW came to a halt, turned to face them and revved its engine very deliberately. Driver with sunglasses.

Ellie grabbed Sylvia's hand and made sure Rebus was on a short lead. 'Let's get inside, before anything else happens.'

Chapter 9

Scuttling away from the car park and the silver BMW and into the pub, Ellie and Sylvia exchanged sheepish glances.

'Wow,' Sylvia said, patting her chest, 'that was a bit menacing.'

'Thank goodness we're inside,' Ellie replied. 'We'll be safe now.'

Deb Hobbs greeted them warmly in the entrance lobby, wiping her hands on a tea towel. She was a cheerful woman with a warm smile, and a practical, homely manner.

A bowl of water was on the floor and a jar of dog treats.

'Come in, come in. Ellie and Sylvia, right? I've got the journals ready for you.' She gestured towards the three cardboard boxes stacked by the window table. 'Terry's gran was meticulous about dating everything. These are 1949 to 1951, which should cover what you're looking for. The others are in the beer cellar for now.'

'This is incredibly kind of you,' Ellie said, examining the boxes. Each was labelled in neat handwriting: *1949,1950* and *1951.*

'Not at all. To be honest, I'm curious myself now. Never really looked through them properly. Felt a bit like prying, if you know what I mean. But given what's happened up at your place...' Deb shook her head. 'Well, if there's something in there that might help, Gran would want it found.'

'What was her surname?' Sylvia asked. 'Your husband's grandmother?'

'Brown. Pritchard before she married. Her daughter married a Hobbs. That's Terry's mum. Mabel worked at the manor from when she was fourteen until she retired. Nearly fifty years of her life, that was.'

'She must have seen a lot of changes,' Ellie observed.

'Oh, she did. She used to tell Terry stories about the family, the servants, the goings-on up there. Some of them were quite...' Deb paused, seeming to search for the right word, 'well, quite shocking, really. Different times, though, weren't they? No employment law and unions like we have today.'

‘I was going to phone my husband about these.’ She explained that Dave was the DCI. ‘Would it be all right if we had a quick look through them here? In the bar? Only, once the police get them, they’ll become evidence, and we won’t be able to see them.’

‘Course you can, love,’ she said casually. ‘I’ll get the fire going properly, make it nice and cosy.'

'I'll text Dave when we leave. Let him know the journals are here so he can collect them. Is that OK?'

'No problem,' said Deb. 'Would you like drinks?’

Twenty minutes later, Ellie and Sylvia were settled at the large table by the fire, the three boxes arranged before them like treasure chests waiting to be opened. Rebus was stretched out on the hearth rug, basking in the heat. Deb had provided a pot of tea and mugs, homemade shortbread, and reading glasses for Sylvia, who’d forgotten hers.

‘Right then,’ Sylvia said, lifting the lid off the 1950 box. ‘Let’s see what Mabel Pritchard had to say about the year Violet Chapman disappeared.’

The first journal was small, leather-bound and with ‘1950’ embossed in gold on the cover. Mabel’s handwriting was neat and precise in places, larger and more scrawling in others, much like Ellie’s own diary. Ellie imagined the young domestic worker writing her entries in her quarters at night, and in private spots around the manor house. The ink had faded to brown in places and was darker in others, presumably where she'd used different pens. The entries were dated and methodical, some neat, some torn and Sellotaped together, recording everything from the weather to social engagements to village gossip.

Ellie flicked through, snapping photos on her phone.

A maple leaf had been pressed between two pages, brittle and papery, now faded to a biscuit colour.

One page had a piece of ribbon in it.

'Listen to this,' Ellie said, reading from the entry dated June 4th, 1950. '"*Young Master Edmund seems quite taken with one of the harvest girls. Cook says she's a pretty little thing from London, very polite and well-spoken for her station. Mrs H is not pleased. There was quite the argument in the library this morning. Voices raised something dreadful*".'

'Mrs H would be Edmund's mother?' Sylvia asked.

'Must be.' Ellie snapped a photo of the entry. 'The judge's wife.'

Ellie turned the page. 'Here's more from June 10th in a different pen. "*The London girl – Violet her name is – was at church again this Sunday. Sat in the back pew with her brother and the other workers, but Master Edmund couldn't take his eyes off her. After the service, I saw them talking by the gate. Mrs H saw too. Her face was like thunder".'*

She photographed this entry too.

The next page was missing, probably dislodged over the years.

Sylvia was reading from a later entry. 'June 30th: *"Terrible row last night. Could hear the judge shouting from the kitchen. Something about family reputation and knowing his duty. Master Edmund's door slammed so hard it shook the whole house. There was no sign of his sister".'*

'Sister?' questioned Ellie. 'Didn't Gideon say Edmund was an only child?' She continued to photograph everything that was relevant.

'That's right. He did. That's strange he got that wrong. He seems so fastidious.' Sylvia returned to the journal entry. "*'Found the master this morning in the garden, looking like he hadn't slept a wink".'*

As they read in companionable silence, the fire crackled in the grate. Customers arrived and ordered drinks, and Deb brought food out of the kitchen.

The journals painted a vivid picture of life at Bramhurst Manor – the strict hierarchy, the gossip among the servants, the growing tension as Edmund's romance with Violet became more serious.

'Oh, this is interesting,' Ellie said, looking up from an entry dated July 15th. 'Listen: *"The judge has forbidden any of the staff to speak to the London workers. Says we're not to encourage fraternisation. But Cook says young Violet still comes to the kitchen door sometimes, asking for scraps for the farm cats. She's a kind soul, that one. It's a shame what's likely to come of all this".'*

'What do you think she means by that?' Sylvia asked.

'That she could see it wouldn't end well?' Ellie suggested. 'The class difference was too great.'

Sylvia turned to the end of August. 'Here we are. August 30th: *"They've gone. Master Edmund and the London girl. Left notes saying they were going to Scotland to be married. The judge is beside himself. Threw everything off his desk and locked himself in the library. Mrs H has taken to her room with one of her headaches. The whole house feels like a storm about to break".'*

'Yet Terry said Mabel didn't believe Violet left the village,' said Ellie.

'Let me see if there's anything else…' Sylvia flipped through the pages. 'Yes, here. September 5th: *"Funny thing. Cook sent me and Nellie to the village for supplies"–'*

'Who's Nellie?'

'Don't know. Another one of the kitchen staff maybe? I'll see if she's mentioned elsewhere…' She carried on reading aloud. '"*and we saw Tommy Chapman at the station. He was alone, carrying a bag, looking like he'd seen a ghost. When I asked after his sister, he just shook his head and got on the London train. Didn't say a word about Scotland or weddings. Something's not right about all this. Nellie thinks so too".*'

Ellie felt a chill. 'I wonder where Tommy was going. And what had shaken him.'

'He looked like he'd seen a ghost,' Sylvia repeated. 'What do you think that means?'

Before Ellie could answer, something fluttered from between the pages of the journal Sylvia was holding. A small, black and white photograph, yellowed with age.

'What's that?' Ellie asked, leaning forward.

Sylvia picked up the photograph carefully. It showed a young woman and a young man sitting on what looked like a stone bridge, their legs swinging over the edge. They were both smiling at the camera, the woman wearing a simple summer dress, the man in shirt sleeves and trousers. Behind them, water sparkled in bright sunlight.

'Is that Mabel?' asked Ellie.

Sylvia shrugged. 'Guess so,' she said softly. 'It's her journal. They look so happy, don't they?'

'Yes. Young and carefree.' Ellie studied the photograph.

The woman was petite and pretty, with dark hair and a bright smile. The man was tall and lanky, with gentle eyes and an almost shy expression. There was something about the way they sat together. Not quite touching, but clearly comfortable with each other, that suggested intimacy. But their clothes made Ellie wonder if the two subjects perhaps *weren't* Mabel and a beau.

'Do you think it could be Edmund and Violet?' she asked.

Sylvia turned the photograph over. In faded pen, someone had written: *"Summer 1950. Remember this day always."*

'The timing would be right.' Ellie observed. 'And if Mabel kept this photo in her journal, she must have thought it was significant. Maybe someone gave it to her, or maybe she found it.'

Ellie took a careful photograph of the old picture. 'We should show this to Gideon. He might recognise the location. That bridge looks local.'

'Good idea. But first, let's see if there's anything else in these diaries.' Sylvia was already reaching for the 1951 box. 'If something happened to Violet in late summer of 1950, there might be more details in the following year.'

They were deep in the 1951 journal when Ellie's phone rang. 'It's Zoe,' she told Sylvia, answering quickly.

'Mum? I've been trying to track down Dr Merrin. I called Kent University and asked to speak to her.'

'And?'

'She's on leave.'

'Yes, on sabbatical in Pembrokeshire.'

'What? No. The department secretary said she's on "indefinite personal leave". Has been for the past month and they're not expecting her back this term.'

Ellie met eyes briefly with Sylvia, who said, 'Sabbatical and personal leave aren't the same.'

'And,' Zoe continued, 'it's a bit weird because they don't know when she's coming back.'

'That *is* interesting timing,' said Ellie.

'That's what I thought.'

Ellie considered the implications. 'Did they give you any other information? A contact number; anything like that?'

'They said all her classes have been reassigned and her research projects are on hold. When I asked if there was any way to contact her, they said they could pass on a message but couldn't guarantee when she'd get it.'

'Call back. Leave a message saying we'd like to speak with her about her research into the role of women's labour. Give my number.' Ellie paused. 'And Zo? See if you can find out anything else about Dr Merrin. Where she lives, family, anything that might help us understand why she was interested in Bramhurst before the remains were found.'

'Already on it. I'll call you back when I've got something.'

After Ellie hung up, she and Sylvia sat in thoughtful silence for a moment.

'How're you getting on?' Deb asked, adding a log to the fire.

'Good, thanks,' Ellie replied. 'Do you happen to know if Mabel had a friend at the manor house called Nellie?'

Chances were, given Mabel had died, Nellie probably had too.

'Yes,' said Deb, 'she did. Nellie Tuppen is her name. Came to Mabel's funeral, she did. She's in a wheelchair now and a resident at Willow Haven in the village.'

'Leonard leads a prayer group there once a month,' Sylvia whispered. 'We could try and talk to Nellie maybe? A lot of the residents in these places are bored stiff. She might relish the opportunity to help, especially since it relates to her time at the manor house.'

'That's a good idea.' Ellie smiled. 'So, Dr Merrin knows something about what's buried in our garden, something that made her decide it was safer to disappear than to continue her research.' Ellie screwed up her nose.

'Or,' Sylvia suggested quietly, 'something that made someone *else* decide she should disappear.'

'Hmm.' Ellie typed out a quick text to Dave, letting him know about Mabel's journals.

Inside, the hearth hummed with warmth, but Ellie found herself drawn to the window. Somewhere out there, a mystery was unravelling, but each answer they found seemed to lead to more questions. And now, it seemed, they weren't the only ones asking them.

Chapter 10

The walk to Bramhurst Farm took Ellie and Rebus through the field at the rear of the chapel and up a gentle rise where the hedgerows gave way to more open countryside. As she strode, she watched Reeby snuffle in the undergrowth. She couldn't help wondering what she might be about to discover.

The farmhouse loomed long and low, its red brick mottled with lichen and soot, with tall chimneys and mullioned windows that caught the light.

Ellie spotted a weathered sign that read 'Bramhurst Farm' in faded green paint. 'Still keeping the old name, then,' she said aloud.

The farmyard was bustling with activity, so Ellie clipped the lead onto Rebus' collar. A man wearing wellie boots and a waxed jacket was directing the movement of a small herd of cattle from one field to another, his voice carrying clearly across the yard as he called instructions to a younger man with a sheepdog.

'Right then, that's the last of them. Get the gate, will you, Toby?'

Ellie walked over, careful to stay well clear of the livestock operation.

The older man noticed her approach and strode over. 'You'll be the lady who rang,' he said with a pleasant smile. 'Giles Finch. Sorry about the chaos. We're getting the cattle settled for winter. Can't afford to hang about once the seasons turn.'

Ellie introduced herself. 'Thank you so much for agreeing to see me. There are two reasons I've come.'

Giles frowned.

'We suspect the remains that have turned up in our garden belong to a seasonal worker from the 1950s. We're trying to understand what life would have been like for them here.'

'Ah yes, the hop and fruit pickers.' Giles glanced back at his cattle operation with the air of a man with plenty to get on with. 'Well, I can show you what's left of their accommodation, though I warn you it's pretty basic. Different world back then.'

As they made their way across the yard, Ellie caught sight of a man in the distance, methodically checking fence posts in a nearby paddock, while another was pressure-washing feed troughs near one of the barns.

'Busy time of year,' Giles explained, following her gaze. 'Getting ready for winter's like preparing for a siege, really. Can't leave anything to chance.' He gestured towards a low building with crumbling walls and a corrugated iron roof. 'That's where they slept – the seasonal workers. We use it for machinery storage now, but the basic structure's the same.'

Ellie gasped as they approached the building. Even converted for modern use, something about the worn path leading to its entrance spoke of the hundreds of people who had passed this way over the years.

Giles opened the door and they stepped inside. The space was filled with modern farm equipment – a tractor, various implements, neat stacks of supplies – but the basics of the old accommodation were still visible. Along one wall, remains of brackets and rusty screws showed where internal partitions had once been.

'Each family would have had a section about the size of that area there,' Giles said, pointing to one of the rectangles. 'Maybe eight feet by ten. Earth floors back then, of course, and they slept on straw.'

Ellie stared at the marked-out spaces, trying to imagine a family of four, five or six people living in such close quarters.

'The youngsters that came on their own, or with siblings, would've been put in a unit the same size. Up to about six.'

Ellie's hand went to her chest. 'It's so small,' she murmured, stroking Rebus' ears.

'That's what I thought when I first saw the old photographs,' Giles agreed. 'Mind you, they weren't here for comfort. It was work, pure and simple. Dawn till dusk in the hop gardens, then back here to sleep. Different priorities.'

'How many families would have stayed here?' Ellie asked, her voice oddly subdued.

'At peak season? Twenty, maybe more. The whole building was divided up like rabbit hutches. No privacy, no proper sanitation or water – they had communal facilities outside.' He shook his head. 'Makes you appreciate what we have now.'

Ellie nodded. She and Dave had struggled with their blow-up mattress at the chapel, but at least they had a choice.

As they left the building, Ellie glanced back over her shoulder. The thought of Violet sleeping in that cramped space, working all hours, seemed to make her more real somehow. Not just a name in a newspaper story, but a young woman who had laughed and worried and dreamed in this very place.

'The hop gardens themselves are long gone,' Giles continued as they walked. 'Same with the fruit orchards. Dug up years ago when mechanisation made the hand-picking obsolete. We've got sheep pasture there now, and some of the higher ground's arable.'

They stopped at a gate leading to a gently sloping field dotted with ewes. In the distance, the spire of Bramhurst Chapel was just visible through the trees.

'Lovely field,' Ellie observed. 'What do you call it?'

'That's Violet's Meadow.'

Ellie looked up sharply. 'You're kidding?'

Giles gave her a puzzled look. 'No. Named after a worker, who disappeared back in the fifties. Not that the previous owners mentioned it when we bought the place. Gideon told me it's been called that for years.' He paused, looking at Ellie with growing curiosity. 'I say, you don't think that's who was buried in the chapel garden, do you?'

'Very possibly,' Ellie admitted. She told him about the alleged elopement.

'Ah.' Giles stroked his chin. 'That would explain it, then. Local memories are long in places like this. Once a field gets a name, it tends to stick.'

Ellie gazed across the peaceful field, imagining it planted with the tall hop vines that would have dominated the landscape seventy-five years ago. 'What do you know about what happened?'

'Only what Gideon told me, I'm afraid. We bought through the solicitors in the village: Morrison, Blake & Associates. Between you and me, I wasn't impressed with their service.' His expression grew slightly grimmer. 'One of their staff was related to the Hollinghursts by marriage, and I got the impression that perhaps they weren't quite as... well, let's just say their professional standards could have been better.'

'In what way?' Ellie asked.

Giles glanced around as if checking they weren't overheard, though the only witnesses were sheep. 'Oh, information that should have been disclosed wasn't. Boundaries that were described one way in the documents but marked differently on the ground. The sort of thing that makes you wonder if everyone's interests were being represented equally, if you catch my meaning.'

A sharp whistle from across the yard interrupted them. Toby was gesturing towards a gate where several sheep had congregated.

'Right, duty calls,' Giles said briskly. 'Look, I hope you find what you're looking for regarding this poor young woman, but I have to say I'm rather glad to be getting on with the business of farming rather than dwelling on former times. The past is the past, isn't it?'

Thinking about Violet, Ellie had almost forgotten the other reason she'd come. 'Before you go – I hope you don't mind. I wanted to ask you about the field that runs along the back of our garden. The one that borders the chapel grounds.'

'Aye, that's mine. Part of the original farm boundaries.' Giles' expression became more businesslike. 'Something wrong with the fencing?'

'No, nothing like that. I was wondering... well, I've got a small campervan, and with the archaeological dig going on in our garden, and the chapel cordoned off, I have no base or privacy. I was hoping I might be able to park the van in your field, so I could have somewhere private to retreat to.'

Giles seemed to consider this, his practical farmer's mind clearly weighing up the request. 'Can't see any harm in it. Field's not in use at the moment, and it's well away from the livestock. How long would you need it for?'

'Just until the dig's finished. A few days, maybe a week at most. I'd be happy to pay you something for the inconvenience.'

'No need for that. We're neighbours, aren't we?' He almost smiled. 'Besides, after what's happened on our properties, I reckon we should all look out for each other a bit more.'

'Thank you,' Ellie said, feeling genuinely grateful. 'That's incredibly kind.'

'Drive along the path from Thimble Lane and park where you want. There's a gate in the hedge about halfway along – been locked for years, but I can sort that out for you. Get it cleared and give you direct access from your garden.'

They said goodbye and Giles was already heading back to his sheep with the purposeful stride of a man with work to do.

As Ellie walked back down the drive towards home, she felt the first stirring of relief she'd experienced all day. Having a bolthole during the excavation would make the whole process much more bearable.

She took one last look at the converted accommodation block. How had the workers stood those cramped units? It was strange. Seventy-five years ago, Violet had been sleeping in there, probably wondering what her future held. And now she had a meadow named after her and, in all likelihood, an archaeological dig in her honour.

Perhaps when it was all you had, you made the best of it. After all – the seasonal workers hadn't really been there by choice. It'd been economic necessity.

Suddenly Ellie felt a desire to know what Violet thought about it all. Where she and Edmund had wanted to live. What their hopes and dreams had been.

'And now we know Morrison, Blake & Associates are, or were, related to the Hollinghursts, that could be significant,' she mused aloud.

Violet's Meadow stretched peacefully behind her.

But Ellie hadn't forgotten that Dave had adopted the campervan as a temporary office and her relief evaporated slightly. How exactly was he going to react to the news that he'd just lost his headquarters?

Chapter 11

Sylvia was spreading strawberry jam on a sponge in the kitchen at the rectory when Leonard emerged from his study, with the satisfied expression of someone who'd solved a particularly tricky crossword clue.

'I've been thinking about your mystery,' he announced, settling onto a stool at the breakfast bar. 'And Violet Chapman.'

'Oh?' Sylvia looked up with interest.

Leonard had a sharp mind and an excellent memory for local history and she was keen to hear his thoughts.

'The thing is, Bramhurst's church, St Mildred's, has always had a strong reputation for record-keeping. Much more so than most village churches.' Leonard reached for the kettle. 'It's partly because of its proximity to Canterbury, of course. The cathedral influence, you might say. Pilgrims and so on. But also because of all the seasonal workers who passed through the area.'

'How do you mean?'

'Well, the church often served as an unofficial registry for the travelling workers. Births, deaths, marriages were recorded as a standard. But they recorded things that might not have been done elsewhere. Like baptisms, christenings, confirmations. The vicars there took their pastoral duties very seriously, particularly when it came to people who might otherwise be overlooked by official channels.'

Sylvia felt a familiar tingle of excitement. 'So, if something happened to the harvest workers... if they died, or got married, or...'

'... or more *minor things...* it would all likely be recorded at St Mildred's, yes.' Leonard smiled at his wife's enthusiasm. 'The current vicar is Jo Smythe. Obliging woman, very dedicated to preserving the church's historical records. I could give her a ring if you'd like an introduction. See if she'll have a chat with you.'

'That would be wonderful. Thank you, darling.'

Half an hour later, Sylvia had parked her car at Ellie's chapel and was walking through Bramhurst village again, this time heading for St Mildred's Church. It sat on a small rise at the far end of the village, its Norman tower visible from the main road. The building was older than she'd expected – parts of it clearly predated the thirteenth century – and there was something solid and enduring about its weathered stone walls. What made her smile, though, was the gleaming, black Harley-Davidson motorbike that was parked at the front of the rectory next door.

As Sylvia approached the church, she could hear voices and laughter from inside. A small sign by the entrance read: "Monday Craft Group – All Welcome".

Sylvia knocked gently and pushed open the heavy oak door. The interior of the church was warm and inviting, with afternoon sunlight streaming through stained glass windows and casting coloured patterns on the stone floor. A group of about a dozen people, mostly women of various ages, sat around tables covered with fabric, needles and craft supplies.

'You must be Sylvia,' said a woman of around Ellie's age, who was approaching with a welcoming smile. She had short, blonde hair and kind eyes, and wore a clerical collar under a shirt and light jumper. 'I'm Jo.'

She seemed familiar.

'Thank you for agreeing to see me,' Sylvia said. 'I hope I'm not interrupting.'

'Not at all. We're just doing some quiet work on our harvest festival decorations.' Jo gestured towards the tables where people were sewing and chatting.

As Sylvia followed the vicar's arm, she noticed that Jo had walking boots on. 'You a fan of the countryside, then?'

Jo beamed. 'You can say that again. I call it my therapy.' She laughed. 'I've got a red setter who needs a lot of exercise. St Millie's has a rambling group if you'd care to join us.'

'Thank you. I'll tell my daughter-in-law. She's got a dog.' Sylvia recalled where she'd seen Jo. 'Think we saw you with your dog actually. Playing in the ford in the village?'

'That was us. Sure that dog has seal genes.' Jo chuckled good-naturedly and led Sylvia to a corner of the church where two comfortable chairs had been arranged near an ancient font. 'Leonard mentioned you were interested in our records from the late 1940s and fifties, relating to seasonal workers.'

'That's right. I'm sure you know remains have been found at the chapel. We're trying to trace a young woman called Violet Chapman.'

Jo's expression grew serious. 'I see. Well, you've come to the right place. In keeping with the interests and values of our patron saint, St Millie's has always prided itself on its compassion and taken special care of the poor and those who felt they were outcasts. St Mildred was renowned for her gentleness, healing, wisdom and peace-making. Her name literally means "peaceful counsel". Her style was one of quiet reverence and local devotion. She had numerous opportunities to take up a life of splendour and chose service instead.'

'That's lovely.'

'Yes. I feel honoured to be the vicar here. The church was founded as a sanctuary for those in need. It's our everyday ethos to care for those who are vulnerable.'

She gestured towards the stained-glass windows, where coloured light depicted figures in medieval dress. 'These windows tell the story of St Mildred, whose origins were in the Kentish royal family of legend. She was born in the seventh century, was educated in France and returned to Thanet, where she served in – and led for thirty years – the abbey her mother founded.' Jo paused. 'She would've been horrified to learn about some of the ill-treatment of the young women and men coming to the village for work.'

Sylvia felt a chill, imagining in her mind the accommodation Ellie had described on the phone in horror when she left Bramhurst Farm.

'St Mildred was opposed to anyone being taken advantage of,' Jo continued. 'Your husband and I have discussed this issue a number of times. It's something he feels very strongly about too.'

'It is.'

'The traditions that St Mildred started continued right through to the twentieth century. The vicars here always felt a special responsibility for the harvest workers. They were young people, coming down from London's poorest areas for seasonal work. They were vulnerable and far from their families.' She shook her head sadly. 'When things happened to them, like workplace accidents, illnesses, fights, unwanted pregnancies and elopements, they would often come to St Millie's in distress, seeking help or sanctuary.' Her voice dropped. 'And occasionally, they would simply... vanish.'

'Really?'

'Yes. One day they'd be here, working in the fields, sending letters and money home, attending Sunday service. The next day, gone. No goodbyes, no word to their families back in London.'

'Did no-one ask any questions?'

'I'm sure they did but they accepted what they were told. Accidents, fights and illnesses did occur.'

'Hmm. What do you know about Judge Hollinghurst?'

Jo's voice grew quieter. 'Probably the same as you. How strict he was.'

'When Violet and Edmund eloped,' asked Sylvia, 'was he thought to have been involved with that?'

'There were rumours. Which was inevitable. Manor house owners were a different class. Their money gave them power and meant they were able to get away with nefarious acts. But it also meant they came under suspicion for things they *weren't* involved with.'

'That's interesting. I suppose working- and upper-class folk both get accused when it comes to crimes, just for different reasons.'

'Indeed,' said the vicar.

'Did Judge Hollinghurst come to church regularly?'

'Every Sunday, front pew, very prominent. Their chapel didn't have a resident vicar. He made substantial donations to the church, and regularly. Had his name on the memorial plaques.' Jo seemed to drift off into thought. 'The thing about power like that is that it comes with expectations...' She peered meaningfully at Sylvia. 'The majority of the congregation in the 1950s were people who depended on the judge for their living, often their accommodation too. They looked the other way, asked fewer questions than they should have.'

Sylvia felt a rush of anger.

'You still get rural communities where people depend on local landowners for work. Wherever you have poverty, you find this same dynamic: those with money have power over those who don't.'

Jo stood up and walked to one of the windows, where the afternoon light caught the deep blues and reds of the glass. 'The vicar here at St Millie's in the 1950s kept very detailed records. Birth certificates for babies born to unmarried workers, burial records for those who died far from home, marriage certificates for couples who wanted to wed before the harvest ended.'

'And records of disappearances?'

'Not official records, no. But notes, observations, correspondence with families in London who were searching for children who'd stopped writing home.' Jo turned back to Sylvia. 'He was a good man, Reverend Matthews. He cared about the workers, tried to keep track of them, tried to help when he could.'

'Those records,' Sylvia said carefully, 'would they still exist?'

'Oh, yes.' Jo's expression changed, becoming somehow more guarded. 'We had an extensive archive going back centuries. Beautifully preserved, meticulously catalogued. It was one of the finest collections of rural social history in Kent.'

'Had?'

'Two weeks ago, an academic came to see me. Dr Elizabeth Merrin from Kent University.'

Sylvia let out a groan at the name. 'Had she come back from Pembrokeshire then?'

Jo frowned. 'What?'

Sylvia summarised what Gideon had shared.

'She didn't mention sabbatical to me. Said she lived locally and was doing research into the history of female labour. Particularly interested in our records from the late forties to the early fifties.' Jo sat back down, her hands clasped tightly in her lap. 'She seemed very knowledgeable, very professional. Had all the proper credentials.'

A shiver of anticipation ran down Sylvia's spine. 'And?'

'She asked if she could borrow the relevant files for her research. Said she'd return them within a fortnight, with copies for our own archive.' Jo's voice was tight with what might have been regret. 'It seemed reasonable. Academic research, contributing to historical knowledge...'

'But she hasn't returned them?'

'No. And when I tried to contact her last week, the university said she was on leave. Indefinite leave.' Jo looked up at the stained-glass windows, where St Mildred gazed down with medieval serenity. 'I'm beginning to think I may have made a terrible mistake.'

Sylvia reached out and touched Jo's arm gently. 'You couldn't have known. Whatever she's up to, she presented herself as a legitimate researcher.'

'But those records, they were irreplaceable. Decades of careful documentation, stories of people who might otherwise be forgotten entirely.' Jo's voice caught slightly. 'If those records are lost...'

'We'll find her,' Sylvia said with more confidence than she felt. 'And the records.'

Jo looked at her with scepticism. 'I hope so.'

Sylvia thought of the photograph they'd found in Mabel's journal, of the young couple sitting on a bridge with their whole lives ahead of them. Of the careful notes about Tommy Chapman looking like he'd seen a ghost.

'Because,' Sylvia said quietly, 'someone needs to speak for these young men and women. Someone needs to make sure their stories are told.'

Jo smiled at her. 'Leonard said you were a woman of conviction.'

Sylvia met her eyes and smiled back.

'Before you go – do you and your daughter-in-law know about the barn dance we've got coming up? It's to celebrate the harvest. Ceilidh band and everything. This coming Saturday at the farm. The marquee will go up at the end of the week.'

'Thank you. I'll make sure Ellie knows.'

Around them, the craft group continued their quiet work, the soft murmur of conversation and the rustle of fabric creating a peaceful backdrop to their discussion. But Sylvia couldn't shake the feeling that Elizabeth Merrin had got too close to the truth.

Had somebody perhaps silenced her?

Chapter 12

While Sylvia was at St Mildred's, Ellie met up with Zoe. Having been to Bramhurst Farm, she was keen to understand the current setup at the old manor house. Rebus was ahead of them as they walked, attention on a trio of pigeons who were pecking at the ground.

'It's completely different from the images I've seen online,' Zoe observed as they arrived. 'Not what I was expecting at all.' She put Rebus on the lead.

'Money,' Ellie said simply as they proceeded through open wooden gates that had replaced the old wrought iron barriers. On tall pillars, either side of the gates, the words "Ashbourne House" were engraved in slate. 'Serious money. This sort of renovation doesn't come cheap.'

The transformation was even more apparent as the two women began looking round. The main change was that where once there had been imposing Victorian grandeur, there was now sleek modern prosperity. Contemporary sculptures sat on manicured lawns. A circular gravel drive centred around an elaborate stone fountain. Through carefully planned landscaping, there were glimpses of a tennis court and swimming pool.

The house itself had been extensively modernised, while retaining its basic Victorian structure. The stonework had been cleaned and repointed, the windows replaced with sleek modern equivalents, and a glass extension had been added to one side, housing an indoor swimming pool. Everything spoke of contemporary luxury rather than historical preservation.

'So, what's our plan?' Zoe asked. 'Just saunter around until someone comes and asks what we're doing?'

'Pretty much. We're new neighbours who've come to introduce ourselves and ask a few questions. If we wander in the direction of the entrance, and manage to get distracted, we'll say exactly that. Nothing threatening or suspicious, just neighbourly interest and appreciation.'

'If you say so, Mum.'

They strolled across the lawns, admiring the landscaping and sharing impressed comments about the obvious expense involved. The old stables had been converted into what looked like luxury guest accommodation, and a new yard had been constructed.

Over stable doors, thoroughbred horses watched two labradors chase a ball. The tennis court was surrounded by perfectly trimmed box hedging that wouldn't have looked out of place at Wimbledon.

'It's beautiful,' Zoe said, then her voice caught slightly. 'The sort of place you'd want to raise a family.'

'Although not exactly a starter home for a young couple.' Ellie's thoughtless sentence was out before she could grab it back. She glanced at her daughter, noting the wistful expression. 'Sorry, lovey. I keep forgetting that you two... Are you thinking about Finn again?'

Zoe's eyes were watery, and her voice unsteady. 'I keep seeing things that make me think of him. Nothing as grand as this, but lovely homes, family spaces. And feeling sad about the future we'd planned together. The house we'd talked about buying, the children we'd wanted...' She trailed off, struggling with her emotions.

'Oh, sweetheart.' Ellie put her arm around Zoe's shoulders. 'I know how hard this is.'

'I just keep wondering if I should have gone with him to Norway for a few months,' Zoe said, wiping her eyes with the back of her hand.

'Why didn't you?' Ellie still had no idea why Finn had decided to vanish off to Scandinavia. She'd tried to ask this before, but Zoe hadn't wanted to talk about it. It was all too raw.

'Because I'm not ready to give up everything I've built here. My work with the animals, my research, my independence. I wanted him to understand that my life matters too, that he couldn't just expect me to drop everything and follow him around the world.'

Ellie squeezed her daughter's shoulder gently. 'That sounds perfectly reasonable to me.'

'But what if I was being stubborn? What if I should have compromised more? Norway is one of the best places to learn lumberjacking. Proper forestry management and sustainable timber practices. Should I have been more supportive?'

That explained Scandinavia.

'Zoe, listen to me.' Ellie turned to face her daughter directly. 'You can't build a life with someone by constantly sacrificing your own dreams for theirs. A good relationship requires both people to respect each other's ambitions and find ways to support them.'

'But what if I've lost him forever?'

'Then that's painful, but it's not the end of your life and it doesn't mean you won't be happy again.' Ellie's voice was gentle but firm. 'All you can do now is get on with your own life, pursue your own goals, and let Finn do the same. You're both young, and you have a vast world to experience. If Finn comes back to Kent and you're both still interested in exploring what you had together, then you'll deal with that when it happens. But you can't put your life on hold, waiting for maybes.'

Zoe nodded, though she still looked heartbroken. 'It's just so hard, seeing couples' homes and knowing he's not going to be part of my future.'

'I know. But the right person *will* be part of that future, when the time comes. Whether it's Finn after he's had his adventures, or someone else entirely.'

She nodded, but Ellie knew she was only semi-convinced.

They walked for a few minutes, eventually finding themselves at the glass extension that housed the indoor swimming pool. The space was impressive – a full-sized pool surrounded by tropical plants and comfortable seating areas, with sliding glass doors that could open to connect it to the outdoor entertainment space.

'Now this is serious luxury,' Zoe said, pressing her face to the glass for a better look. 'Heated pool, spa area, what looks like a fully equipped gym...'

'Can I help you, ladies?' The tone was polite but had elements of concern.

They turned to find a man approaching from the direction of the house. He was casually but expensively dressed. Designer jeans, Ralph Lauren polo shirt, and the kind of confidence that came with significant wealth. His expression was curious rather than hostile, though there was a wariness that suggested he was used to people being interested in his property.

'I'm so sorry,' Ellie said with her most disarming smile. 'We were coming to the front door and got distracted.' She introduced Zoe and herself. 'My husband and I have just bought Bramhurst Chapel.'

The man's expression relaxed slightly. 'Nice to meet you. I'm Simon Stone. My wife and I bought this house three years ago. Sorry to hear about the remains that've been found at your place…'

'Hopefully we'll get to the bottom of whose they are,' said Ellie. 'This used to be Bramhurst Manor, didn't it?'

'That's right. We renamed it when we renovated. You probably know – the manor house, farm and chapel were split up, given their own Land Registry titles, and sold.'

'It's absolutely beautiful,' Zoe said admiringly. 'The work must have been quite an undertaking.'

Simon straightened, pride flickering in the tilt of his head. 'Eighteen months of solid renovation work. We gutted the entire place and started again. Kept the basic structure but modernised everything else.'

'Do you know much about the history?' Ellie asked casually, hoping for a fresh take. 'I heard the original family were quite prominent locally.'

'The Hollinghursts, yes. Though to be honest, we didn't learn much about them during the purchase process. The estate had been sold to distant relatives years ago, and they weren't particularly forthcoming with historical details.'

'Oh, did you buy directly from the family?'

Simon shook his head. 'No, it had been through several hands by the time we found it. We bought through local solicitors who were the executors – Morrison, Blake & Associates in Bramhurst. Same firm that handles most of the estate sales in this area, apparently.'

Ellie's chest tightened slightly. 'They handled the chapel sale too. Although we bought through auction. Did you find them helpful?' she asked, trying to keep her voice casual.

Simon's expression darkened slightly. 'Well, that would be a generous way of putting it. Honestly, we found them rather dodgy. Very evasive about certain details, and we had to keep chasing them up for missing information.'

'What sort of missing information?' She told him about the sub-floor area at the chapel.

'Sounds similar. With us it was lack of information about planning permissions, building consent, historical surveys, that sort of thing. Basic documentation that should have been straightforward to provide.' Simon paused, clearly remembering his frustration. 'At one point we nearly pulled out of the purchase because they couldn't provide clear title documentation for part of the grounds.'

'Did they eventually sort it out?'

'Yes, though it took months longer than it should have. Actually, it was when the farm and chapel were separated from the house and given their own titles. That was finally done. And even then, we discovered after completion that there were several features they hadn't disclosed. Old outbuildings, some sort of family burial plot that had been moved, drainage issues in the lower fields.'

Zoe was listening intently. 'That must have been very annoying.'

'It was. And expensive. We ended up having to do additional surveys and remedial work that should've been flagged before exchange.' Simon looked between them curiously. 'Why didn't they inform you that there was a sub-floor area at the chapel?'

Ellie shrugged. 'We haven't asked them yet. We've only just found out it's there.' She explained about the builders' discovery.

'Must be a crypt.'

'Thing is, we queried it. They said, "no crypt".'

'Goodness.' Simon's expression became sympathetic. 'I'm not surprised. Between you and me, I got the impression they were more interested in pushing sales through quickly than in ensuring proper disclosure. Very much a "buyer beware" attitude.'

'Did you ever meet the actual sellers?' Zoe asked. 'The people who inherited from the Hollinghurst estate?'

'No, but we were given their names on the sales memorandum and my wife googled them. Checked out their social media. Think they live in Australia now.'

Ellie smiled. She had done some googling too.

'Odd bunch, those solicitors, from what we could see. Seemed very eager to get the sale completed. Barely made eye contact. Answered questions with the absolute minimum information.' Simon shrugged. 'It felt like they were hiding something.'

They chatted further. Simon insisted that Ellie and Dave must come for dinner. 'Lovely dog,' he said, giving Rebus a stroke. 'We've got two retriever puppies.' He smiled. 'The house has turned into a puppy crèche.'

'Oh, my days,' said Zoe. 'Adorable.'

'Double trouble,' said Ellie.

'Come and see them sometime,' said Simon.

'Thank you. We will.' Zoe's voice was full of conviction.

They said goodbye.

As Ellie and Zoe walked back towards the chapel, they were both quiet, processing what they'd learned.

'The same pattern,' Zoe said finally. 'Missing information.'

'And in both cases, Morrison, Blake & Associates were involved,' Ellie added. 'Which suggests either they're incompetent, or they're deliberately helping people conceal information about properties in this area.'

'What I want to know is,' Zoe mused as they continued walking, 'what exactly are they all so desperate to hide? And how many other properties in this area have been sold with crucial information deliberately omitted?'

'Or is it just the ones that were part of the Bramhurst estate?'

As they passed through the wooden gates, Ellie couldn't shake the feeling that they'd uncovered another piece of the jigsaw. And that somewhere, someone was still working very hard to make sure the truth about the Hollinghurst family's real legacy never came to light.

Chapter 13

Just as Ellie and Zoe were leaving Ashbourne House, Zoe received a call informing her that a swan had got tangled in fishing line, so they parted ways. Ellie – who was craving some quiet – headed for Bramhurst Books. She'd been bothered by the seasonal workers' cramped living conditions in the barn at the farm.

She settled into a comfortable armchair in the back room with her phone, a mug of tea, and Rebus sprawled contentedly at her feet.

After a few minutes, she checked her notes app and remembered she needed to look up damp proofing specialists.

'Let me try the Bramhurst village Facebook page,' she muttered to Rebus, who was more interested in the chew the shop owner had given him.

The page was exactly what she'd expected – a mixture of local recommendations, community announcements, and the inevitable village drama that seemed to plague every British online community. She scrolled through recent posts.

'Can anyone recommend a reliable damp specialist? Thirteenth- century property, stone walls...' she typed, then paused to read through other requests.

There was Mrs Patterson asking for a reliable plumber (two people had immediately recommended themselves and another had recommended her husband); someone seeking a dog walker (with seventeen enthusiastic volunteers, ranging from lots of experience to none 'but I really like dogs'); and a heated debate about parking outside the village shop that had already attracted forty-two comments, most of them increasingly passive-aggressive. There was a post from Reverend Jo, informing people that the church cinema group were going for a meal before the next film at the Curzon. That sounded fun.

Ellie began to recognise key players on the Bramhurst page. There were self-appointed village guardians who policed every post with woke commentary. One lady couldn't resist turning every innocent query into a lecture about environmental responsibility, neurodiversity or social justice. Someone called Colin Weatherby had managed to hijack a post about lost car keys into a diatribe about car dependency and climate change.

But what she also saw was that the community rallied around anyone in genuine need. There were posts offering help to elderly residents, congratulating local children on school achievements, and sharing genuine concern for anyone going through difficult times. And there was a whole thread of people offering shopping help to a man who'd taken a tumble and broken his hip while walking the dog.

It struck her that village life remained remarkably consistent across time and geography. The same mix of kindness and pettiness, community spirit and small-minded judgement, that had probably existed when Violet Chapman first arrived here in 1950. Perhaps that consistency was both comforting and slightly depressing. Human nature, it seemed, didn't change much, even with the arrival of social media to amplify both the best and worst of it.

Ellie ran a few searches for damp proofing contractors and screenshot the names and numbers of the ones that seemed like genuine recommendations, and the ones that were repeatedly mentioned favourably. A couple of them she'd heard of from their old village, so that was good news.

Then she set about calling each one. She wanted to get three opinions on the damp, and three quotations. That would give her enough to discuss with Dave so they could make a decision about how to proceed.

'There you are,' Sylvia said, striding towards her. 'I've been looking everywhere for you. Where's your phone?'

Rebus hurled himself at Sylvia, as though he hadn't seen her for a century and was convinced she'd died.

The shop was about to close; the owner was tidying up and switching off lights, and in the café, a staff member had stacked the chairs for the cleaners and was wiping down the coffee machine.

'Sorry. I wanted somewhere quiet.' Ellie switched off mute on her phone and whispered, 'After the farm, Zoe and I nipped over to the manor house.'

'Oh? I'm all ears.'

'Fifteen minutes, ladies,' called the bookshop owner from behind the counter. 'You can come back tomorrow.'

'Won't be a minute,' Sylvia said over her shoulder.

'Not here,' said Ellie. 'They're closing anyway. Let's go back to the pub. Get settled.'

Fifteen minutes later, they were once again in the Hop Picker's Rest, at their favourite table by the fire.

'Fill me in then,' said Sylvia as she seized the dessert menu. 'I can't wait much longer.'

Ellie had already described the seasonal workers' accommodation but hadn't said much more about the farm. 'No crops there now. All livestock. Interestingly, both Giles Finch *and* the new manor house owner found Morrison, Blake & Associates shady. Both said they conveniently 'forgot' to hand over important details. When I've got a minute, I'll be paying the auctioneers in Canterbury a visit, and the solicitors. Find out why we were told the chapel did *not* have a crypt.'

'Hmm.' Sylvia frowned. 'It's odd behaviour. And hardly likely to inspire client confidence. Whether by neglect or design, I wouldn't want to deal with a solicitor who didn't get the details correct.' She gave a loud tut. 'What's the manor house like now? Daphne said it's all modern and got a new name.'

'Yup. Simon Stone and his wife have renamed it Ashbourne House.'

'That's got a nice sound to it.'

'The workers' conditions were a surprise, but it was seeing them for myself and imagining the young workers there that upset me.'

They discussed the subject for a few minutes, and Sylvia changed the topic to Reverend Jo's dog and the church rambling group.

'What fun,' said Ellie, smiling. 'I'll pop in. Say hi. St Millie's – I love that name.' She remembered the post about the cinema club meal. Ellie had a good feeling about their new vicar. 'Did you get any relevant information from Reverend Jo?'

Sylvia's eyes were gleaming with mischief. 'Elizabeth Merrin has been *very busy indeed*.'

She told Ellie about Jo's revelations regarding the church's historical role, and most importantly, about the missing archives.

'Wow,' said Ellie. 'Elizabeth *is* on a mission. I'd really like to see the church records, and they need to go to the police. But did Elizabeth take the whole lot?' Her voice rose slightly.

'Everything relating to the late 1940s and early fifties.'

Ellie pulled out her phone. 'We need to find Elizabeth, and we need to find her fast. She's either *in* trouble, or she *is* trouble.'

She quickly typed a text to Zoe: *Can you find an address for Dr Elizabeth Merrin? Need to speak to her urgently. Also, any info on where she might be staying if not in Pembrokeshire.*

'I wonder why Elizabeth hasn't returned the records?' Sylvia said.

'Mm. And why take indefinite leave right after taking them, and go incommunicado on the people who've helped you?' Ellie added. 'I guess there might have been a family emergency.'

Sylvia shrugged. 'Possible.'

A troubling thought occurred to Ellie. 'What if she knew something was about to be discovered?'

'You mean the remains at the chapel?'

'Uh-huh,' said Ellie.

'How could she know about that, though? Perhaps someone put the frighteners on her...?'

'I don't know,' replied Ellie. 'Her timing can't just be a coincidence, surely?'

Ellie's phone buzzed with a reply from Zoe.

On it. Elizabeth's Facebook profile says she lives in Whitstable. Going to check census and electoral register. Also checking university records for any recent research applications or funding requests. Will call you back.

'Whitstable,' Ellie said, showing Sylvia the text. 'That's only fifteen minutes away.'

'I need to get back to the rectory,' said Sylvia. 'Leonard wants me to witness a compliance form for him. If we can confirm her address, and that she's there not Pembrokeshire, we could drive over tomorrow.'

'If she's not avoiding visitors.' Ellie looked around the cosy pub, then back at Sylvia. 'Speaking of avoiding things, I'm dreading tonight.'

'Why?'

'Sleeping in the campervan with Dave and Reeby, plus whatever police equipment he's moved in there.' Ellie sighed.

Rebus raised his head, hearing his nickname, but not seeing or smelling any food, he returned to his snooze by the fire.

Sylvia winced sympathetically. 'I must admit. It wouldn't be my idea of fun. You're welcome to both come and stay at the rectory with us.'

'Thanks, but I suspect Dave will want to stay on site.'

'How's he going to handle having his work and home life literally in the same space?'

'I don't really know. He keeps saying it'll be over soon, but he also keeps telling me I can't touch anything or move anything, or even look at anything too closely.' Ellie rubbed her temples. 'I suppose what he means is the archaeology-crime-scene part will be over soon. The chapel renovation is clearly going to take forever.' She let out an anguished sigh.

'He's like his father, I'm afraid: once he gets started on a case, it eclipses everything.'

Sylvia's late husband had also been a detective.

'Dave and I have been back together four months, and we're about to find out if our relationship can survive living in a space the size of a garden shed while he investigates a death that might've happened in our garden.'

'Well, when you put it like that...' Sylvia chuckled. 'You'll be fine. You're stronger than ever.'

Ellie recalibrated. 'You know, I've been thinking about organising a coffee morning to get to know some of the locals. Find out who lives where, who does what, what's going on that I can get involved with, what tradesmen people use and ...' Her sentence trailed off.

'What a good idea. If you say you're the lady who's bought the chapel with her husband, you're bound to get people coming along with stories of the place.' Sylvia's eyes lit up. 'I'll mention it to Daphne at the village shop. She'll round a few up.'

'The bookshop would be a good place to have it.'

'Don't forget to invite Jo. She'll introduce folk to you, I'm sure, and bring people from the church.'

'I'll see if I can arrange it for Wednesday morning. Bit short notice, but some people might come.'

Ellie's phone rang. 'That's Zoe. Hopefully with good news.' She answered. 'Hi, love, what have you found?'

'Quite a lot, actually,' came Zoe's voice through the speaker. 'I've found where Dr Merrin lives in Whitstable. She's got a photo of her house on Facebook and her street address is on the electoral register.'

'Nice work.'

'I've also found something interesting about her research. She submitted an application for additional funding three months ago, specifically to investigate *"the role of women's labour in Kent, 1945-1955".*'

Ellie and Sylvia swapped a glance.

'Three months ago?' Ellie repeated.

'Yes. And get this: the application mentions recent discoveries that suggest differential treatment of male and female workers in rural communities. Three months later, Rebus finds the remains of a young woman.'

A chill ran over Ellie.

'What kind of recent discoveries?' Sylvia shouted.

'That's what I'm trying to find out. But it sounds like she already suspected women and men weren't being treated equally. The question is, what evidence did she have, and where did she get it?'

After Ellie hung up, she and Sylvia sat in thoughtful silence for a moment.

'Three months isn't long,' said Sylvia. 'She's either a very good researcher who stumbled onto something significant, or she knows something that we don't.'

'I agree.' Ellie glanced at her watch. 'Ah. I need to get going. I've got a yoga class in Harbledown.'

'*Yoga?* Now? D'you want me to take Reeby?'

'Please. I'll collect him after the class.'

'Shame. I was about to suggest some wine.'

'I'm not really going for the exercise,' Ellie said with a slightly guilty expression. 'I recognised one of the cars up at the chapel today. It belongs to Penny Wilkins. She's a forensic anthropologist who sometimes works with Kent Police. We do yoga together on Mondays.'

Sylvia raised an eyebrow. 'And you're hoping to accidentally pump her for information about the remains?'

'I prefer to think of it as friendly conversation with a professional colleague,' Ellie said primly. 'But yes. It's too good an opportunity to miss. If anyone knows what's going on in the soil at Bramhurst Chapel, it's Penny.'

Chapter 14

Half an hour later, Ellie was on her mat in the village hall in Harbledown. They'd done Warrior pose, Plank and were now doing Downward Dog. Ellie was trying to look casual while keeping an eye on Penny Wilkins.

She was a small, precise woman with a quiet intensity and observant eyes.

After the class, as they rolled up their yoga mats, Ellie made her move.

'Penny, lovely to see you. How are you? I didn't make it last week.'

'Oh, you know, the usual. Human bones and teeth.' Penny secured her mat with an elastic band. 'Actually, I was called out to your new place today. Bramhurst Chapel?'

'What've you found?' Ellie tried to sound relaxed.

Penny glanced around the nearly empty hall, then moved closer to Ellie. 'Well, I probably shouldn't say too much, but seeing as Dave knows anyway – the remains are definitely historical, probably early 1950s, as you'd expect from the boot you found with them. But here's the interesting thing…' She paused, and Ellie held her breath. 'The soil around the burial site seems to have been disturbed recently. Have you seen anyone in that part of your garden?'

'Oh, wow, no. I don't think so, only the dog.' She was pleased to be able to answer Penny's question, as it wasn't so obvious that she wanted information herself. 'Disturbed how? By an animal?'

'No. I don't think it's an animal. The telltale signs are missing. This is as if someone has either been digging there or laying fresh soil.'

'Really?' Ellie tried not to sound too excited.

'Looking for something, perhaps, or checking on something.' Penny shouldered her yoga bag. 'Of course, it could be perfectly innocent. But the pattern of disturbance suggests human activity. And we saw footwear marks. Obviously, animals don't leave those. The CSIs have taken photographs and lifted prints.'

'How recently?'

'Hard to say exactly. I'm more the bones lady. Charlotte's the soil woman.'

Charlotte was Dr Charlotte Greaves. Archaeologist.

'She'll know how fresh it looks. But from the conversations I've had with her, she's said within the last few weeks.' Penny looked at Ellie curiously. 'So, you definitely haven't noticed any signs of digging?'

'No,' Ellie said carefully. 'But then, we only moved in recently, and the garden is so overgrown, we haven't touched it yet. Only ventured in this morning as Rebus found the boot and bones.'

'Well, the soil certainly raises questions and so does the...' Penny broke off, perhaps realising she'd told Ellie more than enough.

Ellie waited to see if she'd continue.

'Dave said you don't have any CCTV.'

'No. The place is such a state, we didn't think there was any point.'

'One thing that might help – we've recently been awarded funding for equipment that does facial reconstruction. And, of course, we have the skull...'

'Ooh.' Ellie had seen this on the TV.

'It's partly to help us in our work,' Penny continued, 'and to contribute to our academic research at the university.'

They chatted for a few more minutes and left.

As Ellie drove to collect Rebus, Penny's words echoed in her mind. Had someone been digging in the garden where Violet Chapman – or whoever she was – had been buried? Had that person known, or suspected, there were remains in that spot? Could they have placed them there recently? Removed some of them? The questions went on and on...

If so – who? What had they been doing? And why?

And perhaps most importantly: what was Dr Elizabeth Merrin's role in what was buried in the garden of Bramhurst Chapel?

Chapter 15

'I'm telling you, the panna cotta was miles better,' Dave told Ellie as they walked back from Giovanni's to the chapel, their hands linked in the cool evening air. 'Lighter, more delicate. The tiramisu was too heavy.'

Dave had Rebus on the lead.

'You're completely wrong,' Ellie replied, squeezing his hand. 'The tiramisu had the perfect coffee-and-mascarpone balance. Tangy, complex, satisfying. The panna cotta was only marginally better than blancmange from the packet... just wobbly cream.'

'Wobbly cream?' Dave laughed. 'That's harsh.'

'Yep. And I'm sticking with it.' Ellie chuckled, feeling some of the tension of the day melting away.

It had been Dave's idea to have dinner at the village's Italian restaurant. A proper date night, he'd called it. The bare minimum of discussion of the chapel sub-floor and the human remains, more about the two of them relaxing and getting to know their new community.

'Thank you for tonight,' she said as they approached the campervan, which sat like a small metal island in the sea of police tape and archaeological equipment. 'I needed that.'

She hadn't moved the campervan to the farmer's field yet as she hadn't broached the subject yet of Dave's site office.

'We both did.' Dave's expression grew more serious. 'Seriously, Ells, I know this isn't what we were hoping for...'

'Well, we've certainly made an impression on the neighbours. I can feel the glances in the high street.'

They could see lights still on in some of the houses in Thimble Lane, and Ellie wondered what the residents of Bramhurst made of having their quiet village turned into an archaeological dig.

After all the activity of the day, it was eerily quiet.

'Right,' Dave said, pulling out his keys, 'let me just move all the work stuff so we can get the bed sorted. Won't take a minute.'

Ellie groaned. 'Oh, Dave. Haven't you done it?'

He gave her a sheepish look. 'Sorry – was about to and the anthropologist caught me.'

'I'll wait out here with Reeby,' Ellie said, taking his lead from Dave. 'Get some fresh air.'

Dave disappeared into the campervan and started clattering about. As long as there was room to put the bed down, for tonight at least, she didn't care. Her head was ready for the pillow.

Ellie found a relatively comfortable spot to the side of the van and sat down, Rebus settling beside her with a contented sigh.

The evening was clear and cool, but not cold, with stars just beginning to appear above the village. In the distance, she could hear the gentle sound of water running in the ford, and somewhere an owl called from the ancient oak trees. It was peaceful, almost impossibly so given what they'd discovered here.

She pulled out her phone and opened the snap she'd taken of the old photo from Mabel's journal. The young couple on the bridge looked so happy, so full of hope. "*Summer 1950. Remember this day always.*" Was it too much of a stretch to hope it was a photo of Edmund and Violet? And if so, what had happened to destroy that happiness?

Her mind wandered to the day's revelations. Elizabeth's investigations. Mabel's friend in the care home. Edmund's sister. The fresh soil.

Then there were the irreplaceable church records which had vanished, along with their collector.

But something else was bothering her, something that had been nagging at the back of her mind all evening.

They'd been quick to cast Judge Hollinghurst as the villain of the piece. Powerful man, harsh temper, family reputation to protect. It all fitted the narrative of an authoritarian, aristocratic father disposing of his son's inconvenient romance.

But what if they had it wrong?

What if someone had wanted it to *look* like the judge was responsible?

Ellie sat up straighter, her mind racing. The timing mattered – and so did the truth. When exactly had the body been buried in the flowerbed? Had someone murdered Violet and hidden her body?

Alternatively – what if the burial had happened much later? What if someone had killed Violet elsewhere and then moved her body to the chapel grounds specifically to implicate the Hollinghurst family?

The recent soil disturbance Penny had detected – had someone moved a body to the chapel in the last few weeks?

'All sorted.' Dave's voice came from the campervan doorway.

She stood up, brushing dust from her jeans, and joined him in the campervan, her mind still spinning with possibilities. 'Dave, can I ask you something about the investigation?'

'You know I can't–'

'Not specifics. Just... timing. Is there any way to tell when the remains were actually buried here? I mean, not when the person died, but when they were put in this specific location?'

Dave looked at her carefully. 'That's an interesting question. Why do you ask?'

'Just something that occurred to me.'

'Well, soil analysis can sometimes help with that. Dating layers, looking at root growth patterns, that sort of thing.' He held the van door open for her. 'But I can't discuss the details with you.'

'I know. I was just curious.'

The campervan's interior looked much more civilised now that Dave had cleared away his work materials. The bed had been pulled out from the wall, and he'd even managed to make it up with their own sheets and pillows. It looked almost cosy – if you ignored the fact that it was parked in the middle of a crime scene.

'Home sweet home,' Dave said with forced cheerfulness. 'Let's get a good night's sleep. We've got a big day here tomorrow.'

Rebus immediately jumped onto the bed and settled himself squarely in the middle, taking up most of the available space.

'Rebus, down,' Ellie said half-heartedly, but the dog just wagged his tail and made himself more comfortable.

'He's had a stressful morning, the rascal, digging up bones,' Dave said, folding back the duvet and squeezing under it, beside the dog. 'I think we can make an exception... As long as he's not on *my* side.'

Ellie gave him a playful slap and climbed in on the other side, and for a few minutes they lay there in contented silence, listening to the sounds of the village settling into night. Despite everything – the cramped conditions, the ongoing investigation, the uncertainty about their future living arrangements – there was something nice about being close together like this.

'I'm afraid I have something to confess,' said Ellie.

'Oh no. What?'

She told him about asking the farmer if she could put the campervan in his field. 'So, I'm really sorry. You'll need to get a Portacabin tomorrow to use as your office.'

'Fair enough,' he said begrudgingly.

'Thank you. What time are the teams arriving tomorrow?'

'9am kick-off,' Dave replied, his voice already drowsy.

'When this is all over,' Ellie said quietly, 'and we can actually live in the chapel properly, it's going to be worth it.'

'Absolutely. Beautiful house, lovely village, interesting neighbours. What more could we want?'

'A slightly less dramatic introduction to the community?'

'Where's the fun in that?'

Within minutes, Dave's breathing had deepened into sleep, and Rebus was snoring softly between them. Ellie lay awake for a while longer, staring at the small window above their heads and thinking about the day's events.

Eventually, exhaustion won out, and she drifted off to sleep.

She woke sometime later to the sound of Dave's voice.

'What the heck is that?' He swatted at something on his neck.

A whining sound reverberated in the small space.

Then something crawled on her face. She brushed at her cheek. Something buzzed near her ear – a high, thin sound that made her skin crawl. 'Mosquitoes. That's what they are.'

She sat up and switched on the lamp as another one buzzed around her head.

All of a sudden, the high-pitched whining sound multiplied. In the dim light filtering through the windows, Ellie could see small dark shapes flying erratically around the van's interior.

'Oh, for crying out loud,' Dave said, fully awake now and rubbing his neck.

'Where are they coming from?' asked Ellie.

Rebus, disturbed by their movements, stood up and began snapping at the air, his tail wagging as if this were a wonderful new game.

'Did you leave a window open?' Ellie asked, slapping at her arm where she felt a sharp pinch.

'Yeah. I thought we'd be roasting.' Dave was fumbling for his shoes. 'Two of us in here and the dog panting.'

The light revealed a scene of chaos. Dozens of mosquitoes filled the small space, attracted by their warmth and the carbon dioxide from their breathing. Rebus was leaping around, trying to catch them in his mouth, while Dave and Ellie swatted frantically at the air.

'This is ridiculous,' Ellie said, pulling the sheet over her head. 'Where did they all come from?'

'I'd guess – the water in the village,' Dave suggested, closing the window he'd left open. 'The ford. It's still mild in the daytime, and there are lots of streams running alongside the lanes…' He grabbed a newspaper and began methodically hunting mosquitoes.

For the next twenty minutes, they waged war against the tiny invaders, armed with tea towels, a rolled-up magazine, and Rebus' enthusiastic but largely ineffective assistance. By the time they'd eliminated the last one, they were both covered in bites and wide awake.

'Well,' Dave said, surveying the carnage of dead insects and dishevelled bedding, 'this is definitely not how I expected the evening to end. Don't suppose you've got any anti-histamine cream?'

'Yeah. In my wash bag in the chapel.' Ellie scratched a bite on her elbow. 'Shall we sneak inside? Forget we're not meant to be in there and get on our mattress?'

'Can't, Ells. I'm the SIO. I'd get a disciplinary for that.' Dave switched off the light, and they settled back into bed, Rebus once again claiming the spot in the middle, oblivious of the mayhem.

'I was just thinking…' Ellie said into the darkness.

'If you're about to tell me there are more mosquitoes, I don't want to hear it.'

'About fresh starts and how nothing ever goes according to plan…'

'And? Are you having second thoughts already?'

Here they were, squeezed into a campervan with a dog, parked next to an active crime scene, covered in mosquito bites and probably destined for several more nights of similar discomfort.

'No,' she said firmly. 'But I am wondering if we've made a mistake, buying this place. Perhaps we should've gone for a nice bungalow in a quiet cul-de-sac...'

'Very funny. Anyway – it's too late now.'

Next time we move house, we definitely should not buy at auction, she thought. Then, as she finally drifted off to sleep: *hopefully there won't be a next time*.

Outside, the village of Bramhurst slept peacefully under the stars, keeping its ancient secrets safe for one more night.

Chapter 16
TUESDAY

Ellie woke to the sound of rain pattering on the campervan roof and an empty space where Dave should have been. She could hear Rebus whining softly from his position at the foot of the bed. When she checked her phone, it was barely seven in the morning.

'Come on then, boy,' she whispered. 'Let's get you sorted.'

She pulled on jeans and a waterproof jacket, clipped Rebus' lead firmly to his collar – the last thing they needed was him discovering more buried remains – and stepped out into the drizzly morning.

The chapel grounds looked different in the grey dawn light. The white tents were dark with rain, and the archaeological grids had turned into small pools of muddy water. It was hard to believe that, only a day ago, this had been their dream renovation project.

She found Dave sitting in his car, speaking on his phone and looking like he'd been up for hours.

'Right, yes, I understand that, Penny,' he was saying as she approached. 'We need an ID. Any chance we can get the DNA fast-tracked?' He saw Ellie and held up a finger, indicating he'd be finished soon.

Rebus did his business efficiently, clearly as eager as Ellie to get back into the warm, dry van. They waited under the eaves of the chapel porch until Dave finished his call.

'Morning,' he said, getting out of the car and giving her a quick kiss. 'Sorry I wasn't there when you woke up. Early start.' His cheeks were creased, and his eyes were small. Ellie couldn't help wondering if he'd vacated the campervan and slept in his car.

'I gathered. Everything all right?'

'Just trying to speed things up.' Dave rubbed his face tiredly. 'So far, everyone's coming this morning to check the excavations. No-one's cancelled.'

'Thank goodness for that.'

'I'm going to head to the station for a shower and some breakfast that doesn't come from a packet.' He looked apologetically at the campervan. 'This won't go on much longer, Ells. I promise.'

‘I hope not. And don’t forget the Portacabin.’

After Dave left, Ellie was settling down with a cup of coffee and her phone when Zoe called.

‘Mum? I’ve got news.’

‘About Elizabeth?’

‘Yes. I think we should go there today. Like, *this morning.*’

‘What’s the urgency?’ She told Zoe about the teams arriving.

‘I’ve been doing more digging into her background. Academic papers, university records, that sort of thing. Found something interesting in her PhD thesis from five years ago.’

Ellie waited.

‘Her thesis was on *“Lost Voices: Investigating the Role of Women’s Labour in Rural Post-war England.”* And in the acknowledgments, she thanks her family for their support, particularly in sharing “painful family history” that inspired her research.’

‘Family history?’

‘Exactly. I’m wondering if Elizabeth’s research into women’s labour isn’t just academic ... but personal.’

Chapter 17

Ellie was attempting to make another coffee on the campervan's temperamental gas ring when a cheerful voice called out, 'Hello? Anyone home? Well, I say "home"...'

She peered through the tiny window to see a petite woman standing outside, wearing shorts and a hoodie, wielding a squeegee like a baton. A van parked behind her proclaimed 'Kersey's Windows – we'll make them crystal clear' in enthusiastic purple lettering.

'Sorry, just a minute,' Ellie called, abandoning the coffee and stepping out into the morning sunshine. Rebus immediately bounded over to investigate the newcomer, tail wagging furiously.

'Oh, what a lovely boy.' The woman bent to fuss over Rebus, who was already presenting his belly for rubs. 'I'm Belinda Kersey, Belle to my friends. I'm the village window cleaner, and I always offer new residents a free window-clean as a welcome gift.' She straightened up and looked from the campervan to the chapel with its ancient, mostly broken windows, then back to Ellie. A grin spread across her face.

'Although I'm now realising this might be the first time my welcome offer is completely useless.'

Ellie burst out laughing. 'I was just about to say… the campervan windows are about the size of postage stamps, and the chapel… well…'

They both turned to look at the gothic windows, several of which were boarded up, while others featured more gaps than glass.

'I could give those a go,' Belle said with mock seriousness, 'but I reckon more water would end up inside than out. Might improve the damp situation though – give it a good flush through.'

'Oh crikey, don't mention the damp,' Ellie groaned. 'We've just discovered it's so bad the render won't stick to the walls.'

'Sounds about right for a building that age. My husband's the local chimney sweep – you should see some of the medieval disasters he's dealt with. Chimneys that haven't been swept since the actual Middle Ages, birds' nests the size of Smart cars.' Belle paused. A furtive blush spread over her. 'I'm also being a bit nosy, if I'm honest. The whole village is talking about you finding those bones. Thought I'd come and see if you needed anything. Proper help, I mean, not useless window cleaning.'

Ellie felt a wave of warmth towards this straightforward woman. 'That's really kind. I'm Ellie, by the way. Would you like a coffee? Fair warning. I'm making it on a camping stove that requires an engineering degree to operate.'

'Love one. And don't worry, I'm a dab hand with temperamental gas rings. The hubby and I are campers.'

Five minutes later, Belle had somehow coaxed two decent cups of coffee from the rebellious equipment and they were sitting on camping chairs outside the van, surveying the archaeological chaos of the garden.

'You weren't kidding about the bones then,' Belle said, nodding towards the white tent. 'Human?'

'Unfortunately, yes. Young woman, we think.'

Belle gave a low whistle. 'No wonder the gossips have got going. Daphne Henderson at the shop will be in her element. She'll have convened her Neighbourhood Watch team and solved it by lunchtime.'

Ellie snorted. 'I've heard about Daphne. She seems... thorough in her information gathering.'

'That's diplomatic. She once tried to steam open my post because she was convinced I was having an affair. I wasn't – I was ordering a birthday present for my husband online. But she'd seen parcels arriving when he was at work and drew her own conclusions.'

'What did you do?'

'Started having everything delivered to her shop for collection. Drove her mad not knowing what was in them.' Belle's eyes twinkled with mischief. 'The kicker was when I ordered a fireman's calendar – you know, hunky men with strategically placed hoses. She nearly combusted with curiosity.'

Ellie was properly laughing now. 'That's brilliant.'

'You know her son's the true crime chap, don't you? Rory.'

'Yes, found that out yesterday. That explains the super-speedy village grapevine. He was in the field behind the chapel very quickly, broadcasting live on TikTok. Daphne told my mother-in-law about the police vehicles, so she must have alerted Rory too.'

'Undoubtedly. And the rest of the village.' Belle stretched out her legs, careful not to disturb Rebus. 'Thirty-seven years I've lived in this village. Born here, raised here, briefly escaped to Brighton for a wild youth, then came back and married a man who spends his days covered in soot. Living the dream.'

Ellie smiled. 'Do you like village life?'

'It's like living in a soap opera where everyone knows your lines before you do. But yeah, I love it. Where else would someone nearly run you off the road in a flash BMW, then twenty minutes later you see them skulking around the chapel like they're casing the joint?'

Ellie sat up straighter. 'Silver BMW?'

'That's the one. Total muppet. Sunglasses so dark I'm surprised he could see anything. Came racing round the bend by the ford, had to swerve into the hedge to avoid him. My van's got scratches all down one side now.' Belle seemed to notice Ellie's expression. 'You've seen him too?'

'Yes. He seems very interested in the chapel. Or us. Or something.'

'Well, if you need backup, just shout. My husband's built like a rugby player – occupational hazard of hauling ladders around all day. Speaking of which, if you ever need to borrow any – ladders, not husbands – just ask. We've got enough to reach the moon. Comes in handy for a place like this.'

She gestured at the chapel's tall walls and unreachable windows.

'Very kind. Thank you,' Ellie said, genuinely touched. 'I feel like we're going to need all the help we can get.'

'That's what villages are for, isn't it? Everyone knowing your business but also bringing casseroles when things go wrong.' Belle stood up, brushing dust from her shorts. 'Actually, someone else nearly bought the chapel about six months ago.' She paused by her van door. 'All very hush-hush it was. The estate agent wouldn't say who, just that it was a "private buyer with specific requirements". Then suddenly the whole thing fell through, no explanation, and it went to auction instead. Daphne nearly drove herself mad trying to find out who it was, but even she couldn't crack that mystery.'

'I wonder who it was? And why they didn't go through with it.' Ellie was trying to think who might know. Gideon, perhaps?

Belle shrugged. 'Right, I'd better get on. Mrs Fortescue in the dry cleaners gets upset if her windows aren't done by ten. She's convinced dirty windows affect her psychic abilities.'

'She's psychic?'

'She's *something*.' Belle snorted. 'Personally, I wonder if she drinks the dry-cleaning chemicals. Last week she predicted I'd come into money. I found a pound coin down the back of the sofa, so maybe she's onto something.' Belle grinned. 'Though I notice she didn't predict you'd find human remains in your garden, so her range might be limited.'

As Belle headed back to her van, she turned. 'I mean it about the help. This village can be a bit overwhelming at first – everyone having opinions about everything you do. But most of them mean well. And the ones that don't? Well, that's what friends are for. To tell you who to avoid.'

'I think we're going to get on well,' Ellie said impulsively.

'I should hope so,' Belle replied. 'I've just made you coffee and offered you my husband's ladders.' She climbed into her van, then leaned out the window. 'Oh, and when you do get proper windows in that chapel, I'll clean them for free. Might take me a year to do them all, mind you, but I'm nothing if not persistent.'

Ellie smiled, delighted to have met her.

'Oh, before I forget,' Belle called out, 'this weekend's the harvest festival barn dance at the farm. Saturday night. It's the big event of autumn.'

'Thanks. Reverend Jo mentioned it.'

'Everyone goes, even the people who claim they can't dance. There's a proper ceilidh band coming from Canterbury, and Terry at the pub always does the bar.' She grinned. 'You and the dancing detective should come.'

Ellie frowned. Was Belle referring to Dave's Morris dancing? How did she know about that?

She winked. 'Little birdy told me. Someone from the same side. Going back to the barn dance – it's the best way to meet everyone when they're relaxed and slightly tipsy on Terry's punch. Plus, watching Paul from the bakery's attempt at Strip the Willow is worth the ticket price alone.'

As the van pulled away, revealing a bumper sticker that read 'Honk if you love clean windows', Ellie found herself grinning again, despite everything. Between the bones, the damp, and the mysterious BMW driver, she'd been feeling overwhelmed. But Belle's visit reminded her that village life had compensations.

Rebus barked approvingly, as if reading her thoughts, then promptly went to investigate something in the hedge.

'At least one of us has settled in,' Ellie muttered, digging out her keys so she could move the campervan into the farmer's field before Dave changed his mind.

She had a feeling she was going to need more coffee to get through whatever today would bring.

Chapter 18

Once the campervan was safely installed in the neighbouring field, Ellie and Zoe set off for Whitstable, leaving Reeby having a snooze on the bed. It was a short journey, and they were soon driving past the harbour. The sea air was distinctly briny, and seagulls squawked as they swooped overhead. Workmen were stocking their stalls with fresh oysters and whelks.

Leaving the colourful beach huts behind, Ellie turned into the narrow back streets. Elizabeth Merrin's address turned out to be a small, terraced house two roads back from the seafront, with a white front door, terracotta window boxes full of pink and mauve cyclamen and a potted olive tree in the front garden.

'Her car's here,' Zoe observed, pointing to a little green Peugeot parked outside. 'I recognise it from Facebook.'

'Right then,' Ellie said, checking her reflection in the wing mirror. 'Let's see if she's ready to tell us what she knows.'

The woman who answered the door was younger than Ellie had expected, probably mid-thirties, with chestnut hair pulled back in a ponytail and intelligent brown eyes that had a worried expression. She was wearing jogging bottoms and a university sweatshirt.

'Dr Merrin?' Ellie said. 'I'm Ellie Blix, and this is my daughter Zoe. We were hoping we could talk to you about your research.'

Elizabeth's face went pale, and she seemed to freeze. 'How did you find me?'

'The electoral register,' Zoe said gently.

Elizabeth frowned.

'We're private investigators,' Ellie added quickly. 'We're not here to cause trouble. My husband and I have bought Bramhurst Chapel. We just want to understand what's been happening there.'

'You've seen the news, I take it?' said Zoe.

Elizabeth nodded. For a moment, she looked as if she was deciding between bolting and closing the door on them.

'Can you tell us what you know about Violet?' said Zoe quickly, before she did. 'Violet Chapman.'

Elizabeth's shoulders sagged slightly, and she stepped back. 'You'd better come in,' she said quietly. 'I knew when the chapel went up for auction, it was only a matter of time.'

Ellie wanted to ask, 'before what?' but instinct told her to let Ellizabeth relax. Hopefully she'd tell them everything.

The interior of the house was cosy. Books and newspapers were scattered across a dining table at one end of an open plan room, and the smell of toast lingered, making Ellie hungry.

Elizabeth gestured for them to sit on a worn sofa at the other end while she perched nervously on the edge of an armchair. 'You're investigating the remains found at Bramhurst Chapel,' she said.

It wasn't a question.

'Only informally,' Ellie said carefully, then explaining Dave was a detective. 'We understand you've been researching women's labour.'

'For quite some time, yes.'

'And that you collected historical records from St Mildred's Church just before you went on leave.'

Elizabeth's hands twisted in her lap. 'I had to. I couldn't risk them disappearing or being destroyed.'

'Destroyed?' asked Zoe. 'Who by?'

Elizabeth was quiet for a long moment, staring at her hands. When she looked up, her eyes were glassy with tears. 'By whoever doesn't want the truth to come out.'

Ellie waited.

'My grandfather was Tommy Chapman,' she said with quiet emotion. 'Violet was my great-aunt.'

The words hung in the air like a confession.

Ellie felt pieces clicking into place in her mind: the personal motivation, the detailed research, the urgency of collecting evidence.

'You've been trying to find out what happened to her,' Zoe said gently.

'All my adult life. Even more than that – from when I learnt of her disappearance.' Elizabeth's voice was barely above a whisper. 'My grandfather never got over what happened in Bramhurst. He went back to London alone and was... broken. Used to have nightmares. Would wake up screaming about things he'd seen and heard.'

'We're extremely sorry. Did he ever say what those things were?'

'Not directly. But he and his wife believed Violet never ran away. They thought she was dead, and that powerful people had killed her.' Elizabeth wiped her eyes with the back of her hand. 'Of course, no one believed him.' She gave a cynical laugh. 'A working-class boy from the East

End, making accusations against a high court judge? It was unthinkable.'

'But you believed him?'

'I grew up with the stories. Tommy would come and visit when I was little. He eventually married but never got over Violet's death. He died three years ago.'

'Really sorry.'

'He used to tell me about Violet, about how clever and kind she was, how she deserved better than what happened to her.' Elizabeth stood up abruptly and walked to the window. 'When I became an academic, I decided to investigate properly. To find evidence that would prove Tommy had been telling the truth.'

'And you found that evidence?'

'Oh, yes. Enough to know that Violet was made to disappear.'

She turned back to them. 'I was so close to having everything I needed to go public with the story. Had a journalist at *The Observer* ready to write a piece.'

'*Was?*' Ellie asked.

Elizabeth walked to a desk in the corner and picked up a piece of paper. Her hands were shaking as she handed it to Ellie.

It was a typed note, printed on plain white paper, with no identifying marks:

"Dr Merrin,

Violet Chapman met her end five-and-seventy summers past, and there's nowt to be gained from rooting through her shadow. Folk here have long memories. If you don't drop this meddlin o yours, you'll be joining her in the chalk. Barrel ash don't lie."

Ellie felt a chill run down her spine. She fixed her gaze on Elizabeth. 'When did you receive this?'

'Two weeks ago.' Elizabeth's voice was barely steady. 'It was left in the letterbox flap when I was out.'

'That's why you've been hiding...'

'Yes. I went over St Mildred's, collected the records from the vicar, went on leave, and I've hung onto them while I've been trying to decide what to do.'

'I gather you asked Gideon if he would collect Mabel's journals from Terry for you. What happened there? Why didn't you ask for them yourself?'

'Oh, I felt more comfortable asking the vicar as I'd corresponded with her. I knew she respected my academic credentials...'

That had been true.

'Whereas I was worried the Hobbs might think I was being a busybody.'

'And *were* you in Pembrokeshire?'

'That was a fib, I'm afraid. I hoped it would make Gideon more likely to help me if he thought I was a long way away.'

Ellie nodded.

'Well, the police will need to see the church records. We'll take them with us. And the note – it's such a weird way to write, in dialect.'

Elizabeth shrugged. 'I've already shown them the note. They weren't particularly interested. Couldn't get any prints. No CCTV outside.' She looked between them desperately. 'They might not have been concerned, but I am. Don't you see? Someone knows I've been investigating. Someone who's still alive, is still protecting the secret of what happened to Violet.'

'It's not just that,' said Ellie. '"*You'll be joining her in the chalk.*" Whoever sent this knows Violet was buried in the ground – either at our chapel or somewhere else.' Thoughts clicked into place.

Elizabeth's eyes welled up with tears. 'I know.'

'I didn't see a doorbell camera...?'

She shook her head. 'I don't have one. I've ordered one, though.'

'Do any of your neighbours?'

'No. The kids round here vandalise them. It's why I haven't bothered before.'

Zoe leaned forward. 'Elizabeth, you can't let them intimidate you. If you've got evidence of what happened to Violet–'

'I know, but it was seventy-five years ago...' Elizabeth shook her head.

'Well, someone alive today is willing to kill to keep whatever happened secret,' said Zoe. 'That means the story isn't finished. It means there's something contemporary about this, something that threatens – or bothers – someone still living.'

Ellie thought about the recent soil disturbance; about Elizabeth's research beginning months before the discovery; about her systematic collection of evidence.

'Do you think someone moved Violet's body to the chapel grounds?' she asked carefully. 'Recently, I mean. To make it look like the Hollinghursts were responsible?'

Elizabeth stared at her. 'What makes you ask that?'

'Something about the timing. About how convenient it was that the body was found just as you were getting close to the truth.'

'I...' Elizabeth sat down heavily. 'I hadn't thought of that. But it would make sense, wouldn't it? If someone wanted to pin the blame on a family member that's been dead for decades, make sure the real culprit was never discovered.'

'The question is,' Zoe said thoughtfully, 'who benefits from that? And who's still alive to send threatening notes?'

Silence lay between the three women for a few minutes.

It was time to leave.

'Could we get the church records, please, for the police?'

Five minutes later, they left Elizabeth's house with the box of notebooks and made their way back to the jeep.

Outside, the seagulls' cries echoed like lost memories on the wind.

As they walked, Ellie realised they were no longer just investigating a historical mystery. They were dealing with someone who was very much alive, determined... and who might be dangerous.

Her phone pinged with a message from Dave.

Are you about? The chief archaeologist wants to speak to us at 10.30am.

Chapter 19

Before the meeting with the archaeologist, Ellie made a quick dash to the rectory at St Mildred's with the church's records.

Bramhurst's rectory was a comfortable Victorian house with worn Persian rugs, leather sofas, and mirrors.

Jo led her into a cosy sitting room where sunlight streamed through floor-to-ceiling windows.

'I'm so grateful to you for getting these back,' Jo said, as she took the box of files from Ellie and placed it on a sideboard in the lounge. She settled on one of the sofas. 'When Elizabeth disappeared with everything, I thought we'd lost Reverend Matthews' records forever.'

'She's convinced someone is after them,' Ellie replied, 'and could potentially destroy them.'

'Oh, goodness.'

Ellie told Jo about the threatening note.

'Ah, I can see now why she was worried.'

She explained that the police needed to see Reverend Matthews' records. 'Is it OK for me to take them with me and hand them over?'

'Of course.'

'They've got Mabel's journals now. She and Reverend Matthews are contemporaneous witnesses, and saw first-hand what was going on at Bramhurst Manor and Farm. Hopefully, they'll be useful.'

'Absolutely. I'm curious about what he recorded. Shall we have a quick look before you take them?'

Ellie smiled.

Jo opened the first notebook carefully, a substantial volume bound in brown leather with 'Parish Records 1950' embossed in faded gold lettering. 'These are his *official* records,' she explained. 'Births, deaths, marriages, that sort of thing. All the formal church business.'

They spent ten minutes flicking through the entries, which painted a picture of a busy rural parish serving both the established village community and the seasonal workers who arrived each summer. Matthews had recorded everything meticulously: marriage banns for young couples, baptisms for babies born during the harvest season, funeral services for elderly villagers, and confirmations for teenagers ready to commit to their faith.

'He was clearly very thorough,' Ellie observed, noting the careful handwriting and detailed descriptions of each ceremony.

'But look at this,' Jo said, reaching for a second notebook. Smaller, less formal, bound in simple black cloth. 'This is his personal journal. Where he recorded... well, everything else.'

The contrast was immediately apparent. Where the official records were formal and structured, the personal journal revealed a man deeply troubled by what he was witnessing in his parish. The entries were more emotional, more immediate, written in the same careful hand but with an urgency that spoke of real concern.

'Listen to this,' Jo said, finding an entry dated July 15th, 1950.

'"Mrs Fletcher came to me again today regarding the wages owed to her daughter, Annie. The girl has worked three weeks at Bramhurst Farm but has received only half the promised payment. When she complained, she was told the rest would be docked for 'accommodation and meals,' though the accommodation is little better than a barn and the meals are bread and dripping twice daily."'

'Wage disputes,' Ellie said grimly. 'Taking advantage of people who had no recourse.'

Jo turned several pages and read:

'"July 22nd: 'Found young Tom Harrison sleeping rough behind the church again. Says he was dismissed from the farm for 'insolence' after questioning why the workers were locked in their quarters at night. Gave him shelter in the vestry and what food I could spare.'"'

'Locked in their quarters?' Ellie shivered. 'That's not employment, that's imprisonment.'

The journal entries painted an increasingly worrying picture. Matthews had recorded thefts from seasonal workers, their few possessions stolen while they slept, their wages mysteriously reduced or withheld entirely. But more troubling were his observations about injuries.

'August 3rd, 1949,' Jo read aloud. '*"Simon Williams attended morning service with visible bruising to his arms and face. When I approached him after the service, he became frightened and insisted he'd fallen. His friend Angus whispered that Simon had been beaten by the farmer for eating an egg."'*

'He was documenting neglect and abuse,' Ellie said quietly.

Jo turned to an entry a year later, dated August 10th. '*"The workers gathered at the church gates this morning, carrying wild flowers and singing that hymn they love, 'Abide with Me.' They were mourning young Tilly Moore, who they say got consumption and passed away. They left the flowers at St Mildred's shrine and asked me to say a prayer for her.'''*

Tears pricked in Ellie's eyes. 'They held a memorial service for their friend.'

'Here's another one the following year,' Jo said softly, turning to September entries.

'''*September 15th, 1951: Another protest at the gates today. The workers are demanding to know what happened to their friend who failed to turn up for work the past month. They speak of 'Lookingbane Hall' with such fear in their voices. I have asked around the village, but no one will tell me what this means.'''*

'Lookingbane Hall,' Ellie repeated. 'What's that? What a strange name.'

Jo shrugged. She continued reading.

'''*September 20th, 1950: Request for food from the Harrison family. Five children and the father out of work after questioning conditions at the farm. Gave them what I could from the rectory pantry.'''*

The journal was filled with similar entries: requests for temporary shelter, for food and clothing, for shoes for children whose families couldn't afford proper footwear. But threaded through these practical concerns were Matthews' prayers and reflections on the plight of the seasonal workers.

'"*September 1st ,1948*,"' Jo read, her voice growing emotional. '"*I have prayed again for the souls of those who were injured on the farm these last six months. Jenny Suggs, Danny Porter, and little Sid Baxter who was no more than fourteen. Their friends speak their names with love and sorrow. Lord, grant them peace, and grant us the strength to protect those who remain.*"'

'Awful,' said Ellie. 'I know times were different but...'

'And look at this entry from November,' Jo said, turning towards the back of the journal. '"*Great relief in the parish today. Arthur Brown and his new wife Mabel (née Pritchard) have been appointed as live-in housekeepers at Bramhurst Manor. Mrs Hollinghurst insists on having married couple supervision of all household staff and visiting workers. Perhaps now the vulnerable will have some protection.*"

'Mabel and her husband moved into the manor? I didn't know her husband even worked there.' Ellie felt a surge of hope. 'That must have made a difference.'

'It seems to have,' Jo confirmed, reading the next entry. '"*December 15th: Mabel reports that conditions at the manor have improved considerably since she and Arthur took up residence.*"'

They sat in thoughtful silence for a moment, absorbing the implications of what they'd read.

'So, the mistreatment stopped when Mabel moved in,' Ellie said finally, her hand on her chest. 'Thank goodness.'

'Which suggests Mrs Hollinghurst either didn't know what was happening,' said Jo, 'or didn't have the power to stop it until she had allies in the household.'

'And it explains why Mabel's diaries from 1950 were so detailed about the family dynamics,' Ellie added. 'She was observing everything because she knew how dangerous the situation could be for vulnerable workers.'

'But it still doesn't tell us exactly *who* was responsible for Violet's death,' Ellie said. 'Though it's becoming clearer that it wasn't necessarily the judge himself.'

Jo turned back to one of Matthews' earlier entries. 'Look at this again. The reference to "Lookingbane Hall". *Lookingbane.* The workers were afraid of the place itself, not necessarily just one person. It suggests the whole establishment had a reputation for exploiting vulnerable people.'

'A reputation that continued until Mabel and her husband moved in and Mrs Hollinghurst finally had the support she needed to change things,' Ellie concluded.

As they prepared to close the journals, Jo paused at one final entry by Reverend Matthews that made them both catch their breath.

'"January 1951,"' she read. '"*I have learned the meaning of 'Lookingbane Hall.' The workers use this name because they say those there who are wicked, watch and wait for the weak and the alone. They speak of it as if the very stones are predatory. God help us all if such treachery has taken root in our parish, and God grant that it dies with this generation.*"'

'Evil that dies with this generation,' Ellie repeated thoughtfully. 'But what if it didn't die? What if it just... changed hands?'

Chapter 20

Ellie stuffed Reverend Matthews' church records in the jeep to give to Dave and zoomed back to the chapel with a minute to spare.

Dave was on their improvised bench – a plank balanced between two crates – watching the archaeological excavation of their new garden with a mixture of fascination and frustration. The morning was crisp and bright, perfect for outdoor work, though not exactly *this* sort of work.

Ellie joined him.

'It's like watching paint dry,' Dave muttered, taking a sip from a polystyrene cup. 'Except paint drying would probably be faster.'

The archaeologists worked with painstaking precision. Every few minutes, work would stop entirely while someone photographed a particular area, made detailed notes, or carefully bagged what looked to Ellie like nothing more than dirt or a tiny stone.

'Look at that,' she said, pointing to where a young archaeologist was using what appeared to be a paintbrush to clean a small section of soil.

'She's been working on that same patch for over an hour,' Dave said. 'Method in the madness, though. If they miss something or contaminate the evidence, we'll never get proper answers about what happened here.'

The main excavation site was now a complex arrangement of white tents, measurement grids and carefully labelled sections. Archaeological tools were arranged with military precision on folding tables. Trowels, brushes, measuring tapes and cameras.

Dr Charlotte Greaves, the lead archaeologist, moved between the various excavation points with the confident authority of someone who'd spent decades coaxing secrets from the earth. She wore practical field clothes, boots, a hard hat and a high-vis top.

'At least they're thorough,' Ellie observed, watching Charlotte crouch down to examine something that was invisible to the untrained eye. 'Though I'm beginning to understand why archaeological projects take years rather than weeks.'

'Speaking of which,' Dave said, checking the calendar on his phone, 'we still don't know how much longer this is going to take. I keep asking whether we're talking days or weeks and the answer is always, "we don't know yet," which isn't particularly helpful for planning purposes. Hopefully she's about to tell us.'

Rebus, who had initially shown great interest in all the digging, had long since become bored and was now sleeping peacefully in a patch of sunshine, occasionally opening one eye to check whether a walk was imminent, treats might be emerging, or his humans had wandered off.

Ellie and Dave watched as one of the team members carefully sieved soil through a fine mesh, separating out anything that might be significant. Another archaeologist was taking soil samples and sealing them in labelled containers.

'Look,' said Ellie. 'She's measuring the exact position of that tiny piece of... what is that? Metal?'

'Probably a button or a buckle,' Dave said. 'Could be from the 1950s, could be from last week. But they'll analyse it anyway, just in case.'

Charlotte had been working at the far end of the site for most of the morning, directing the careful removal of soil from an area that had been marked with particularly dense flagging. Ellie had noticed increased activity around that section, with several team members taking photographs and making detailed sketches.

As if sensing their attention, Charlotte straightened up and walked over to where they were sitting.

'Sorry to keep you waiting. How are you holding up?' she asked, settling onto another crate. 'I know this is rather more disruption than you bargained for when you bought the place.'

'We're managing,' Ellie said diplomatically. 'Any sense of how much longer this might take?'

Charlotte's expression became more serious. 'Well, that's what I wanted to talk to you about, actually. We're going to need to extend the excavation area.'

Dave set down his coffee cup. 'How much of an extension are we talking about?'

'Another section towards the eastern boundary of the property. We've found traces of additional remains.'

Ellie's heart sank. 'More bodies?'

'Fragments, at this stage. Bone material that Penny's examined and confirmed as human, but...' she eyed them both with seriousness, 'from a different individual than the first remains.'

'Oh?' Dave's professional interest was immediately engaged.

'Penny's still analysing the fragments, but they're definitely from another person. Whether they're related, we don't know yet.'

'So, we're looking at multiple people?' Ellie asked.

'Possibly.'

Ellie stifled a gasp.

'We know a little of the history here,' Charlotte continued. 'It could be Edmund Hollinghurst. We don't know if he died at the same time as Violet.'

'It won't be Tommy, Violet's brother,' Ellie told her.

Dave's eyebrows shot up.

'We've just been talking to... er... a relative of his, and he survived,' she continued, aware of Dave's stare on her. 'Died three years ago.'

'*Ellie.* You promised–'

'I know. I was coming to tell you all about it. I've just been to collect evidence to give you,' she said. 'It's in the jeep boot.' She paused, letting Dave absorb the information. 'Actually, there's more I need to tell you.' She was thinking of the threatening note. The police had seen it apparently, but that didn't mean Dave had.

Dave groaned and returned his attention to Charlotte. 'What else can you tell us?' He was making notes in his phone.

'The fragments are small and scattered. The soil patterns we mentioned suggest significant disturbance in that area. It's possible someone has been digging there relatively recently. Within the last few weeks, possibly even more recently than that.'

'Do you mean someone's been moving bodies around?' Dave's voice had taken on the sharp edge it acquired when he was processing serious information.

'We don't have evidence of that yet, but it is possible. The soil stratification is all wrong for an undisturbed burial site. There are layers mixed up that shouldn't be mixed up, and the bone fragments are scattered in a pattern that suggests they've been... redistributed.'

Dave pulled his fingers through his hair. 'Good grief. This keeps getting worse.'

Ellie was shaking her head. 'So, someone might have moved remains from somewhere else and buried them in our garden?'

'Or,' Charlotte said grimly, 'someone removed remains that were originally buried here and relocated them somewhere else. Which raises the obvious questions...'

'Who, why and where to?' Dave finished.

They sat in contemplative silence for a moment, watching the archaeologists continue their meticulous work.

'So,' Ellie said finally, 'instead of having our garden back in a few days, we're looking at...?'

'A couple more days after that,' Charlotte said apologetically. 'We need to map the entire disturbance pattern, excavate the extended area, and try to understand what's been moved and when. Plus, if we find evidence of recent activity, that becomes part of DCI Blix's investigation.'

'Which means even more specialists, even more time, and even less chance of us completing the work on the chapel this year,' Ellie said with resignation.

Charlotte looked genuinely sympathetic. 'I know it's frustrating. But if someone has been using your property to hide evidence – whether historical or contemporary – we need to understand the full scope of what's happened.'

'And,' Dave added grimly, 'we need to find out who's been moving soil around.

Ellie's stomach crunched. She needed to tell Dave what they'd learnt from Elizabeth.

As Charlotte returned to her excavation, Ellie and Dave remained on their makeshift bench, watching their garden slowly reveal its secrets. The archaeological process was fascinating, but the implications of what they were finding were becoming increasingly disturbing.

'You know what the worst part is?' Ellie said eventually.

'The fact that we're going to be living in temporary accommodation probably until Christmas?' said Dave.

'No. The fact that someone's been treating our garden like a... like a body storage facility. Possibly for decades.'

Dave reached over and took her hand. 'Hey. We'll get through this. And when it's over, we'll have the most thoroughly-investigated garden in Kent. Plus, some very unique dinner party stories.'

'That's assuming we ever get to the dinner party stage,' Ellie said. 'At this rate, we'll still be sleeping on a blow-up mattress when we're eighty.'

'Now – about that sleuthing you promised you wouldn't do...' Dave switched into his DCI role.

Ellie knew she had some explaining – and apologising – to do.

'I want to know who you've spoken to and what you've discovered.'

Ellie filled him in on Elizabeth being Violet's great-aunt, about the church records and the threatening note.

'You promised you wouldn't interfere...' He wasn't just annoyed. There was hurt in his eyes.

Ellie shook her head. 'I know. I'm sorry.' She told him about crossing her fingers behind her back. 'Talking about it now, it was childish.'

She paused, gathering her thoughts and frowning. 'It was as though something took over and I'd done it before I thought about it. There seems to be a drive in me that means I cannot stop myself from investigating when something happens to someone who matters to me. The chapel... the young girl, Violet...' Ellie covered her mouth with her hands. She'd hated not being honest with Dave. Hadn't approved of her crossing-her-fingers trick.

Dave rubbed his chin. 'It's really inconvenient for me, especially with this new DCI role... But – I can see that investigating is part of your DNA.'

'I'm sorry.'

He shrugged. 'If I'm, honest, it's part of why I love you. You've got such a big heart. You get much more emotionally involved in these cases than I do.'

'I'm really sorry.'

'You need to promise that you will keep me informed of all your discoveries. Yes?'

Ellie nodded.

'And hand over – promptly – all evidence that comes your way?'

'Yes. In that case – you'd better get Reverend Matthews' records from the boot of my car.'

Chapter 21

Bramhurst Books was quickly becoming one of Ellie's favourite shops in her new village. The Victorian building had high ceilings with cornicing, plenty of adjoining rooms and comfortable furniture. It had the kind of peaceful atmosphere that came from decades of being a place for people to browse, buy and discuss books.

'The coffee morning's sorted for tomorrow,' Ellie told Sylvia as she settled into a comfy armchair in the back room, where they couldn't be overheard. Rebus sat next to her chair, seemingly undecided about who or what he wanted to observe.

'That's good. Leonard is at a diocesan meeting in Canterbury,' Sylvia explained. 'So, I can come along, and don't have to rush back. It'll be more private here than the pub, and certainly more comfortable than your campervan.'

'Yes,' Ellie said. 'I've had to come clean with Dave about us investigating.' She told Sylvia how she'd let the cat out of the bag when they were talking to the archaeologist. 'I'm relieved not to be lying. Quite apart from the morality of it, and the stress – I'm a useless liar.'

Sylvia chuckled. 'I can vouch for that. D'you remember that time, years ago, when I caught you and Dave drinking cider? You tried to tell me it was apple juice.'

They both laughed.

Ellie relayed what she'd agreed to: updating him on developments and handing over evidence.

'Fair enough,' said Sylvia.

While they waited for Zoe to arrive, Ellie pulled out her phone. 'I need to ring the structural engineer about the chapel. Check he's coming tomorrow morning for the sub-floor inspection.'

The engineer picked up after several rings.

'Ah, Mrs Blix,' said Mark Stevens. 'I was going to call you. The situation's become more complicated.'

Ellie braced.

'Although the chapel isn't a listed building, it's historically significant, so I've liaised with a conservation architect about the best way to proceed with our survey.'

'What does that mean for our timeline?'

'Well, the archaeologist will be doing a thorough check of the sub-floor area tomorrow, in case there's been a crypt there. And… in case there are any remains down there…'

'Good grief. I hope not.' She told him no crypt had been mentioned when they bought the property.

'That doesn't mean much I'm afraid. Auction houses are only required to insist on the bare minimum of information on each property. Unfortunately, many people don't bother to obtain a structural survey in case they don't win the auction.'

Ellie groaned.

Obviously, if there's a crypt down there, there may be bodies there legitimately.' Mark paused. 'And given your dog found remains in the flowerbed, it's important to consider whether there are any more.'

'Of course.'

'I'm afraid it could take longer than we first thought.' He sounded genuinely apologetic. 'It's not what you want to hear, I know, but I've asked the conservation architect to accompany me tomorrow, if that's OK. Be on the safe side.'

'Of course.'

They finished their conversation, and after Ellie hung up, she and Sylvia sat in glum silence for a few moments.

'Well,' Sylvia said with determined cheerfulness, 'at least you'll have time to solve the mystery properly before you move in.'

Ellie snort-laughed. 'That's one way of looking at it.'

Zoe arrived five minutes later, carrying her laptop bag and looking flushed and flustered. 'Sorry I'm late. Traffic was dreadful through Canterbury, and I had a fox in the van. Had to drop it off at the rescue centre.'

'No worries,' Sylvia said. 'We were just discussing the latest delays to the chapel renovation.'

'Oh no, how long now?'

Ellie passed on the news and smiled at the barista who'd arrived with their coffee and cakes. Lemon meringue pie for Zoe. Coffee cake for Sylvia and banoffee pie for Ellie. They waited for the young girl to leave before discussing the case.

Rebus' nose twitched at the smell of food.

'Onto the case,' said Ellie. 'We need to evaluate what we've learned from Elizabeth.'

They discussed Elizabeth's relationship with Violet.

Sylvia tilted her head with interest. 'That explains the personal investment. Is Tommy's wife alive still?'

'Actually, Gran, that's a good question,' said Zoe. 'We didn't think to ask. She might have information.' She turned to her mum. 'We need to know right away. I'll ring her.' She already had her phone out. She dialled the number and put the call on loudspeaker.

Elizabeth answered.

Zoe asked how she was and explained what they wanted.

'Yes, Gran's in Lark View in Canterbury. She and Granddad were both there.'

'Would it be OK if we visited her?'

'Sure. Her name's Ida. Ida Chapman.'

Zoe thanked her and rang off. 'I suggest we pop along at some point and see what she knows. I can't do this afternoon. I've got two more pickups to do: a hedgehog and a beaver.'

Ellie agreed and moved on. 'Still on the subject of Elizabeth,' she said to Sylvia, 'here's the crucial part.' She showed Sylvia the photo on her phone of the note that had been pushed through Elizabeth's door.

'That's pretty fancy language,' said Sylvia. 'Who speaks like that?'

'We were wondering that too,' replied Ellie. 'Certainly, nobody writes like that. Unless they're a poet, maybe? Or someone deliberately trying to make their language sound old, rural and Kentish?'

Zoe was already opening her laptop. 'This changes everything. If there's someone alive today who's willing to threaten violence to keep whatever happened quiet, they must have a strong reason.'

'I agree. It means that identifying who's actually buried in our garden becomes critical,' Ellie finished. 'We've been assuming it's Violet, but we need to know for certain.'

'Any ideas how we can find that out?' Sylvia asked.

'Dave was chasing an ID first thing this morning, but the police aren't going to reveal it to us. I might be able to get some unofficial information.'

Ellie mentioned Penny Wilkins, the forensic anthropologist, who she'd already pumped for information at yoga, and Charlotte Greaves, the archaeologist. 'I could try to get them talking. I didn't promise Dave not to prise information from people.' She grimaced, guilt nipping at her.

'That sounds like a plan,' Zoe said. 'What about Elizabeth?'

'I was thinking of taking her to see Gideon,' Sylvia said. 'Show him that photograph from Mabel's journal. If anyone would recognise Edmund Hollinghurst, it would be him. And Elizabeth might spot details we've missed.'

'Ask him if he can find out anything about Edmund's sister,' said Elllie. 'Is there a reason why he thought Edmund was an only child? Was the sister ill or something?'

'That's a really good point,' replied Sylvia. 'I'll ask him about Mabel's friend, Nellie, too.'

'Good idea.' Ellie was making notes on her phone. 'We need to approach this systematically. If someone's watching Elizabeth, we can't afford to make mistakes. Or put her in danger.'

Zoe was quiet for a few minutes, staring at her laptop screen. 'I've been doing some research,' she said, 'on the potential reasons why a young harvest worker might end up buried in a garden rather than a proper graveyard.'

'Go on,' Sylvia encouraged.

'Well, there are several possibilities.' Zoe turned her laptop round to show them a list she'd been typing. 'First, she could have been working for the farmers, and died. An injury, perhaps. The employers could have buried her with or without permission from her family.'

'That's possible,' Ellie said. 'And quite common.' She told them about Reverend Matthews' records from the time. 'Especially in poor families who couldn't afford a funeral.'

'Second, illness. Something like tuberculosis was common then. Typhoid, measles, smallpox. There were sometimes restrictions on where victims with infectious diseases could be buried.'

Sylvia nodded thoughtfully. 'The church records wouldn't show those if the person was buried unofficially.'

'Third, religious reasons. If she wasn't baptised, or was of a different faith, she might not have been allowed in consecrated ground. So, a garden somewhere, or private land, might've been the only option.'

'Also possible,' Ellie agreed. 'And might explain the flowerbed.'

'Fourth,' Zoe continued, 'she could have died in circumstances the family considered shameful. Unmarried pregnancy, for instance, or if she'd taken her own life.'

'Hence the secrecy,' Sylvia said sadly.

'Fifth, murder. Someone killed her and needed to hide the body quickly.'

The word hung in the air between them.

'And sixth,' Zoe said, her voice dropping slightly, 'she could have been connected to the Hollinghursts in some way that made her burial there... *significant*.'

'Connected how?' Ellie asked.

'Well, that's the sixty-million-dollar question, isn't it?' Zoe looked between her mother and grandmother. 'If she was just a seasonal worker, why bury her on family property? Unless she meant something to someone in that family – and we know Violet did. Or her death was somehow their responsibility.'

Ellie shuddered.

Sylvia set down her cake fork. 'What are you thinking?'

Zoe closed her laptop. 'That a young woman ended up buried in the private grounds of a powerful family, and that seventy-five years later, someone's still willing to threaten – even kill – to keep it secret.'

The room was silent.

'Whatever the connection was, it was important enough to hide then, and it's still important enough to protect now.'

The three women sat in the peaceful room, surrounded by books, each lost in their own thoughts about what that connection might have been, and what it meant for their investigation.

Chapter 22

'This is Dr Merrin,' Sylvia told Gideon, as he opened the door of Wisteria Cottage.

'How nice to meet you finally,' he said.

Elizabeth looked uncomfortable, glancing at Sylvia for support. 'I'm sorry about my... er... unconventional approach. Things became complicated.'

'Please, come in, both of you.'

Gideon ushered them into his sitting room, where the fire was roaring and textbooks lay in piles on every available surface. 'I was just working on my notes for next month's historical society lecture. Perfect timing for a break.'

Sylvia settled into the familiar armchair while Elizabeth perched nervously on the edge of the sofa. She still had the hunted look of someone expecting bad news, despite Sylvia's reassurances during the drive over.

'Gideon,' Sylvia said, 'we have something we'd like to show you. Something that might be connected to the Hollinghurst family.'

'Indeed?' Gideon's eyes lit up with curiosity. 'I do love a good historical puzzle.'

Elizabeth pulled out her phone and opened the photograph Ellie had sent her – the image of the old picture from Mabel's journal. 'This was found in the journal of someone who worked at Bramhurst Manor from the late 1940s onwards. We were hoping you might be able to identify the people in it.'

Gideon accepted the phone and studied the photograph carefully, his expression growing more interested by the moment. He reached for his magnifying glass and examined it again.

'Fascinating,' he murmured. 'Absolutely fascinating.' He looked up at Elizabeth. 'Whose journal was it?'

'Mabel Brown. She was a cook at the manor. The entry was from 1950.'

'I remember that name from my research.' Gideon handed the phone back but continued to study Elizabeth intently. 'Dr Merrin, may I ask why you're so interested in this particular photograph? In your original correspondence with me, you mentioned research into women's labour history, but this seems rather more specific.'

Elizabeth looked at Sylvia, who nodded encouragingly.

Elizabeth explained her relationship to Tommy and Violet. 'I've been trying to find out what really happened to her.'

Gideon's expression softened immediately. 'Ah, I see. A family matter, then. That explains the personal investment.' He leaned back in his chair. 'Well, I can certainly help with the identification. The young woman in the photograph is definitely Violet Chapman.'

'You're certain?' Sylvia asked.

'Yes. I've seen other photographs of Violet. There's one in the village archive, taken at a harvest festival. Same features, same smile. It's definitely her.'

Elizabeth's eyes lit up. 'And the young man?'

'That's Edmund Hollinghurst,' Gideon said without hesitation, 'heir to the family fortune and the apple of his father's eye... until this romance, of course. Before he lost his father's favour, there were portraits everywhere. I've seen several, and this is unmistakably the same person.'

'I agree,' Elizabeth said, studying the photo again on her phone. 'It definitely isn't my grandfather. Tommy was stockier, and shorter, with different features entirely. A thicker face and neck, stronger build.'

Sylvia had been doing calculations in her head. 'Gideon, if this photograph was found in Mabel's journal from 1950, and the inscription says: 'Summer 1950,' when exactly could it have been taken?'

'Well, the harvest season typically ran from July to October, so sometime in that period. Which isn't particularly helpful.'

Elizabeth was staring at the image with growing confusion. 'Look at them. They're clearly together, clearly happy. It looks like...'

'Like a photograph taken during a settled relationship,' Sylvia finished. 'Like two people who were comfortable with each other, who had time to pose for a camera.'

'The inscription.' Elizabeth read aloud: '"*Summer 1950. Remember this day always.*" That sounds like someone marking a special occasion, not someone about to run away.'

Gideon was quiet for a moment, studying their faces. 'What exactly are you suggesting?'

'Well,' Sylvia said carefully, 'according to Mabel's journal, the official story was that Edmund and Violet left notes saying they were going to Scotland to be married. But what if they never actually left Bramhurst at all?'

'You think the elopement story was fabricated?'

'I think,' Elizabeth said slowly, 'that someone wanted it to look like they'd run away together. But they could still have been in the area after they were supposed to have left.'

Gideon reached for a leather-bound notebook and began flipping through pages covered in his neat handwriting. 'You know, there's something that's always bothered me about the timing of events that summer, which could mean that what you're suggesting is true.'

'What sort of thing?'

Gideon cleared his throat. 'Well, the official story was that Edmund and Violet wrote their goodbye notes and disappeared on August 30th. But I found a reference to Edmund being seen in early September. The 2nd or 3rd, something like that.'

Sylvia's breath caught. 'He was still in Bramhurst then?'

'The entry is ambiguous, and I always assumed it was a mistake in the dating. But now...' Gideon looked at the photograph again. 'What if it wasn't a mistake? What if Edmund was still here because – as you suggest – he'd never left?'

Elizabeth stared at the image on her phone. The young couple sitting happily on a bridge, their futures ahead of them. 'You're saying they were both killed, and someone made it look like they'd run away to cover it up?'

'It would explain why your grandfather Tommy came home alone,' Sylvia said gently to Elizabeth. 'And why he was so traumatised. If he saw something that concerned him... or had suspicions...'

'He might have known they were dead, but been powerless to prove it,' Elizabeth finished, her voice barely above a whisper.

Gideon closed his notebook slowly. 'But look at that photo. Wheat and barley harvests are complete by the end of August. You can see an orchard and an apple cart. That was taken in late August or early *September*.'

Elizabeth gasped. 'Golly. You're right.'

'There's something else,' said Gideon. 'Something I've never been able to verify, but which might be relevant now.'

They waited.

'There were rumours – just rumours, mind you – that Judge Hollinghurst received some sort of communication about his son's death sooner than he claimed. Not a few years after the supposed elopement, but a few *weeks*.'

'What kind of communication?'

'Notification from authorities. But it was quickly hushed up.' Gideon looked frustrated. 'I still cannot verify this.'

The implications hung in the air. Someone had spent considerable time and effort creating the fiction of Edmund and Violet's elopement.

'In which case, who benefited from that deception?' Elizabeth asked quietly. 'And why are they – or their descendants – still protecting it seventy-five years later?'

Outside Wisteria Cottage, somewhere, someone who knew that truth was watching, waiting, and preparing to do whatever it took to keep it buried.

Chapter 23

Sylvia left Elizabeth and met Leonard at Willow Haven care home in the village to talk to Mabel's friend, Nellie Tuppen.

'This is exactly what we need,' Leonard told Sylvia cheerfully as he locked the car. 'A complete change of pace from all this business with threatening notes and mysterious BMWs.'

Sylvia nodded, checking they had with them the small gifts they'd prepared: homemade biscuits and chrysanthemums from the garden. 'Nellie must be ninety. I do hope her memory is still clear.'

The care home was a neat and sprawling modern building surrounded by well-tended gardens. The sound of singing could be heard from the moment they stepped through the front door. A cheerful receptionist directed them towards the main lounge, where about twenty residents were gathered in a circle, enthusiastically working their way through what appeared to be a repertoire of 1950s favourites.

"How Much Is That Doggie in the Window?" was just finishing as they entered, conducted with great enthusiasm by a member of staff.

'Oh, how wonderful,' Sylvia exclaimed, immediately recognising several faces from her previous visits to the home with Leonard. 'May we join you?'

'The more the merrier,' called out a sprightly eighty-year-old who'd been the village hairdresser for thirty years. 'We're just getting to the good ones now.'

Leonard, who had a pleasant baritone, immediately threw himself into the next song with typical enthusiasm.

Sylvia sat next to two older residents. One was a tiny, bird-like woman with bright, intelligent eyes who was keeping perfect time with her fingers on the chair arm.

'Is that lady Nellie Tuppen? Sylvia asked during a brief pause between songs. She gestured to a woman in a wheelchair – which Deb had mentioned – by the patio doors.

'That's her,' the tiny woman replied.

Sylvia went over. Sat down next to Nellie and introduced herself.

'Oh yes, dear,' said Nellie. 'I remember you from when you lived in Bramhurst. Though that must be a while ago now.' Her voice was thin but clear, and her smile was warm. 'How nice to see you again.'

"We'll Gather Lilacs" proved popular with the group, and even some of the care staff joined in from doorways and corridors. There was something deeply moving about hearing these voices, some wavering with age but all filled with joy, singing songs that had accompanied them through their youth.

After another twenty minutes of music, the session wound down and residents began to disperse for lunch. Leonard was immediately surrounded by several elderly ladies who were clearly delighted to have a vicar to chat with, and they began asking him whether he liked Halloween, whether it was Christian and whether it was acceptable to dress up for it.

This left Sylvia free to settle in with Nellie.

'I hope you don't mind me asking,' Sylvia began gently, 'but I understand you used to work at Bramhurst Manor with Mabel Brown, née Pritchard?'

Nellie's face lit up. 'Oh yes, dear Mabel. Able Mabel, I called her. I do miss her. I might not remember everything but the day we started at the manor is still clear as day.' She smiled nostalgically. 'We were in service together when we were both fourteen. She began as a kitchen maid; I was a housemaid. Worked there for nearly fifty years, we did.'

'It must have been quite a household to work in.'

'Well, it had its moments,' Nellie said, lowering her voice slightly and glancing around to make sure they weren't overheard. 'The family were... complicated, shall we say.'

'How do you mean?' prompted Sylvia, hoping she would reveal something new.

Nellie was quiet for a moment, as if deciding how much to share. 'The judge was a hard man, very demanding. We were all a bit scared of him, to tell the truth. And Mrs Hollinghurst, well, she was nervous as a cat most of the time. Lived on her nerves, that one did.'

'And their son, Edmund?'

'Poor boy. Gentle as a lamb, nothing like his father. You could see the judge despaired of him sometimes.'

'And Edmund's sister?' Sylvia held her breath, waiting to hear what Nellie would say, and realising they'd forgotten to tell Gideon about her.

'Rosa. Took after her mother, she did. Highly strung. Sickly. Died young, unfortunately. Used to go on trips with her mother. I don't know if it was a doctor she went to...' Nellie shrugged. 'We were never told.'

This was the first they'd heard of Edmund's mother and sister going on trips.

'A carriage took them both to the station one day with another young lady, but where they went, we never knew.' Nellie's expression grew troubled. 'Didn't improve the judge's demeanour, I'll tell you that much. In fact, it was the judge himself that worried us most, especially over Violet Chapman.'

Sylvia felt the thrill of excitement. 'Go on... Did you ever see anything specific?'

'Not with her.' Nellie was quiet for a long moment, her fingers working at the edge of her cardigan. 'I shouldn't really say. It was all so long ago, and I might have been wrong...'

'Nellie, please. My family and I are trying to find out what happened to Violet, so whatever was going on at the manor house could be very important.'

She gave a sad nod. 'Well, one morning, must've been late summer, 1950 or thereabouts. I'd been sent to fetch eggs from the farm. As I was walking up the path, I saw one of the boys who worked there leave one of the old barns. The ones they used for equipment and such. His clothes were all dishevelled, his hair messed up something dreadful, like he'd been in a fight.' Nellie shook her head sadly. 'Then I saw the judge leaving the same barn.'

'Go on.' Sylvia was thinking that, given the judge owned the farm, he could've been there legitimately.

Nellie dropped her voice to a whisper. 'The judge saw me watching and his face went black as thunder. Told me to mind my own business and get about my work.'

'Did you tell anyone?'

'I mentioned it to Mabel, of course. Didn't say anything to anyone because we needed our wages.'

'And this was around the time Violet Chapman was working there?'

'Oh yes, dear Violet. Such a sweet girl, always polite, always grateful for any kindness.' Nellie's eyes grew sad. 'We were all so shocked when she disappeared like that. Though between you and me, Mabel and I weren't entirely surprised something had happened to her.'

'Why?'

'Because young Edmund was clearly smitten with her, and we'd all seen the angry way the judge looked at her.' Nellie gripped Sylvia's hand suddenly. 'You don't think... you don't think the remains they found at the chapel might be her?'

'We think they might be, yes,' Sylvia said gently. 'Which is why it's so important that we understand what really happened back then.'

Nellie was quiet for a long moment, staring out at the care home gardens.

'If it is poor Violet,' she said finally, 'then someone needs to answer for what was done to her. Even after all these years.'

Leonard appeared at Sylvia's shoulder, having finally extricated himself from his admiring audience. 'How has your chat been?' he asked kindly.

'Very enlightening,' Sylvia said, giving Nellie's hand a final squeeze. 'Thank you so much for sharing your memories.'

As they prepared to leave, Nellie caught Sylvia's sleeve while Leonard went ahead.

'Be careful, dear,' she said quietly. 'If the judge really got rid of poor Violet, then there might be others who helped him cover it up. And some secrets are worth killing for, even after all these years.'

Outside in the car park, Leonard already had the engine running. He pushed the passenger door open for Sylvia when she approached. 'Just seen your silver BMW.'

'You're kidding?'

Leonard shook his head. 'Pulled into the kerb and drove off when I got out and walked over.'

Sylvia gasped. 'Did you get a look at who it was?' She shut the car door.

'Unfortunately not.' He clicked the central locking on and changed the subject. 'Did you learn what you needed to know?'

'I learned that Judge Hollinghurst could get physical,' Sylvia said grimly. 'And that the servants knew it but were powerless to stop him.'

'And now?'

'Now we have to prove it, before whoever sent that threatening note decides to do more than just write letters.'

But there was something else on Sylvia's mind – why Gideon had forgotten that Edmund had a sister.

Chapter 24

While Sylvia and Leonard were at the care home with Nellie, Ellie and Elizabeth had just pulled up in the car park of Kent Archaeology Services. The laboratory was housed in a modern, single storey building on the outskirts of Canterbury, surrounded by security fencing and CCTV cameras. It looked more like a high-tech office complex than the kind of place where decades-old mysteries were solved.

'Are you absolutely certain about this?' Ellie asked Elizabeth. 'I mean, we're essentially members of the public gatecrashing their laboratory.'

Elizabeth checked her reflection in the wing mirror and straightened her shoulders. 'Penny Wilkins works for the police, but she's also an academic. I've corresponded with her, and she understands the importance of family connections to historical cases.' She looked at Ellie with determination. 'I'm here to inquire about remains that might belong to my great-aunt. I have every right to know the truth.'

'Alright then,' Ellie replied, sighing and getting out of the car.

At the reception desk, Elizabeth explained they were here to speak to Drs Wilkins and Greaves regarding the Bramhurst Chapel remains. The security guard made a phone call, and within minutes Penny appeared in the lobby, wearing a white lab coat and looking surprised but not unwelcoming.

'Elizabeth. I wasn't expecting to see you here.' Penny's eyes moved to Ellie. 'And Ellie.'

'I'm sorry to turn up unannounced,' Elizabeth said, 'but I need to know. About the remains. Whether they're...' She paused, gathering herself. 'Whether they're my family.'

Penny's expression softened. 'Of course. I understand completely. Charlotte and I have just left the site to run a few analyses while the team does some more excavation.' She glanced around the lobby. 'You'd better come through.'

She led them through a series of corridors lined with laboratories and offices, each visible through large, shiny windows. Ellie glimpsed technicians in white coats working with microscopes, computers and equipment she couldn't begin to identify.

'This is our main anthropology lab,' Penny said, opening a door marked "Authorised Personnel Only." 'Where we do most of the bones analysis.'

The laboratory was smaller than Ellie had expected but packed with sophisticated equipment. Stainless steel tables held various bones laid out in anatomical order, while computer workstations displayed complex imaging software on huge screens. The smell of chemicals and disinfectant hung in the air.

Charlotte Greaves looked up from a computer terminal as they entered, and said warmly, 'Elizabeth, good to see you again. And Ellie.'

'Thank you for allowing this,' said Elizabeth. 'I know it's not standard procedure.'

'Well,' Charlotte said with a slight smile, 'academic curiosity tends to override bureaucracy when we're dealing with historical cases. And Penny's told me about your family connection. That makes this a rather special case.'

Penny gestured towards a workstation where a skull sat on a specialised mount, illuminated by powerful LED lights. 'We've been conducting a full osteological analysis of the remains. Based on the pelvic structure, skull characteristics, and bone measurements, we can confirm the individual was female, approximately 18-25 years old at the time of death.'

'How long ago was that?' Elizabeth asked quietly.

'The bone chemistry and preservation state are consistent with death around 1950,' Charlotte added. 'Which fits with your family timeline.'

'But you can't be certain it's Violet without additional evidence,' Ellie said.

'Exactly.' Penny moved to another workstation where small bone samples sat in labelled containers. 'Which is why we began DNA extraction yesterday. The older the remains are, the more challenging it is, but we've had some success.'

'DNA extraction?' Elizabeth leaned forward with interest.

'We drill tiny samples from the densest parts of the bones – usually the petrous part of the temporal bone,' Charlotte explained. 'It's where DNA is most likely to be preserved. Then we use specialised techniques to amplify any remaining genetic material.'

'And?' Elizabeth's voice was tight with anticipation.

'We've extracted some DNA, but what we have is degraded and incomplete so we're trying a range of samples,' Penny said. 'We have a comparison sample from a family member. Your grandfather kindly made sure his DNA was on file in case a discovery was made.'

Elizabeth nodded immediately. 'Excellent. Grandad believed Violet was murdered.' She was matter of fact. 'We just need to prove it.'

At one of the computer workstations, Charlotte was concentrating on a screen. 'While we're waiting for the DNA results – which will take a few days – we've been working on some craniofacial reconstruction and superimposition.'

'Is this the equipment you were telling me about?' Ellie asked Penny.

'Yes. We've had it for about a year,' she replied.

Charlotte turned the computer screen towards them. 'What we've done is create a 3D model of the skull and we're comparing it with photographs of known individuals from the period.'

The screen showed a detailed computer model of a skull, rotating slowly to display every angle. Beside it was a second window showing facial reconstruction software, building layers of virtual tissue and muscle over the bone structure.

'It's remarkable what technology can do now,' Ellie said, watching the computer work in fascination. 'My daughter would love this.'

'We can essentially rebuild a face from skeletal remains,' Charlotte told them. 'Do either of you have photographs of Violet?' she asked.

Elizabeth pulled out her phone and scrolled through her photos. 'I have these two.' She showed them the bridge photograph and another image, a formal portrait of a young woman with dark hair and intelligent eyes, wearing what looked like her best dress.

'And I've got this one which my daughter found on the internet,' said Ellie. It showed a young woman on a makeshift swing in the chapel garden, hair in the breeze, head thrown back in laughter. Under the image, a caption said, "*Violet Chapman, seasonal worker from East London, catching a rare moment of play – summer 1950.*"

'Perfect,' Charlotte said. 'Could you both send the images to this email address?' She pointed to a piece of paper with the department email details. 'And I'll upload them into the software.'

A few moments later, everything was done.

'Now we can do a direct comparison,' Charlotte told them.

They watched as the software overlaid the reconstructed facial features onto the skull model, adjusting proportions and angles. The process took several minutes. They watched while Charlotte made fine adjustments to the positioning and scale.

'OK. The facial reconstruction is largely complete,' she announced. 'Now for the moment of truth.'

She brought up the bridge photograph on one side of the screen and the reconstructed face on the other. The resemblance was immediately apparent: the same delicate bone structure, the same proportions, the same distinctive jawline.

'If you look at the orbital spacing,' Penny said, pointing to the computer screen, '... and the nasal aperture width, the measurements are almost identical.'

Charlotte fine-tuned the comparison, overlaying the reconstructed face directly onto the photograph. The alignment was near-perfect.

'And now the formal portrait,' she said, switching to Elizabeth's second photograph.

Again, the match was striking. The computer-generated face fitted the photograph like a template, every major feature aligning precisely.

Elizabeth stared at the screen, her hand covering her mouth. When she finally spoke, her voice was barely above a whisper.

'It's her. It's definitely her.'

'Let's try the third,' said Penny. 'On the swing.'

Charlotte repeated the process and rotated the orientation.

Another match.

'There's consistent alignment across multiple landmarks in both frontal and lateral views,' said Charlotte. 'In my professional view, the craniofacial superimposition strongly suggests these remains belong to Violet Chapman,' Charlotte said formally. 'Combined with the age, time period, and location, I'd say – pending DNA confirmation – we have a positive identification.'

'I suspect Grandad was right,' Elizabeth said, tears starting to fall. 'Poor Violet never left Bramhurst. She never ran away with Edmund. She died here.'

Penny moved back to the skull under the bright lights. 'Charlotte is still running analyses on the soil. It *is* possible the young woman was killed elsewhere and brought to Bramhurst for burial...'

'You said "killed"...'

'Indeed. There's something else you'll want to know. Something that might help explain what happened to her.'

Penny adjusted the angle of the skull, zoomed in and pointed to an area on the frontal bone, just above where the eyebrow would have been. 'Do you see this depression here? There's distinctive damage.'

Elizabeth and Ellie leaned forward to look. There was indeed a clear indentation in the bone, roughly crescent-shaped and about two inches long.

'What caused it?' Ellie asked.

'The shape and depth are consistent with a blow from a curved blade,' Penny explained carefully. 'Something like an agricultural tool such as a sickle, a scythe or a billhook. The angle of impact suggests she was struck from above.'

Elizabeth's face went pale. 'A sickle?'

'It's a working hypothesis,' Charlotte added quickly. 'The damage could theoretically be from other causes, but the pattern is quite distinctive.'

'But a sickle...' Elizabeth's voice was barely a whisper. 'That's not something she could have done to herself.'

'No,' Penny agreed. 'A blow of this nature, to this location, is very unlikely to have been self-inflicted, so it rules out suicide. It was either an accident or...' She paused.

'Or someone hit her,' Elizabeth finished.

'We can't definitively say it was murder,' Penny said carefully. 'It could have been a tragic accident. Perhaps she was struck during farm work, or there was some kind of mishap with equipment.'

'But you don't believe that?' Ellie said, reading Penny's expression.

'The location of the burial suggests this wasn't treated as an accident,' Charlotte said diplomatically. 'If someone had died accidentally, there would typically be records, family involvement, proper burial arrangements.'

Ellie reached out and squeezed Elizabeth's hand. 'I'm so sorry.'

'Don't be sorry,' Elizabeth said, wiping her eyes but with a determined expression. 'Now we have confirmation: Violet died from a head injury, and someone buried her in secret.'

Charlotte was already printing out copies of the comparison images. 'These will serve as documentation for the official report. And Elizabeth, when the DNA results come back, you'll have scientific proof of what your family has always known.'

'How long for the DNA?' Elizabeth asked.

'Forty-eight to seventy-two hours,' Penny replied. 'But based on what we've seen today, I don't think there will be any surprises.'

As they prepared to leave the laboratory, Ellie found herself looking back at the skull, illuminated under the bright lights. It was no longer just an archaeological specimen. It was Violet Chapman, a young woman who had come to Kent looking for honest work and had instead found death.

'What happens now?' she asked Penny.

'We will prepare a full forensic report for DCI Blix and the investigating team,' the anthropologist replied. 'They will now treat the discovery as a suspicious death, and it will become a cold case murder investigation. The head injury combined with the irregular burial circumstances need thorough investigation.'

Outside the laboratory, as they walked back to the car, Elizabeth was quiet for a long moment. 'Thank you,' she said finally. 'For coming here with me to find the truth about Violet.'

'You're welcome,' said Ellie. 'Would you like to go for a coffee or something?'

Elizabeth looked back at the laboratory building, then at the photograph on her phone showing Violet's smiling face. 'I'm not sure. The investigation has become a lot more dangerous. Right now, I could do with a brandy.'

Chapter 25

Sylvia met Ellie and Elizabeth at the Hop Picker's Rest. The three women sat at a corner table. Rebus was on the floor, his head on Ellie's foot.

'We definitely need something stronger than coffee,' Sylvia said.

The pub was busier than Ellie had seen it before. Customers were tucking into meals and ordering drinks at the bar. The atmosphere was warm and convivial, a stark contrast to the sterile forensic laboratory they'd just left.

And not at all how the women were feeling.

'I can't quite believe it,' Elizabeth said, still clutching the printed photographs from the craniofacial analysis. 'After all these years, we actually know for certain. Violet was killed.'

They were still chatting when Zoe joined them, carrying a brown, furry bundle in her arms. Presumably, one of her rescues.

'Sorry I'm late,' she said, slightly breathless, showing them the chocolate-coloured animal in her arms. 'I'd arranged to collect this little one from a breeder near Canterbury. She's thirteen weeks old and just been returned by the family that bought her. They said she was too boisterous for their lifestyle.'

The puppy gave a soft whuffle and wriggled in Zoe's arms.

Hearing another dog, Rebus was quickly on his feet and pushing his nose at the brown bundle.

Zoe stroked Rebus' ears. 'I've been so lonely with Finn gone, I said I'd take her.' She glanced round the table, and squidged in next to Ellie. 'Everyone, meet Marple.' She glanced at Rebus. 'Reeby, this is your niece.' She plonked a kiss on each of the dog's noses.

The puppy began an enthusiastic tour of the corner seat, climbing over laps with confidence and curiosity, tail wagging and bottom wiggling. Her chocolate-brown curls were impossibly soft, and her amber eyes sparkled with mischief.

'Oh, my goodness,' Elizabeth cooed, as Marple settled briefly in her lap before launching herself towards Sylvia. 'She's absolutely adorable.'

'Cockerpoo, like Reeby,' Ellie observed, gently stroking the puppy's silky ears. 'Good choice for someone who understands the breed.'

'She's supposed to be very intelligent,' Zoe said.

As if on cue, Marple dropped down from the seat and lolloped off towards the bar.

Ellie just managed to grab Rebus' collar to stop him following her.

'Marple!' Zoe leaped to her feet, charging after her. 'Marple, come.'

Terry's laughter erupted behind the bar, followed by the sound of something being dragged.

'Hey, you little monkey.'

Marple reappeared moments later, with a bag of cheese and onion crisps clamped firmly in her tiny jaws.

'She pulled the box out,' said Terry, chuckling.

Marple trotted proudly back to their table, tail going like a propeller.

Terry came running after her.

'Well,' Sylvia said, laughing as Zoe gently extracted the crisp packet from the puppy's mouth, 'she's certainly got initiative.'

'And cheese and onion?' said Ellie. 'Can I just say: Marple's got taste.'

They all laughed.

'I'll pay for the crisps,' Zoe told Terry. 'They're covered in puppy slobber.' She scooped Marple up and carried her back to the table, Terry behind her.

He greeted them with his usual welcoming smile. 'Afternoon, ladies. What can I get you? A nice bottle of wine to share?'

'Oh, no,' Sylvia declared. 'We aren't celebrating. We're here for fortification. How about brandy?'

They all nodded.

'Four brandies, please.'

Zoe sat back beside Ellie. She clipped a lead on Marple's collar. The puppy climbed over Ellie's legs and settled on Sylvia's lap.

As Terry bustled away to prepare their drinks, the women sat in contemplative silence for a moment. The weight of the afternoon's discovery hung over them like a cloud.

A few minutes later, Terry returned with a tray of tumblers containing amber liquid. 'There we are.'

They sipped their drinks.

'You know what I keep thinking about?' Zoe said, her voice slightly louder than before. 'Violet was younger than me. She came here looking for honest work and–'

'... and we're going to get justice for her,' Ellie added.

'Yes. Let's drink to justice,' Sylvia raised her glass in a toast. 'To Violet Chapman, and to the truth finally coming out.'

They clinked glasses.

Zoe's phone buzzed on her lap. 'Sorry. Need to check in case it's work.' She put her tumbler on the table and swiped the phone screen.

Sensing anxiety on her daughter's part, Ellie glanced at Zoe's phone. New texts showed the sender's name in bold. Zoe scrolled past these to Finn's name and groaned when she saw there were no new messages from him.

'Lovey, what's up?'

Zoe's face crumpled. She shoved her phone back in her pocket, her voice becoming wobbly. 'It's Finn. He said he understands if I want to move on and go out with someone else while he's away.' She wiped her nose with the back of her hand.

Ellie was trying to process the remark before commenting again. It didn't sound like the considerate Finn they'd known for four years.

'But that's just his way of saying he wants to be free to meet Norwegian forestry girls, isn't it?' Zoe continued. 'I mean, who tells someone they love that they'd "understand" if they dated other people unless they want to do the same thing?'

Ellie and Sylvia met eyes briefly. This was the first time they'd heard this.

Zoe hiccupped. 'When he told me he wanted to go, he made it sound all reasonable. He said he loved me, but wanted to broaden his experience and career opportunities while he was still young.'

Ellie was gathering her thoughts. She didn't like the "but" in that sentence.

'And telling me I'm free to move on…?' She spluttered: 'What does that mean?'

'Oh, sweetie,' said Ellie, pulling Zoe into a hug.

Marple climbed onto Zoe's lap, stood on her hind legs and reached up to her upset owner.

Zoe stroked her. 'It's OK, sweetie.' She turned to the group of women. 'I don't know if I'm supposed to – *hic* – wait for him or forget about him or what. He's left me completely – *hic* – confused, and I've been telling everyone he – *hic* – dumped me because it's easier than explaining that my boyfriend has basically – *hic* – given me permission to see other people while he's off having adventures in – *hic* – Norway.' She made a sweeping gesture with her hand, almost sending her brandy glass flying.

'Finn is an idiot,' Sylvia declared with righteous indignation. 'He'll be back.'

'It's not uncommon for someone of his age to want to further their professional life,' said Ellie, 'but I don't understand the other comments about dating other people. Let's discuss it when we're not drinking.' Ellie didn't want to say anything that would upset Zoe further.

'The only thing I can suggest is to try not to dwell on it,' said Sylvia. 'He said he loves you, so it's not as if that's changed. And it can, when it's one of your first serious relationships.'

Was Zoe's relationship over? Ellie didn't know what to advise. 'I agree. Focus on work. The case. Your gorgeous puppy. Your family and friends.'

Zoe sniffed, brightening slightly.

'We should probably get going,' Ellie said, checking her watch. 'I need to get to the auction house in Canterbury.'

They left their cars in the pub car park and set off on foot towards the chapel, arms linked for mutual support and singing a folk song that had been playing in the bar. Zoe was on one end of the row, Marple trotting along beside her on the lead, Ellie on the other with Rebus.

As they approached the chapel grounds, Ellie pressed her finger to her lips. 'Shhh,' she told the women in a voice that was much louder than she realised. 'We need to be quiet. This is an active crime scene.'

'Right, yes, quiet,' Zoe whispered loudly, immediately tripping over her own feet and stumbling.

'We're professionals,' Elizabeth added, also not particularly quietly.

They could see lights on around the chapel and the sound of voices coming from near the main entrance. As they got closer, they could make out Dave's familiar figure.

'There's my husband,' Ellie announced cheerfully, waving enthusiastically and beginning to regret not having had some food with her brandy. 'Yoo-hoo, Dave.'

'Can't wait to introduce him to Marple,' said Zoe.

It was only as they stumbled into the site lights that Ellie realised Dave wasn't alone. He was standing with three other people – a stern-looking woman in an expensive suit, a man with a clipboard and official air, and another woman wearing an English Heritage badge.

'Hi, Dad.' Zoe hiccupped, giggled and pointed at the brown bundle by her feet. 'This is Marple.'

Rebus, who didn't know what was going on but had seen Dave, started squealing and wriggling.

Dave stared at them. Silent. His face went through several expressions in rapid succession – surprise, recognition, and then something approaching horror.

'Uh-oh,' said Zoe. 'I feel like I'm – *hic* – in front of the headmaster.'

'What are you ladies doing here?' he said through gritted teeth, focusing his gaze on Ellie.

'Going to the campervan,' she announced brightly, as if this were the most reasonable thing in the world. 'This is Elizabeth Merrin, by the way,' she added, gesturing grandly. 'She's Violet Chapman's great-niece.'

'She's wh–?'

'We've just been at the archaeology lab,' Elizabeth added, interrupting him. 'With Penny and Charlotte.'

Dave's face became thunderous. 'You've what? Ellie, I thought you–'

'Don't get cross with Ellie,' Elizabeth told him. 'It wasn't her idea. It was mine. I wanted to know if the remains belong to my great-aunt.'

Dave frowned.

'They've confirmed her identity by cranio-facial-super-imposition.'

Ellie smiled at the way Elizabeth enunciated the word slowly and carefully.

'After that,' Elizabeth continued, 'we went to the pub for a fortifying brandy and...' Her sentence trailed off.

Dave's jaw was moving, as though he was choosing his words carefully. 'Ladies, I'd like you to meet Detective Chief Superintendent Williams.' His voice was icy. 'My new boss.'

Oh, goodness. Dave was going to be furious.

'And Miss Patterson from the council's conservation team, and Dr Clarke, the CEO of English Heritage.'

'Oh dear,' Ellie said, the gravity of the situation penetrating her consciousness. 'We're going to be in trouble...'

'We were just conducting a site assessment,' Dave continued, his voice dangerously calm.

'Are you making good progress?' Sylvia asked brightly, either oblivious to the tension or pretending to be.

Detective Chief Superintendent Williams looked the four women up and down with barely concealed disapproval. 'DCI Blix,' she said coldly, 'I wasn't aware that family members had ongoing access to an active crime scene. Or...' she glared at Rebus and Marple 'pets.'

'They don't,' Dave said quickly. 'This is highly irregular. Ladies, you need to leave immediately.'

Zoe chose that moment to hiccup again, loudly, which set off a chain reaction of poorly-suppressed giggles from the other three women.

'This is a crime scene,' Miss Patterson said sharply, 'not a social gathering.'

'We know it's a crime scene,' Elizabeth said with earnest intensity of someone who cared about the case. 'That's why we're here.'

Dr Clarke from English Heritage was taking notes on a tablet, and Ellie had the uncomfortable feeling that none of this was going in their favour. She attempted to look sensible and responsible. 'We'll go.'

'Yes,' Dave agreed tightly, 'you absolutely should.'

As they turned to leave, Sylvia called back cheerfully, 'Nice to meet you all. Good luck with the field work.'

They made it about fifty yards before dissolving into helpless laughter and stumbling back towards Thimble Lane.

'Did you see Dad's face?' Zoe gasped between giggles.

'He looked like he wanted the ground to swallow him up,' Elizabeth added.

'Or us,' said Ellie. 'Poor Dave. I think we might have just set back his career by several years.'

'Oh well,' Sylvia said philosophically, 'at least we confirmed Violet's identity. That's got to count for something. And you've brought him up to date now – which is what he asked you to do.'

Ellie nodded, swallowing down the uncomfortable feeling that she was going to have a lot of explaining to do.

Chapter 26

'I think it's probably best if I give Dave some space for a few hours,' Ellie told Elizabeth as they walked along Thimble Lane towards the high street. 'He looked like he wanted to throttle the lot of us in front of his boss.'

Zoe and Marple had left. Sylvia had taken Rebus home.

'You're welcome to stay at mine,' Elizabeth offered. 'I've got a spare room, and honestly, I could use the company after everything that's happened.'

'I'll have a ponder, thank you. Dave will need to sleep somewhere so I don't want to abandon him. And I can understand him being furious about us turning up like that.' She was dreading the conversation they would need to have. 'I'd love a shower though.'

'That's fine. Do you want to come back to mine now and have one?'

They decided on that.

As they made their way through the quiet streets, Elizabeth continued chatting. 'How are you finding Bramhurst?'

'Apart from the remains in the garden, we like it very much.' She didn't mention the builders and the renovation as it was their choice to take on the project, and she knew they were lucky to be able to afford to do it.

They passed the bookshop and Ellie thought about the open mic nights, poetry slams and author readings she'd seen advertised. She mentioned these to Elizabeth.

'How lovely,' she said.

'Yes. The owner seems to have a knack for bringing the artistic community together.'

They passed Giovanni's restaurant, where candlelit tables were visible through the windows.

'Ah,' said Elizabeth. 'I came here with a friend recently. The restaurant has a delicatessen attached to it with seating. They do themed events on specific days of the week. Friday Fizz – prosecco and antipasti. Wellness Wednesday, with those trendy Buddha bowls everyone's obsessed with. Tapas nights on Saturdays.'

'Oh, wow. I'll definitely be trying those. Bramhurst has everything.'

Ten minutes later, they were on the bus heading down the hill into Whitstable, the sea in front of them.

'I can't believe we finally identified Violet today,' Elizabeth said. 'After all these years of wondering, of following dead ends and incomplete records...'

When they reached their stop, they got off the bus and began walking along Elizabeth's road. As they approached the house, Elizabeth stopped walking, her face draining of colour.

'What is it?' Ellie asked, following Elizabeth's gaze.

There, tucked into the letterbox flap was a white envelope. Even from the pavement, it looked ominous. Too deliberate, too carefully placed to be junk mail or a friendly note from neighbours.

'Oh no,' Elizabeth whispered, clutching Ellie's arm. 'That's where they left the last one.'

'We should call the police,' Ellie said.

'And tell them what? That someone left me a note?' Elizabeth's voice was shaky but determined. 'They'll say the same thing they said about the last one – no fingerprints, no witnesses, no way to trace it.'

'But if it's another threat–'

'Then I need to know what it says.' Elizabeth took a deep breath and released Ellie's sleeve. 'Come on. Let's get this over with.'

They approached the front door cautiously, as if the envelope might explode. Elizabeth pulled out her phone and took several photographs of it in situ.

'Put your hand inside this,' Ellie told her, handing Elizabeth a fresh dog poo bag from her pocket. 'The police will want prints.'

Elizabeth slid her hand in the bag before carefully removing the note from the letterbox.

Inside the house, with all the lights on and the curtains drawn, Elizabeth opened the envelope with shaking hands. The paper inside was the same plain white as before.

Ellie read it aloud: '*"Told you afore, din't I? But you wouldn't do as you was told. I tell you agin; leave Violet Chapman be. Dig no more – or you'll be cold in the ground, cellar deep, same as she."*'

Both women stood still.

Silent.

'It's the same rural dialect,' Elizabeth said finally. 'What's that about?'

'Sounds like it's from someone around here,' Ellie replied. '"*Din't I*" and "*same as she*"... Or someone trying to write in Kentish dialect.' She studied the message more closely. 'Or someone educated, trying to sound local. To throw us off.'

'Either way,' said Elizabeth. 'They know the remains belong to Violet. That's only possible if they're involved somehow. We only left the laboratory a few hours ago.'

The implications were chilling.

'I think you need to take this seriously,' Ellie said carefully. 'Maybe stay with a friend for a few days. Or family?'

'I can't run away every time someone tries to scare me,' Elizabeth said, though her voice lacked conviction. 'Violet deserves better than that.'

'Violet's been dead for seventy-five years. You're alive, and I'd like you to stay that way.' Ellie sat down next to her. 'And you've got a pet to think about.' She gestured to a small, black cat which was dozing in a basket of washing.

'That's Socks,' said Elizabeth.

As if on cue, the animal arched its back and jumped into Elizabeth's arms.

'I'm not being chased out of my home,' Elizabeth said finally. 'I'll lock the doors and stay here tonight and think about it in the morning.'

'We'll need to give Dave this note – and the other one. They're death threats. They need to know you've received another one.'

Elizabeth nodded.

Ellie took a couple of snaps of the message on her phone and pinged them over to Dave. She looked at the note again, with its crude threats and dialectal spelling. 'I think we're getting close to something. Someone's scared enough to risk exposure by threatening you directly.'

While Ellie had a shower, Elizabeth had a nap on the sofa.

Ellie was drying her hair on a towel when her phone buzzed.

Dave's name appeared on the screen, and she felt a flutter of guilt about their embarrassing encounter at the chapel.

'Hi,' she said cautiously, going into the kitchen so as not to disturb Elizabeth.

He thanked her for sending over the snaps of the note then switched his voice to carefully neutral. 'I'm sorry about earlier. I was a bit sharp with you.'

Ellie leaned against the doorway, watching the street through front window. 'No, you were right to be annoyed. We were completely inappropriate, turning up like that when you were with your superiors. I'm sorry.'

'Well, what's done is done.'

She could hear him sighing.

'Right: Elizabeth. We'll be over there shortly. Can you stay with her until we get there? Or tell her to go inside and lock the doors?'

'Will do.'

'Oh, and I've been thinking about the accommodation situation. The campervan isn't ideal. I've managed to get hold of a decent camping tent with a proper mosquito net. We could set it up in the chapel grounds, if you fancy it.'

'I think we should stay at the pub. More comfortable than camping.' As Ellie spoke, she froze. Because, across the road, something was moving in a rhododendron bush...

And minutes earlier, someone had just left a death threat in Elizabeth's letterbox.

Chapter 27

Ellie kept her eyes peeled for movement in the rhododendron bush as she finished the conversation with Dave and rang off. She opened the front door and glanced left and right. Putting the latch on, she strode over. As she approached, a large ginger cat shot out and dashed under a parked car.

Relieved, Ellie returned inside.

Elizabeth was awake and reassured to know the police were coming.

'Shall we see if any of your neighbours saw who delivered this charming message?' Ellie asked her. 'We'll see the police when they arrive.'

The street was a quiet row of Victorian terraced houses, each with its own small front garden and a window overlooking the road. If someone had been skulking around, delivering threatening notes, there was a reasonable chance a neighbour had noticed.

They started with the house immediately to the left. Number 47. A neat property with a freshly painted, green front door and window boxes full of red geraniums, which were still going strong.

The woman who answered was in her seventies, with carefully permed purple-grey hair and the watchful air of someone who missed very little of what happened on her street.

'Mrs Patterson?' Elizabeth said. 'I'm sorry to bother you, but I wondered if you might have seen anyone around my house earlier today?'

Mrs Patterson's eyes immediately sharpened with interest. 'What sort of someone, dear? Not burglars, I hope?'

'Nothing like that,' Elizabeth assured her quickly. 'Just someone who might have left something at my door.'

'Well, I've been in most of the day,' Mrs Patterson said, glancing between them curiously. 'I was doing my ironing. Always do it by the front window. Best light, you know. But I was in the back garden earlier pinning up the washing, and got chatting over the fence.'

'Thank you anyway,' Ellie said pleasantly. 'If you do remember seeing anyone, could you let Elizabeth know?'

'Of course, dear. Is everything all right?'

'Just a minor delivery issue,' Elizabeth said with a reassuring smile.

The house on the other side, number 51, was a stark contrast. The front garden was overgrown, the paintwork peeling, and it took several minutes of knocking before the door was opened by a dishevelled young man wearing a stained t-shirt and an expression of barely concealed irritation.

'What?' he said by way of greeting.

'I'm from number 49,' Elizabeth said politely.

'I know who you are.'

'I was wondering if you might have seen anyone around my house earlier today?'

The man squinted at her as if she were speaking a foreign language. 'Nah. Been asleep, haven't I? Work nights.' He started to close the door, then paused. 'What's it about then?'

'Someone left something at my door,' Elizabeth explained. 'I'm trying to find out who.'

'Right.' He seemed to lose interest immediately. 'Can't help.' The door closed with a decisive click.

'Charming,' Ellie murmured as they walked back to the pavement. 'Very neighbourly.'

The houses on the other side of Elizabeth's yielded equally little information. The door of Number 52 was answered by a harried young mother with a toddler on her hip and another child clinging to her legs. She'd been dealing with a nappy emergency and hadn't looked out of the window all afternoon.

Number 54 housed an elderly gentleman who was clearly hard of hearing and seemed confused about what they were asking. Number 56 was empty, according to the neighbours. The owners were away visiting family in Scotland.

'This is rather dispiriting,' Elizabeth said as they stood on the pavement, having exhausted the obvious possibilities. 'I suppose whoever it was chose their timing well.'

'Let's try a few more,' Ellie suggested. 'Sometimes people notice things without realising they've noticed them.'

Number 58 was a beautifully maintained house with a seagrass-green front door and a garden that looked like something from a lifestyle magazine. The woman who answered was wearing gardening clothes and carrying a pair of secateurs.

'How nice to meet you properly,' she said when Elizabeth introduced herself. 'I'm Annabel. I've seen you coming and going but we've never had a chance to chat.'

Elizabeth repeated her question about the door. 'Did you see anyone?'

Annabel's expression became more thoughtful. 'Earlier today... let me think. I was dead-heading the roses about ten o'clock, and then I was planting some bulbs...' She shook her head apologetically. 'I'm sorry, I was rather focused on the garden. I probably wouldn't have noticed if a brass band had marched past.'

'That's alright,' Ellie said. 'Thank you for thinking about it.'

'Is everything okay?' Annabel asked, genuine concern in her voice. 'It's not anything worrying, is it?'

'Just trying to track down a delivery,' Elizabeth said diplomatically.

They were about to give up when Elizabeth remembered the house at the end of the terrace. Number 60, which was set slightly apart from the others and had a clear view down the entire street. The front garden was immaculate, with geometric flower beds and a perfectly trimmed hedge.

The woman who answered the door was smartly dressed, with short, blonde hair and a confident manner. 'I'm Amanda,' she said when they'd introduced themselves. 'I'm just about to start a Zoom call. How can I help?'

Elizabeth explained the situation.

'Actually,' Amanda said, her expression brightening, 'you might be in luck. My son, Charlie, was coming home from his job at the garden centre at lunchtime, and he mentioned something odd when he came in.'

Ellie felt her pulse quicken. 'Oh?'

'Well, apparently, he bumped into a friend of his who was leaving the street looking rather flustered. Charlie said it was all a bit awkward because the other boy clearly wanted to get away quickly, but Charlie was pleased to see him and kept trying to chat.'

'Did your son say what his friend had been doing?' Elizabeth asked, trying to keep her voice casual.

Amanda nodded. 'That's what made it strange. Charlie asked, and the boy said he'd been delivering something. But when Charlie offered to walk with him, the friend made some excuse and hurried off in the opposite direction.'

'Did Charlie say which house his friend had been near?' Ellie asked.

'He wasn't sure exactly, but he thought it had an olive tree out the front.' Amanda gestured vaguely towards Elizabeth's end of the street.

'That's mine,' said Elizabeth. 'I've got an olive in a pot. It's quite big now.'

'Charlie said his friend seemed on edge about something, kept looking over his shoulder.'

'Do you know the friend's name?' Elizabeth asked.

Amanda hesitated. 'No, but I can ask Charlie and let you know.' She swiped her phone screen. 'What's your number?'

'I'll give you mine, if that's OK,' said Ellie. 'We're not looking to cause problems for anyone.' She conveyed her phone number. 'We just want to understand what happened.'

Amanda gave a polite smile. 'Charlie was puzzled by the whole thing,' she continued. 'He said his friend's usually chatty and friendly. Made Charlie wonder what he'd been up to and why all the secrecy.'

'How old is Charlie?' Ellie asked.

'Eighteen. The other lad is the same sort of age.'

After thanking Amanda and promising to let her know if there was anything she should be concerned about, Ellie and Elizabeth walked slowly home.

'So, either a teenager is threatening you,' said Ellie, 'or someone *got* a teenager to drop the note off. Who?'

'And why?'

'Was the teenager acting on his own initiative, or did someone put him up to it? Pay him, even?'

They paused outside Elizabeth's front door, both lost in thought about what this revelation might mean.

'What do we do now?' Elizabeth asked.

'The police will follow things up. They won't tell us what they find out, so I suggest you keep chasing Amanda for the name of her son's friend. Because anyone involved with Violet's death needs investigating.'

Ellie looked back down the quiet street. Over at number 51, the stained t-shirt guy was peering round the curtains.

She did not like this one bit. She steered Elizabeth back over to the sofa. 'I'll put the kettle on and wait with you until an officer arrives.'

Chapter 28

It wasn't long before a uniformed officer arrived with a CSI, so Ellie left Elizabeth, got the bus into Canterbury and headed for the auctioneers, determined to find out why she and Dave had been given false information about the crypt.

She stepped carefully over the uneven cobbles, the soles of her shoes registering each dip and ridge of the narrow street. The ancient buildings leaned in around her, timber-framed and close enough to whisper their secrets. Their upper stories jutted out like curious onlookers.

The cathedral bells rang out behind her, low and sonorous.

Ellie paused for a moment, letting the sounds settle in her chest. It was different here. The city had a rhythm of its own, brisk and layered, like a fugue. Not the slow, lolloping pace of Bramhurst.

A burst of coffee aroma drifted from a shop tucked between a jeweller and a bookbinder. Rich, with a hint of cinnamon. Ellie glanced through the window. Warm light, polished wood, a barista with a topknot and a milk jug mid-pour. She felt the tug of temptation but kept walking.

This couldn't wait.

The street widened out, the cobbles still wet from the earlier rain. Her foot slipped slightly, and she steadied herself against a flint wall, fingers brushing moss. Ahead, lights were on in the Catholic church.

Canterbury was beautiful, but it seemed to press in. The village breathed out.

She reached the corner where the auctioneers' brass plaque gleamed against old brick. A delivery van rumbled past, and the bells tolled again, softer now, as if marking her arrival.

From the street, Canterbury Auction House looked like any other modest Canterbury shop front. Whitewashed brick, a bow-fronted window with leaded panes, and a painted sign just beginning to flake at the edges. Ivy crept along the lintel, and a narrow blue door was slightly skewed in its frame.

Ellie squared her shoulders, took a breath and stepped inside.

It was exactly as she remembered it from the auction day: a bustling Victorian building filled with people buying and selling everything from furniture to fine art. The reception was a snug, wood-panelled space with a faint scent of old paper and furniture polish, its windows mottled with condensation.

'Mrs Blix.' The property coordinator, a cheerful woman called Hilary recognised her immediately. 'How lovely to see you again. You've got all sorts going on at the chapel, I gather. Saw it on the local news.'

'That's actually why I'm here,' Ellie said, keeping her tone friendly but purposeful. 'We've discovered some significant structural features that weren't mentioned in any of the documentation or plans.'

Hilary's smile faltered slightly. 'Oh dear. What sort of features?'

'A crypt beneath the chapel floor, for starters. Something that's had quite an impact on our renovation plans, as you might imagine.'

'A crypt?' Hilary looked genuinely surprised. 'That certainly should have been mentioned. Let me check our files.' She disappeared into a back office, returning with a thick folder. 'I'm looking at the description now, and you're absolutely right. There's no mention of any sub-floor structures.'

'So, the question is, where did that information come from originally? And who was responsible for ensuring its accuracy?'

Hilary flipped through several pages, looking increasingly uncomfortable. 'Well, the property details were compiled from information provided by the sellers and their representatives. But for something this significant...' She paused, clearly out of her depth. 'I think you need to speak with Mr Vale, our senior auctioneer. He handled the chapel sale personally.'

Ten minutes later, Ellie found herself in a small office overlooking the main auction floor, facing a distinguished man in his sixties who was examining the chapel file with growing concern. She remembered him from the auction day.

'This is most irregular,' Mr Vale said, adjusting his glasses. 'A crypt has clear historical significance and should absolutely have been disclosed. It affects both the structural integrity and the heritage value of the building.'

'So where does that leave us?'

'Well, legally speaking, *caveat emptor* applies to auction sales...'

'What does that mean?'

'Essentially – buyer beware. But there are still obligations regarding material non-disclosure.' He looked up at Ellie seriously. 'The question is whether this was an innocent oversight or a deliberate omission. For that, you'd need to speak with the sellers' solicitors. They handled all the legal paperwork on behalf of the Hollinghurst estate. Morrison–'

'... Blake & Associates in Bramhurst. Thank you.'

Half an hour later, Ellie was back in the village, walking down the high street. Morrison, Blake & Associates occupied a handsome Georgian building between the village shop and a hairdresser. Outside, brass nameplates gleamed in the sunshine, giving an air of established respectability.

The reception area was all polished wood and leather chairs, designed to impress potential clients with the firm's tradition and reliability. The receptionist looked up from her computer with a professional smile.

'How can I help?' she asked crisply.

'I'm Ellie Blix. My husband and I recently purchased Bramhurst Chapel through yourselves. I need to discuss an issue with the property particulars.' Ellie articulated the next sentence slowly. '*A serious omission.*'

The receptionist blushed and her expression became guarded. 'I see. Well, the sale completed several weeks ago, which means you accepted the property information as presented. If you have concerns now...'

'I have concerns about information that was *omitted* from the particulars,' Ellie interrupted, her tone remaining pleasant but becoming noticeably firmer. 'Specifically, a crypt beneath the chapel that wasn't mentioned anywhere in the documentation.'

'As I said, completion means acceptance–'

'Completion means we accepted the information we were given,' Ellie said, her voice taking on slight irritation. 'We could hardly accept information we didn't know existed, could we?'

The receptionist blinked, seemingly not used to being challenged. 'Well, I... that is to say...'

'My question is simple,' Ellie continued. 'Who was responsible for ensuring the accuracy of the information in the listing and supporting paperwork? Your firm, the sellers, or both?'

'I'm not qualified to answer legal questions about–'

'Then perhaps you could find someone who is,' Ellie said with a smile that didn't quite reach her eyes.

The sound of raised voices had apparently attracted attention from the back offices. A door opened and an overweight, rather sweaty, man in his mid-fifties emerged, wearing an expensive suit and the slightly irritated expression of someone whose afternoon had just been disrupted.

'Is there a problem, Jennifer?' he asked, glancing between the receptionist and Ellie.

'Mr Morrison,' Jennifer said with obvious relief, 'this lady is asking about the Bramhurst Chapel sale. Something about missing information in the particulars.'

'I see.' Mr. Morrison's expression became more professional. 'I'm Hugh Morrison, senior partner. Perhaps you'd better come into my office, Mrs...?'

'Blix. And thank you.'

Morrison's office was impressively appointed with law books and oil paintings. He gestured for Ellie to take a seat. 'Now then, what seems to be the issue with the chapel sale?'

Ellie explained about the discovery of the crypt, the structural implications, and the complete absence of any mention in the auction particulars.

Morrison listened carefully, occasionally making notes on a legal pad. 'That is certainly a significant omission,' he agreed when she'd finished. 'Let me find the file and see exactly what due diligence was conducted.'

He disappeared into an adjoining room, returning with a thick folder that he spread across his desk. 'Here we are. Bramhurst Chapel, sold on behalf of the executors for the Hollinghurst estate.'

'Are there any living relatives? I understood the family had died out.' Ellie tried to keep the annoyance out of her voice.

'Yes, distant relatives of the original family. The property had been in their hands since the main line died out.' Morrison was flipping through documents. 'Now, let me see... the new title register and plan... local authority searches... contract... survey... planning permission for change of use... restrictive covenant...'

He paused at a particular document, frowning. 'Ah. Here's the issue. We did conduct inquiries about sub-floor structures and potential archaeological features.'

'And?'

Morrison looked up, his expression troubled. 'According to our file, we specifically asked the sellers to confirm whether there was a crypt or burial vault beneath the chapel. They signed a declaration stating categorically that there was no such structure.'

'Except there is. Our builders nearly fell into it.' OK. That wasn't strictly true but...

'Indeed.'

'So, did the sellers lie?'

'Without speaking to them to clarify, I can only think that they were genuinely unaware of its existence.' Morrison leaned back in his chair, distinctly uncomfortable. 'This puts us in a very difficult position. We relied on their representations in good faith.'

'And it puts my husband and me in an even more difficult position,' Ellie pointed out. 'We've bought a property with significant undisclosed features that affect both its structural integrity and its renovation difficulties. Not to mention costs.'

Morrison nodded grimly. 'Indeed. This could constitute grounds for a misrepresentation claim. Though I should point out that pursuing the sellers might be... complex.'

'Why?'

'Because according to our records, the Hollinghurst family's executors completed the sale and then immediately wound up the estate. The individuals involved have moved abroad...'

Ellie stared at him. 'How convenient.'

'... to Australia.'

'Oh, great.'

'It's most unfortunate...' he muttered.

'With respect, you're going to need to do better than that.' Ellie was aware that their sleepless night was getting the better of her. 'My husband and I will be taking legal advice, and you will need to hand over all the details. Names, addresses. The lot.'

As Ellie walked back down the high street, she reflected on what she'd learned. The sellers had deliberately concealed the existence of the crypt, then immediately made themselves unavailable for any comeback. It suggested a level of planning and foreknowledge that was deeply troubling. If they'd they known about the crypt, and everything was legitimate, why didn't they disclose it? Was there something down there they didn't want people discovering?

Ellie was walking back to the bus stop when her phone rang.

Sylvia.

'Hello, Ellie, lovey.' Her voice was bright with excitement. 'I've just had the most interesting call from Leonard. He's been chatting with Reverend Jo about local history events, and apparently Gideon Marsh is giving a talk to the WI tonight.'

'Oh? What about?'

'It's part of their "Women in Kent" series, and it's on the role of seasonal labour in Kent's agriculture. It was going to be at Gideon's antique shop but there's been a change of venue. Not sure why.'

'Space?'

'Yes, probably. It's being held in the function room above the Hop Picker's Rest. Rather appropriate, given everything we've been discussing about the harvest workers.'

Ellie felt a spark of interest.

'Leonard mentioned it because he thought I might be interested, but the moment I heard the topic...' Sylvia paused. 'I think we should go. Both of us. The more eyes and ears the better.'

'That could be very relevant to our investigation,' Ellie agreed.

'At the very least we'll see how people in the village react when the subject of seasonal workers comes up in public,' Sylvia added.

Ellie considered this. After the earlier discovery of the threatening note which linked Elizabeth and Violet, she was even more determined to find out what was going on. 'When does it start?'

'Six-thirty. But I suggest we get there early, say, six-ish, so we can watch people arrive and choose our seats strategically.'

'Good thinking. I'll bring Elizabeth with me, if that's all right. Given her family connection to all this, she might pick up on things we'd miss.'

'Excellent idea. I'll bring Reeby with me. I'm not sure Leonard is up to having him sleeping on our bed otherwise.'

Ellie chuckled. They arranged to meet at the campervan and walk up to the pub together.

'Perfect. If there are people in the village who know more than they've been letting on, a public talk about seasonal workers might just prompt them to reveal something interesting.'

'Let's hope so. We could certainly use a breakthrough.'

After hanging up, Ellie rang Elizabeth.

They greeted each other.

'Fancy an educational evening?' Ellie asked her. 'How about a WI meeting in Bramhurst?'

Chapter 29

Sylvia and Leonard had walked Rebus, so Ellie fed him and got him settled in the campervan and walked up to the Hop Picker's Rest with Sylvia.

The function room above the pub had been transformed for the evening's event. Folding chairs were arranged in neat rows facing a small stage area where Gideon Marsh was setting up his laptop and projector. The walls were decorated with vintage agricultural posters and old photographs of hop picking, lending an appropriately rustic atmosphere to the proceedings.

Elizabeth had already arrived.

The three women positioned themselves near the back where they could observe both the speaker and the audience.

'I asked Gideon why he'd forgotten about Edmund's sister, Rosa,' Elizabeth told them, her voice low.

'Well done,' said Sylvia. 'What did he say?'

'He admitted he had, and said it was probably because she didn't figure much in people's stories...'

'Which is true,' said Ellie. 'Nellie Tuppen said Rosa was ill a lot.'

Deb Hobbs had been bustling about setting up chairs and checking the tea urn, playing the perfect host.

'Good turnout,' Elizabeth murmured as women began filing into the room.

The audience was a mixture of ages, from young mothers who looked like they'd escaped from domestic duties for an evening out, to elderly ladies who'd clearly been pillars of the WI for decades.

Gideon looked very much at home in front of his audience, dressed in a tweed waistcoat and corduroy trousers, and wearing the slightly theatrical air of someone who genuinely enjoyed sharing knowledge and telling stories.

Behind him, the projector displayed a sepia photograph of workers in a hop field, their faces serious beneath straw hats and flat caps.

Terry arrived, looking unusually irritated, and as soon as the clock hit six-thirty, he introduced Gideon.

'Good evening, ladies,' Gideon began warmly. 'Thank you for inviting me to speak about something that's very close to my heart: the forgotten stories of the seasonal workers who helped shape Kent's agricultural heritage.'

He clicked to the second slide, showing a map of migration routes from London's East End to the hop fields and fruit farms of Kent.

'For over a century, every summer saw an extraordinary migration. Thousands of working-class families would leave the crowded terraces of Whitechapel, Limehouse, Poplar, Bethnal Green and Stepney for a few weeks in the Kentish countryside.'

An interested silence fell on the room.

'They came to pick hops, harvest fruit, and earn money that would see them through the leaner winter months.'

The next slide showed photographs of women, children and elderly relatives all dressed in their working clothes and carrying bundles of possessions.

'But this wasn't a holiday,' Gideon continued, his tone becoming more serious. 'These workers were entering a complex social hierarchy that relegated them to the very bottom. They were essential to the agricultural economy, but they were also vulnerable and not always popular. They were essential but expendable, welcomed but not quite trusted, needed but not necessarily protected. Street-wise and city-smart, they attracted attention and mixed feelings.'

Mutters went round the room, and Ellie noticed several women in the audience nodding knowingly.

'Far from home, dependent on their employers for both work and accommodation, with little legal protection if things went wrong.'

An elderly woman in the front row raised her hand. 'My mother used to talk about the hop picking. She said it was hard work but good for the children. Fresh air and physical exercise.'

'Indeed,' Gideon nodded. 'For many families, it was their only chance to experience country air and outdoor rural work. However, the social dynamics were complex. You had the landowners at the top. Often titled families with vast estates. Below them, the tenant farmers who actually ran the agricultural operations. Then the permanent staff, the seasonal supervisors, and finally the casual workers themselves.'

Ellie was as fascinated as the WI ladies.

Gideon advanced to a slide showing a grand manor house alongside a photograph of basic worker accommodation.

'This is a manor house in Harbledown.' He moved onto the next slide. 'This one's in Faversham.' He clicked through several more photos showing large estates. 'Rough Common... Tyler Hill... Bridge... Bishopsbourne.'

Ellie had got out her notebook and was making careful observations about who seemed most engaged with the topic.

'Now,' Gideon continued, 'I'd like to talk about how these dynamics played out in our own area. Bramhurst Farm, for instance, and this very pub, were part of the Bramhurst estate. The farm employed seasonal workers for hop picking and fruit harvests throughout the early twentieth century.'

This was their cue to ask questions which might promote new information.

Elizabeth raised her hand. 'Mr Marsh, in your research, have you come across any accounts of a young woman called Violet Chapman?'

A subtle tension seemed to ripple through the room. Several women shifted in their seats, and Ellie noticed one of the helpers pause her tea preparations.

'I have, yes. And her brother, Tommy.' While he elaborated, Ellie, Sylvia and Elizabeth studied the room.

A woman in her sixties, sitting halfway back, leaned forward. 'There were plenty of rumours about Judge Hollinghurst,' she said cautiously, 'but they weren't all accurate.'

Ellie felt the tickle of excitement.

'I know because my grandmother worked on his farm, and she had some tales to tell.'

'Can you share any?' said Ellie.

The woman, who was dressed in trendy clothes and had her silver-blonde hair swept up in a turban, stood up. 'I'm Linda. My grandmother was Ruby Henley, and she came down from Bethnal Green to work at Bramhurst Farm in 1952.'

'That would've been after Violet Chapman's time,' Gideon observed.

'Oh, it was. Nan said that made a difference. She worked at the same farm, stayed in the same accommodation, but by then the atmosphere had changed completely.'

'In what way?' Elizabeth asked.

Linda looked around the room, clearly comfortable with having the attention of the group. 'Well, according to Nan, she had no issues at all with the judge. Or Mrs Hollinghurst.' Her tone was important. 'She was apparently a kind woman who made sure the workers were treated fairly and paid properly. Especially the women.'

Ellie wondered what Linda was about to tell them.

'Always checked on their welfare, she did. Made sure the accommodation was as good as it could be. Provided blankets and extra food.'

'That's interesting,' Ellie said. 'What about the other people involved in running the operation?'

Linda's expression darkened. 'Nan said the farmer himself – the man who actually employed the workers – was odious.'

'In what way?' This came from several women in the audience simultaneously.

'Right bully he was,' Linda said bluntly. 'Nan said he made life miserable for anyone who wouldn't do what he said.'

There were mutterings of 'disgraceful' and 'awful'.

'All the workers were afraid of him. He'd dock their pay for any excuse, make them work in dangerous conditions. That sort of thing.'

An uncomfortable murmur ran through the room. This was clearly hitting close to home for several audience members.

'Did no-one report his behaviour?' Elizabeth asked gently.

Linda gave a bitter laugh. 'Report to whom? The farmer was connected to all the local authorities. The magistrates; police; councillors. Who was going to listen to working-class youngsters from the East End of London, with no proof of anything?'

The room was very quiet now, the earlier comfortable atmosphere replaced by something more tense and thoughtful.

'Mrs Henley,' Ellie said carefully, 'do you happen to know the name of this farmer? The one your grandmother found so troubling?'

Linda pursed her lips grimly. 'Oh yes. Nan never forgot his name. Gibson, it was. Ernest Gibson. And according to Nan, he got away with his behaviour for years because nobody with any power cared what happened.'

Ernest Gibson.

In the sudden silence that followed, Ellie became acutely aware of Gideon, standing frozen by his projector, face pale and his hands gripping the edge of the table.

Had Judge Hollinghurst not been part of it then? If he hadn't, had he known what was going on?

And why was Gideon acting strangely?

Chapter 30

The bar at the Hop Picker's Rest was warm and inviting. In the fireplace flames licked quietly at logs, and the low-beamed ceiling created an intimate atmosphere that made Ellie feel cocooned from the chaos of the past few days.

Dave had checked himself, Ellie and Rebus into one of the pub's three guest rooms, and the relief of having a proper bed and bathroom was almost overwhelming.

'This is more like it,' he said, settling into the worn leather of a corner booth. 'No mosquitoes, no cramped spaces, no archaeological equipment to trip over.'

Gideon Marsh was at the bar, deep in conversation with Daphne Henderson, their heads bent together over what looked like an old photograph album.

Ellie couldn't help remembering how pale his face at been at the end of his WI talk, when one of the women had mentioned Ernest Gibson, and how he'd seem to freeze. Something about his manner had aroused her curiosity.

The distinctive crack of pool balls drew Ellie's attention to where two women were engaged in what appeared to be a highly competitive game. She caught a glimpse of purple hair under the light as the woman lined up a shot.

'Those are the women who run the pottery studio,' Ellie whispered to Dave.

'Why are you whispering?'

Deb Hobbs appeared at their table with menus. 'Evening, you two. Lovely to have you staying with us.' She gave them a warm smile. 'So funny how your dog went straight over to the hearth rug.'

She gestured to Rebus, who was stretched out in front of the fire with another couple, bothering only occasionally to check Ellie and Dave were still there.

'He knows what he likes,' said Dave, laughing.

'Terry's gone to Canterbury for supplies,' Deb continued, 'but I've got the kitchen running smoothly with a bit of help from Ryan. Tonight's specials are on the board there.'

Ellie glanced at the chalkboard. 'The clam chowder sounds perfect.'

'Sausage and mash for me,' Dave said. 'With onion gravy?'

'Of course. I'll get those started for you.'

They ordered drinks and as Deb headed back to the kitchen, Ellie began to get a sense of the normal rhythm of the pub. The gentle hum of conversation, the clink of glasses, the occasional burst of laughter from the pool table where one of the sisters had apparently just beaten the other. It all felt wonderfully ordinary after the extraordinary discoveries of recent days.

Their food arrived promptly, and Ellie's chowder was thick with clams and potato, and delightfully creamy. Dave's sausages were bursting with herbs and properly caramelised.

They ate in comfortable silence for a few minutes, then Dave nodded towards the wall. 'Look at that.'

A chalkboard listed the dessert options in neat handwriting. Sticky toffee pudding with clotted cream. Blackberry and apple crumble with vanilla ice cream. Lavender and elderflower posset. Dark chocolate torte with salted caramel.

'The posset sounds intriguing,' Ellie mused.

'It'll be crumble for me. Can't beat a classic.' Dave pointed to another board nearby. 'Quiz night every Thursday. We should put together a team.'

'You're already planning our social calendar?'

'Why not? We live here now. Might as well get involved.' He grinned. 'Besides, with me on crime, you on Kent life, Mum on cooking, Leonard on religion, we'd be formidable.'

'Add Zoe for anything about animals or social media...'

Deb returned to clear their plates.

While waiting for their desserts, Ellie noticed some black and white photographs lining the walls that she hadn't ever spotted before. She stood to examine them more closely, and Dave followed.

Rebus watched them carefully, still not moving though.

'Look at these,' she said, peering at a faded image of workers in a hop field. 'Lots are from the 1950s.'

The photographs were arranged chronologically along the wall, each with a small brass plaque beneath. The earliest showed Victorian-era workers with their long skirts and cloth caps, but as they moved along, the images became clearer, the clothing more familiar.

'Here we are.' Dave pointed to a group photo dated 1950.

The spidery, faded writing beneath said: *Bramhurst Farm Harvest Workers* and listed names: *Ernest Gibson, Arthur Brown, George Pimm, Harry Craddock, Albert Tilling, Sid Hood, Walter Rill, Ernie Brissenden, Frank Nye, Charlie Crocker.*

'Here's Gibson, the farm manager.' Ellie leaned closer. The man in the photograph held a sickle with casual authority, his expression stern even in the formal portrait.

They moved to the next photograph. More workers, but this time Ellie recognised a name: 'Mabel and Arthur Brown, Housekeepers.'

'That's Terry's gran,' Ellie said. 'Look how young she is here.'

It was fascinating to put faces to the names she'd been discussing with Sylvia and Zoe. Made the characters more real.

Mabel's face was kind even in the grainy photograph, standing beside a tall man with a mark on his cheek. They looked directly at the camera with the steady gaze of people who knew their worth, despite their station.

'Strange to think Mabel made such detailed notes about everything,' Dave murmured. 'Shows she knew something was wrong even then; even if it seemed like the norm at the time.'

They studied each photograph in turn, searching for other faces they might recognise, names that might mean something. The seasonal workers looked tired but proud, their clothes worn but clean, their faces telling stories of hard work and hope.

'All these people,' Ellie said softly. 'Coming here year after year, trusting they'd be safe. That they'd earn enough to see their families through winter. And they weren't treated well.'

On another wall, the images of people were mixed with documents. An alcohol permit. A poster from VE Day, announcing the end of rationing. A lease of some sort for the pub. A newspaper clipping showing a man next to barrels and holding a pint of beer. Public house rules. Harvest quotas.

Ellie took a few photos on her phone to look at later.

Their puddings arrived so they sat back down. The posset was silky and delicate. The lavender didn't overpower the elderflower, and both flavours danced on Ellie's tongue. She tasted Dave's crumble, which was tart from the blackberries, sweet from the apples, and had a buttery topping that crumbled perfectly.

'You know what I keep thinking about?' Ellie said, savouring the last spoonful of her pudding. 'Those barns at the farm where the workers slept. Eight feet by ten feet for entire families.'

Dave looked up from his crumble. 'Still thinking about Violet?'

'How can I not be? We're sitting here in comfort, complaining about a few nights in a campervan, when those workers endured conditions we can't even imagine.'

'They were very tough times.'

'Someone robbed her and Edmund of their future...'

Dave reached across the table and took her hand. 'We'll find out what happened. I'll make sure of it.'

From the pool table came a crow of triumph as one of the women from earlier finally potted a ball against the other.

'Come on. Let's focus on something else.' Dave's eyes twinkled. 'Shall we challenge them to pool?'

'I haven't played for years,' said Ellie, laughing. 'I suspect they'll thrash us.'

Chapter 31
WEDNESDAY

The next morning, after a hot shower at the pub, Ellie was quickly dressed and eating porridge with the other B&B guests. Dave had gone ahead to meet the teams who were due to start inspecting the chapel sub-floor at 8.30am.

When Ellie arrived, the grounds resembled a small scientific expedition. Several official vehicles were parked carefully around the building, and she could see people in hi-vis jackets and hard hats moving purposefully between the entrance and various pieces of equipment.

She popped Rebus in the campervan with his breakfast and went to join everyone.

Dave strode towards her, looking more rested than he had first thing. 'Morning. Ready for the grand inspection?'

'As ready as I'll ever be. Who've we got here?'

'Everyone we expected,' Dave said, consulting his clipboard, 'which is good news. Historic England have sent Dr Deborah Whitfield. She's their lead archaeologist for Kent. The structural engineer is Mark Stevens from Canterbury Council – I think you spoke to him – and he's here with their conservation architect. And we've got Dr James Crawford from the Diocese of Canterbury. He specialises in historic church architecture and burial practices.'

Ellie smiled. 'Quite a gathering.'

'And...' Dave turned to a young man in a suit and tie, who looked no older than a sixth-former, 'a reporter from the local newspaper.'

Dr Whitfield approached them, a tall woman wearing practical clothing and carrying what looked like ground-penetrating radar equipment. 'Mrs Blix? Thank you for your patience with all this. I know it's disrupting your renovation plans considerably.'

'Better to get it sorted properly than have the floor collapse later,' Ellie said pragmatically. 'What's the plan?'

'Step by step, I'm afraid. First, we need to assess the structural safety of the floor itself. That's Mark's department. Then we'll use non-invasive techniques to map what's actually down there before we even think about opening anything up.'

Mark Stevens, a slender man, was already setting up equipment near the altar end of the chapel.

'The floor's definitely unstable in places,' he called over. 'I can see where some of the flagstones have shifted, and there's evidence of subsidence around the edges. We'll need to shore up the safe areas before we can work properly.'

Dr Crawford was examining the architectural details around the altar. He was an elderly man with the gentle authority of someone who'd spent decades working in churches.

'This is fascinating,' he told the conservation architect.

Ellie crept over to listen.

'The stonework suggests this was indeed designed as a family chapel with burial provisions. See these carved niches? They're typical of private chapels where wealthy families would display memorial tablets or religious artifacts above their family tombs.'

'So there definitely was a crypt?' Ellie asked.

'Almost certainly. The question is, what's in it now?' He gave her a professional smile. 'The morning will involve a careful process of making the floor safe enough to work on. Mark and his team will install temporary supports and identify areas where it's safe to stand, while Dr Whitfield will methodically scan the sub-floor area with her ground-penetrating radar.'

'Good. Thank you. I'll come back around 12pm. I've got a coffee morning to get to.'

Chapter 32

The morning sunshine streamed through the windows of Bramhurst Books, making the shop look even more inviting than usual. Ellie had arrived early to help Rebecca arrange chairs in a circle near the children's section, where colourful cushions and low shelves created a cosy atmosphere perfect for informal conversation.

'This is such a terrific idea,' Rebecca said, adjusting a display of local history books and stroking Rebus. 'I love organising community events. We should have a welcome coffee morning each time someone new moves into the village.'

Ellie chuckled. She liked Rebecca already. She was friendly, creative, and clearly passionate about bringing people together.

'I just thought it would be nice to meet some neighbours properly,' Ellie said. 'Moving to a new village can feel quite overwhelming, especially when you've lived somewhere all your life and now you're converting a building that's been part of the community for centuries.'

'Well, you've certainly chosen one of the most interesting buildings in Bramhurst,' Rebecca laughed. 'Between the archaeology and the police investigation, you must feel like you're living in a crime drama.' She smiled kindly, interest flickering in her eyes. 'Although, with your husband's job, perhaps you're used to that...'

The first to arrive was Reverend Jo from St Mildred's, accompanied by her dog, who immediately began circling Rebus. Then, noses twitching, the two dogs broke into soft, clumsy play.

Ellie had hoped Jo would arrive on her motorbike, but the dog was more than adequate compensation.

'Lily, get out of there,' Jo said fondly as she eased the setter's nose out of the handbag of one of the women who'd arrived. 'She thinks everyone carries treats.'

'Sounds familiar,' said Ellie, offering the setter her hand to sniff. 'Mine's the same – Rebus. How old is she?'

'Two.'

'Reeby's five. Anyhow, thank you so much for coming. I know how busy you are.'

'Not at all. It's wonderful to know our historic chapel will soon be a home.'

'Not sure about 'soon', but...' Ellie summarised the latest developments.

Over the next twenty minutes, a steady stream of people arrived. Some Ellie recognised from around the village, others she was meeting for the first time.

Rebecca bustled about with a coffee pot and plates of pastries and biscuits, clearly in her element as hostess.

'I'm so sorry about this,' she said quietly to Ellie, as she emptied a packet of chocolate chip cookies onto a plate. 'My usual cake supplier has let me down at the last minute. These are just shop-bought, I'm afraid.'

'Don't worry at all,' Ellie replied. 'Perhaps you should chat to my mother-in-law.' Ellie waved Sylvia over and filled her in. 'Sylvia is an excellent baker.' She remembered the frustrations Sylvia had shared about being a vicar's wife. 'I'm sure she could supply you with some homemade cakes to try out, if you're interested.'

Sylvia's eyebrows shot up and she beamed all over. 'Oh... er... I'd be delighted.'

'Really? That would be wonderful. I'm always looking for local suppliers.'

The two women chatted, and Ellie left them exchanging numbers and discussing Kentish apple cake and gypsy tart.

As people settled into chairs with their drinks, Ellie found herself facing a warm, curious group of about fifteen villagers, including a man who said he was a widower. He ran the locksmith and had lived in Bramhurst for decades. The there was a young mother with a toddler, a retired couple who played bowls, and... Rory the true crime podcaster.

'What's he come for?' muttered Sylvia, a little too loudly.

Rory must've heard. 'Hi... er...'

'You're not going to film, are you?' asked Ellie. 'People are here to relax.'

'No, don't worry. Mum mentioned the coffee morning and...' His sentence trailed off.

He'd come for a nose.

'Well,' Ellie began. 'Thank you all for coming. Do make sure you've got a drink and biscuit.' She introduced herself and talked about the unexpected developments at the chapel, including the crypt and damp walls.

There was nervous laughter around the circle.

'My dear, you've certainly had more excitement in your first two weeks than most of us see in a lifetime,' said a woman with long hair dyed henna-red. 'I'm Cynthia Thornley, by the way. Lived here forty-three years, and I can honestly say nothing this dramatic has happened since the great flood of 1987.'

'It must be fascinating working on such a historic building,' added the young mum, holding her squirming toddler. 'I'm Fiona, and this is my son. We live in Forge Cottage, the former blacksmith's house. These old buildings all have such incredible stories.' She gave Ellie a warm smile. 'Ours has wrought iron additions everywhere, and horseshoes as plant holders.'

'That's exactly what I was hoping to hear about,' Ellie said eagerly. 'Any stories, memories, family tales about the chapel or the manor house or the farm... I'd love to understand more about the history of our new home.'

An older man with a white beard raised his hand slightly, finished his mouthful and swallowed. 'I'm Richard. My grandfather worked on the Hollinghurst estate in the 1950s. General maintenance, bit of gardening and help on the farm. The things he said about that place.'

'What sort of things?' Ellie asked, trying to keep her voice casual.

'Well, we've all heard the rumours for years, haven't we?' replied Richard. 'What I don't understand is – why was nothing ever done?'

A thoughtful silence fell over the group.

Reverend Jo was nodding slowly. 'My predecessor in the 1940s and fifties, Reverend Matthews, kept detailed notes about the harvest workers.'

Ellie had asked Jo if she could help encourage people to tell their stories.

'There are several entries,' Jo continued, 'expressing concern about the way the seasonal workers were treated.'

'Can anyone elaborate?' said Sylvia, who'd been playing with Jo's setter.

The Blixes knew about the issues and wanted to encourage new input.

'My grandmother and her friends used to call that place Lookingbane Hall,' said a woman Ellie hadn't met before. 'Not Bramhurst Manor.'

'Lookingbane?' Ellie glanced encouragingly at the woman who'd spoken. 'I've heard it called that before.' She and Jo had seen the name mentioned in Reverend Matthews' records.

The speaker continued. 'I'm Pat, by the way. Gran worked as a laundress for several big houses in the area. She always said the manor house had an unhappy feeling about it, especially in the later years. She said it was as if the place was cursed.'

Ellie felt a chill run over her.

In the corner, near the books on folklore and Kent legends, the podcaster chap was listening eagerly.

'Did your grandmother ever say anything more specific?' she asked.

Pat shook her head. 'She always warned people to stay away from the master... *and* his young wife. Said she was just as dangerous as him.'

Ellie exchanged glances with Sylvia, wondering whether there was substance to the concerns they'd been hearing about Judge Hollinghurst and his wife, or whether they were normal village gossip about locals from a different class, with a different lifestyle. This was the first time they'd heard Edmund's mother mentioned in negative terms though.

'How horrible,' murmured the young mum, unconsciously pulling her toddler closer.

'Different times,' Cynthia said diplomatically. 'My granddad worked at a neighbouring farm. People were still recovering from the war. All staff had less protection then than they do now, especially the seasonal workers. Contracts were verbal and broken in a flash. Those that couldn't cope with the physically demanding nature of the work were dismissed.'

'From what we've heard,' said Ellie, 'the judge wasn't happy about his son dating Violet Chapman.'

Cynthia sucked in air through her teeth.

'The farm manager, Gibson, was much worse than old Hollinghurst himself,' said Richard, his voice grave and his expression troubled.

Ellie caught his comment. At the WI talk, there'd been concern about Gibson too.

'But surely if something serious had happened, there would have been official investigations?' This came from a middle-aged man Ellie didn't recognise.

Richard shook his head grimly. 'You have to remember, Hollinghurst was one of the most powerful men in Kent. High Court judge, connections everywhere, money and influence. Who was going to investigate him – or his odious farm manager? And lose their job, their income, their home?'

Ellie shot a glance at Sylvia. It was the second time Richard had mentioned Gibson.

'Exactly,' said Jo. 'As Cynthia's alluded to, the power dynamics were completely different then. A man in the judge's position could quite literally get away with murder, especially if the victim was from the most vulnerable parts of society.'

'Is that what you think happened?' Rebecca asked. 'To the person whose remains were found at the chapel?'

Ellie interjected quickly. 'We don't know yet.' If she told them what they'd learnt, it could stop people from sharing new information. 'That's why we're keen to learn more about the people who lived and worked on the Bramhurst estate. To understand the context better.'

'Well, the village has a long memory,' Cynthia said knowingly. 'If there are stories to be told, someone here will know them.'

Rory-the-Podcaster cleared his throat. 'I've been looking into the nickname, Lookingbane Hall. Names like that don't come out of nowhere.'

'They definitely don't,' said Richard.

'It's because a thought or idea has entered the collective unconscious of those around. "Bane" is a word with many layered meanings. It's often used to denote "deadly" or "poisonous". In its oldest usage, it refers to something that causes death or destruction. Think of plant names like wolfsbane or henbane. Both toxic, both deceptively lovely.'

Deceptively lovely?

Like – Criminally Curious?

Ellie chuckled at the thoughts tumbling through her head.

'Bane can also refer to something being the source of distress or ruin,' Rory continued. 'More figuratively, it's used to describe something that brings persistent trouble.'

'The bane of my life...' said Sylvia, as though she was trying the word out.

'It comes from old English "bana", meaning "slayer" or "thing causing death." It's rooted in Germanic languages and often tied to folklore and fatality. "Lookingbane Hall" suggests a place where what you see, or think you see, might be your undoing. It's not just a house with secrets. That "seeing" was two-way. It was a house whose very gaze was dangerous.'

Ellie caught a frown flit across Sylvia's face.

What did he mean: a house whose gaze was dangerous?

Pat spoke before Ellie had time to ask. 'My grandmother always used to say, if you catch your own eye in the glass at Lookingbane, it means trouble's coming.' She took a deep breath. 'As kids, we'd sing: "*Lookingbane's where light goes lame. And true men step into shame*".'

'Can you remember where you got that from?' asked Sylvia. 'Was it something you heard adults saying?'

The expression reminded Ellie of the notes Elizabeth had received.

Pat shrugged. 'I'm not sure I recall.'

As the coffee morning went on, more details emerged: fragments of family stories; half-remembered warnings; pieces of village folklore that painted a picture of a community that had long suspected dark secrets at

Bramhurst Manor, but had been powerless to expose them.

As Ellie listened, she was aware that it was hard to decipher fact from fiction.

When people finally began to leave, promising to think about what other stories they might remember, Ellie felt both enlightened and disturbed. While the judge's reputation for strictness seemed to have been an open secret, there seems to have been a growing pattern of concern about the farm manager, Gibson.

'Thank you so much for organising this,' Jo said, as she clipped Lily's lead on her collar. 'It's important that these stories are finally being talked about.'

'And thank you for coming,' Ellie replied. 'I had no idea there was so much local knowledge about what went on.'

Rebecca was stacking chairs and collecting empty coffee cups. 'You know, I've lived here for eight years, and I'd never heard most of these tales. It makes you wonder what other secrets this village is keeping.'

As Ellie helped tidy up, she reflected on what she'd learned. She was looking forward to discussing the morning with Sylvia.

'Rebecca,' she said, 'would you mind if we did this again? Maybe in a few weeks? I have a feeling there are more stories out there, and people might feel more comfortable sharing them after they've had time to think.'

'Absolutely,' Rebecca agreed. 'I think they feel more relaxed sharing them in front of each other too. Safer. You know?'

'Yes. I'm a newcomer. And although I've lived nearby all my life, I'm not from Bramhurst. That makes absolute sense.'

Chapter 33

Ellie and Sylvia took their time leaving the bookshop. They wanted to get the contact details of people who'd made interesting comments, so they could follow up, if necessary.

They chatted as they walked back along the high street with Rebus.

'That Richard chap mentioned the farm manager *twice*,' said Sylvia. 'Did you hear?'

'Yes. We need to do some more research on him. And interesting that Mrs Hollinghurst was referred to in uncomplimentary terms when at the WI talk, she was described as kind.'

Sylvia nodded. 'Hmm. Hard to decipher. I guess people's opinions of her might have varied depending on what they saw and knew...'

The closer they got to the chapel, the keener Ellie became to find out what the teams had discovered in the crypt.

Penny's Land Rover was parked behind an estate car with ladders on the roof rack.

Dave was standing on the chapel steps, waving her over.

'Shall I put Reeby in the campervan?' asked Sylvia.

'Please.' Ellie handed her the lead and the van key.

'I'll drop the key back in a sec.'

Ellie thanked her and dashed over to Dave. 'Have they found any more remains?' she asked him, giving him a brief hug.

He shook his head.

Relief flooded Ellie. 'That's good news.'

They joined the team at the opening down into the sub-floor area.

'You'll need to stay up there, please,' Dr Crawford told them. 'Don't want to disturb anything.'

'Sure,' said Dave.

'This is interesting,' Dr Whitfield said, studying the readouts on her equipment. 'We're definitely seeing void spaces down here – and substantial ones. Stone walls, what looks like carved stone furniture... certainly a formal burial crypt.'

'Any signs of recent disturbance?' Dave called down.

'Not from these readings. Whatever's down here has been stable for a long time.'

Dr Crawford had been examining historical records on his tablet. 'I've been checking the diocesan archives, and I think I may have found something relevant. There's a record from 2002 of a "disinterment and relocation" at Bramhurst Chapel, conducted under proper legal authority.'

'What does that mean exactly?' Ellie asked.

'It means that any human remains that were originally buried in the crypt were officially exhumed and moved to another location. Possibly the main village graveyard.'

Dave looked up from his own notes. 'As far as I can see, 2002 would be around the time the last known Hollinghurst died.'

'Exactly. It was common practice when private chapels were being decommissioned. Families would arrange for their ancestors to be moved to consecrated ground in the local churchyard.'

Dr Whitfield was still studying her radar readings. 'That would explain what I'm seeing here. The structural elements of the crypt are intact, but there's no evidence of coffins or burial goods. It looks like an empty burial chamber.'

'So, we're not going to find any more bodies?' Ellie asked hopefully.

'I'd say it's very unlikely,' Dr Whitfield replied. 'But we still need to physically access the crypt to confirm its condition and assess any structural implications for your renovation.'

'It's going to take most of the day to complete the process of creating safe access to the crypt,' Dr Crawford told them. 'I'm sure you're both busy, so shall we reconvene at 4pm?'

Chapter 34

An hour later, Ellie and Sylvia were back in Bramhurst high street.

'Right then,' Sylvia announced as they approached the village shops. 'Time for some more introductions. Can't have you living here without knowing the local characters.'

They left Thimble Lane, and Ellie and Rebus followed Sylvia towards the rows of shops that formed the heart of the village.

The day was crisp and bright, and even though she was concerned about the crypt, and what had happened to Violet, she felt a bubble of excitement about continuing to explore her new community.

Their first stop was Paws & Tails, the pet shop. The moment they stepped inside, the shop greyhound rose gracefully from a bed behind the counter and approached with dignified curiosity.

Ellie quickly introduced Sylvia and herself and explained she'd recently moved to the village.

'Nice to meet you,' the assistant replied warmly from behind stacks of dog food. 'I'm Rose, the owner, and that's Duchess. She's very particular about her friends.'

Duchess and Rebus regarded each other with careful politeness. Then, as if some invisible signal had been given, both dogs suddenly launched into a game of chase around the narrow shop aisles.

'Oh dear,' Ellie laughed, trying to avoid being tangled in Rebus' trailing lead as he bounded after the greyhound between displays of squeaky toys and cat scratching posts.

'Don't worry,' Rose replied cheerfully. 'Duchess loves a good game. Here, let me give your boy something.' She produced a chew from behind the counter. 'He OK to have it?'

'Thank you. Yes.'

Rebus accepted the gift with dignity, and Duchess returned to her bed looking happy and exhausted, like a hostess who had successfully entertained a guest.

'I'm sure I'll be back in soon,' said Ellie. 'My daughter's just taken on a puppy.'

'Oh, *do*. We host a puppy club twice a week. I'll give you a leaflet. And we team up with a local dog trainer, if she's interested in classes.'

They chatted for a few more minutes and left.

'Next stop, the village shop,' Sylvia said as they emerged, slightly breathless, onto the pavement. 'Rory's mother has been running it for *forty* years. If anyone knows the history of this place, it's Daphne.'

The village shop and post office occupied a three-storey, red brick building. Inside, an impressive array of goods inhabited a space barely larger than most people's sitting rooms.

'Daphne, I'd like you to meet Ellie,' Sylvia announced to the woman behind the counter. 'She's bought the chapel.'

Daphne was a small, neat woman in her sixties with sharp eyes behind tortoiseshell spectacles. She looked Ellie up and down with the shameless assessment of someone who felt entitled to know everything.

'The chapel, eh? Brave of you. That place has been empty far too long.' She lowered her voice. 'I hope you're not expecting it to be quiet. Old buildings like that, they've got their own sounds.'

'I rather like the idea of living somewhere with character,' Ellie replied diplomatically, smiling inwardly at the way Daphne had whispered to tell them about noise.

'Character it's got, I'll give you that.' Daphne's expression softened slightly. 'My mother used to run this shop before me, you know. She always said the seasonal workers would come in here to post their letters home to London. Bought their stamps right here at this counter.' She stroked it, as though she was imagining one in front of her now, purse in one hand, an envelope in the other. 'Lovely people, most of them. Hard workers.'

'Did she know any of them personally?' Ellie asked.

'Oh, a few. They'd come back year after year. Mum got quite fond of some. Worried about how they were managing back in the city during the winter months.' Daphne adjusted her spectacles. 'You must join our Neighbourhood Watch, Mrs Blix...'

Before Ellie could reply, Sylvia was already steering her towards the door. 'Must be off, Daphne. Next stop is Thrown Together. I've never been in. It opened after Ron and I moved out of the village.'

Thrown Together occupied a converted house. Its large front window displayed an array of bowls, mugs, and vases in earthy glazes. Through the glass, they could see Mel at her wheel, hands moving with practised ease around a growing vessel. She looked up as they approached and waved them in with clay-covered fingers.

'Come in, come in. Don't mind the mess,' she called out, not pausing in her work. 'Nice game of pool last night, Ellie. Sorry. We did rather thrash you and your husband.'

'Ah, the demon pool players,' said Ellie.

The studio was a delightful chaos of works in progress, shelves of finished pieces, and the pleasant smell of clay and wood smoke from a small kiln in the corner. Mel had wisps of strawberry-blonde hair hanging around her face from a loose bun, and clay smudges on her apron.

Ellie introduced Sylvia. Rebus sat between the two Blix women, wondering what was going on.

'We've been hoping someone interesting would take on the chapel before it got derelict.' Mel gestured with her elbow towards the back of the studio. 'Dee. Come and meet Sylvia.'

Dee emerged from the back room, wiping her hands on a towel. Where Mel was earth-toned and serene, Dee was all energy and bright colours – purple hair, multiple earrings, and paint-stained overalls over a vivid green jumper.

'Hi again, Ellie.' Then she turned to Sylvia, grinning. 'I'm the black sheep sister who came crawling back after twenty years in London.'

'Hardly crawling,' Mel protested with fond exasperation. 'More like sweeping back in a whirlwind of chaos and disrupting my peaceful studio.'

'Peaceful is boring,' Dee retorted cheerfully. 'Now then, Ellie and Sylvia, have you ever tried pottery?'

'Er... I–'

Before Ellie could answer properly, Rebus' lead was handed to Sylvia, and she was sitting with her legs either side of a potter's wheel, a lump of clay centred in front of her and Dee's enthusiastic guidance ringing in her ears.

'Right, hands like this. Gentle pressure. Let the clay tell you what it wants to be. No, not that much water. Oh, never mind. It's supposed to be wobbly when you're learning.'

Within minutes, Ellie was covered in clay from wrist to elbow, with splashes on her jumper and face, and a smudge on her nose. The bowl she was attempting looked more like a drunken ashtray than anything functional, but she was laughing too hard to care.

'I'm even worse at pottery than I am at pool,' she gasped as her attempt collapsed entirely.

'Nonsense,' Dee declared, already preparing another lump of clay. 'You just need practice. And possibly protective clothing and goggles.' She let out a hearty laugh. 'Mel, fetch the woman an apron before she ruins that lovely jumper completely.'

'Already ruined, I should think,' Mel observed mildly, but she was smiling as she handed Ellie a clay-stained apron. 'Don't let Dee bully you. She thinks everyone should be as enthusiastic about getting messy as she is.'

'Says the woman who throws perfectly symmetrical bowls without even thinking about it,' Dee snorted. 'Show-off.'

Sylvia had declined the opportunity to try, and was watching and laughing from a nearby sofa.

The playful banter between the sisters was infectious, and Ellie relaxed completely, forgetting all about remains and crypts and damp stonework.

'I lived in Bow for twenty years,' Dee was saying as she helped Ellie attempt another pot. 'Just near the church. The famous Bow Bells of East London. Funny thing about that church – they had memorial lists on the wall. Names of all the local people who'd gone off to work in Kent and Sussex over the years and succumbed to accidents, illness, fights... and not come home.'

Ellie's hands stilled on the clay.

'The families back in London would wait and wait, but...' Dee shrugged. 'Hard times.'

'That's rather sad,' Ellie breathed, thinking of Violet and wondering if her name had appeared on that list, and how her parents must've felt, waiting for news of their daughter.

'That was life then, wasn't it?' Dee said pragmatically. 'These days we've got mobile phones and Facebook – much harder to just vanish into thin air.'

They spent another half hour at the wheels, with Ellie managing to produce one small, lopsided bowl that she was ridiculously proud of. Mel promised to fire it for her, and Dee persuaded Ellie to come back the following week for another lesson and join her adult class if, after that, she still wanted to learn pottery.

'We should have a Bramhurst pottery group,' Dee announced as they prepared to leave. 'Get some of the other village women involved. Make it a social thing. Pottery and wine? I'm sure Belle would be up for it.'

'What could go wrong?' said Mel, chuckling.

'Excellent idea,' Sylvia agreed. 'I haven't touched clay since school, but it looks like tremendous fun.'

As they were saying their goodbyes at the studio door, Dee suddenly snapped her fingers. 'Oh, I nearly forgot. Someone was asking about you yesterday, Ellie.'

'*About me?*'

'Well, about whoever bought the chapel. Odd bloke – dark sunglasses indoors, kept jangling his car keys like he was in a hurry. Wanted to know if you'd been in, asking questions about Bramhurst Manor.'

Ellie felt a small chill. 'What did you tell him?'

'Nothing.' Dee's expression grew slightly more serious. 'To be honest, something about him got my back up. Felt a bit... I don't know. Pushy?'

'Did he give a name?' Sylvia asked sharply.

'If he did, I wasn't paying attention. Why? Should I have been worried?'

'We've seen a similar-looking man around the village a couple of times,' said Ellie. 'He clearly wants something.'

'I followed him out when he left,' Dee said. 'Got into a very swanky silver BMW.'

'That's him,' said Sylvia. 'My husband saw him too.'

'He's clearly used to leaving that thing where he wants,' said Dee. 'It was on the chevrons by the pedestrian crossing. He was lucky he didn't get a ticket. We've got a new traffic warden in the village, and he doesn't take any nonsense.'

As they walked back to the chapel, Rebus trotting contentedly beside them, Ellie's earlier optimism was slightly dimmed. She'd had a lovely time with Mel and Dee, and had felt genuinely welcomed into the community. But the mention of someone asking questions about her made her uneasy.

She looked back at the pottery studio where Mel and Dee were visible through the window, back at their respective wheels. It was fun to be making friends. Even if one of them did seem determined to cover her in clay.

Ellie's phone buzzed. She slid it from her pocket. 'Ellie Blix.'

'It's Belle.' The window cleaner was whispering. 'Look, I'm at the pub, doing their windows. That BMW driver has just walked in. D'you want to talk to him? I'm happy to hang around. Make sure you're safe.'

'I'll be there in ten minutes.'

Chapter 35

Ellie handed Rebus over to Sylvia and charged through the village, her mind racing. Finally, a chance to confront the BMW driver, their mysterious watcher.

When she reached the Hop Picker's Rest, Belle was up her ladder with a chamois and scraper.

'Didn't want to alert him,' she told Ellie as she shinned down to the ground.

They entered the pub together, and Ellie immediately spotted him – fair-haired, wearing chinos and an expensive jacket. He was leaning against the bar, accepting a pint from Terry.

'That's him,' Belle muttered. 'Mr Speed Demon himself.'

They approached, and the man's eyes widened slightly when he recognised them. Up close, Ellie could see he had a tattoo of an axe on his neck.

'Why have you been watching people in the village?' Ellie asked directly. No point in dancing around it.

He blushed but tried to maintain composure. 'I don't know what you mean.'

'And you nearly forced my van into a hedge,' Belle added. 'What's your problem?'

Terry was watching the exchange with interest while polishing a glass.

'I don't have a problem. Just doing a bit of business.'

'What's your name?' asked Ellie.

'Evan.'

'Evan what?'

'Morrison.' His reply was barely audible, as if hoping they wouldn't make the connection.

Ellie's mind immediately went to the solicitors. 'As in Morrison, Blake & Associates?'

His colour deepened. 'It's a common name.'

'So it would seem. Are you related to the solicitors, or not?'

Evan took a long drink of his pint, clearly buying time. 'Does it matter?'

'Given that firm handled the sale of the chapel and forgot to mention a few significant details... like the crypt... yes.'

'I don't know anything about that.'

'Why are you going round the shops, asking questions about me?' asked Ellie.

'Don't know what you're talking about.'

She groaned.

'Where do you *actually* live?' Belle demanded. 'Because it's not in Bramhurst – I know everyone here. And why have you been hanging around?'

'I have my reasons.'

He'd ignored the first question.

'Which are?'

Evan looked between them, seeming to weigh his options. 'Look, in villages like this, lots of people are related. Even people you wouldn't expect.' He eyed Ellie meaningfully.

'What's that supposed to mean?' Ellie asked, relieved Terry was nearby in case Evan got nasty.

He turned to her directly. 'Do you, for example, know what your builder's surname is? Andy, who's been working on your chapel?'

Ellie frowned. She'd only ever heard him called Andy-the-Builder, the way villages identified people by their trades. 'What *is* his surname?'

'Might be worth finding out.' He gave a bored shrug and finished his pint in one long swallow.

Belle and Ellie exchanged glances.

'Andy's surname is Gibson,' said Belle gently.

Evan set down his empty glass. 'And the woman who runs the village shop? Did you know she used to be a Morrison? You might want to be careful about who you trust. This village has more secrets than just the one in your garden.'

'What do you mean?' Ellie's voice sharpened.

He'd set his pint down and was already moving towards the door, but paused. 'Let's just say... the remains you've found? They might not be the only ones.'

'Wait,' Ellie called after him. 'What do you know about other remains?'

But he was already pushing the door open and crossing the car park.

'That went well,' said Belle after a moment.

Terry had moved closer, no longer pretending not to listen. 'I'd leave him,' he said. 'Not worth putting yourselves in danger.'

Ellie nodded.

'How's the investigation going?'

'Slowly,' said Ellie through an irritated snarl.

'The Morrisons have had money for generations,' said Terry.

'Do you know him?' Ellie asked.

'His brother owns the solicitors here.' Terry moved away to serve another customer who'd just arrived.

Belle and Ellie stood at the bar, absorbing the interaction.

Belle shook her head. 'That creep's playing games. Winding people up. Spying. He's best ignored.'

But Ellie wasn't so sure it was a game. Evan had seemed prepared to take risks. Was that what happened when you had money behind you?

And his warning about other remains.

'I need to talk to Dave,' Ellie said.

Chapter 36

Ellie left the pub full of questions. Before heading back to the chapel, she rang Andy Gibson, the builder.

'Alright?' Andy bellowed down the phone.

They chatted for a few moments, and then Ellie said, 'Do you mind if I ask you about Ernest Gibson?' She explained they were investigating the remains in the chapel garden. 'You're his grandson, aren't you?'

He sucked in a pained breath through his teeth. 'Correct.'

'Are you aware of the allegations about your grandfather's treatment of seasonal workers at Bramhurst Manor?'

A regretful sigh came down the line. 'I share genes with him but that's it. The way he treated the workers was disgraceful.'

Ellie waited.

'I'm ashamed. I even contemplated changing my surname but eventually me and the missus decided it was better to clean up the Gibson name. Create a new image for us and the kids and grandkids; one people could rely on and respect. It's partly why I was happy to work for you at the chapel.'

Ellie thanked him for being candid and rang off.

Ten minutes later she was back at the chapel with Dave for the next update on the crypt.

Mark's team had carefully removed several flagstones near the altar, revealing steps leading down into darkness. Powerful LED lights were lowered into the space, illuminating carved stone walls and ornate archways.

'Beautiful workmanship,' Dr Crawford said admiringly, as he descended the steps. 'Thirteenth-century stonework, I'd say, though modified in later periods.'

Ellie held her breath as the specialists conducted their examination below. The wait seemed interminable, filled with the sound of measured footsteps on stone and occasional technical discussions she couldn't quite make out.

Finally, Dr Whitfield's voice called up from below: 'All clear down here. We're ready to give you the report.'

Fifteen minutes later, they were gathered around a table in Dave's incident room, with photographs and diagrams on tablets and laptops.

'Right,' Dr Whitfield began, 'here's what we've found. The crypt is indeed a formal family burial chamber, probably built in the fourteenth century and modified several times over the centuries. It's structurally sound and architecturally significant.'

'And empty of human remains?' Dave asked.

'Completely. Dr Crawford was right about the 2002 disinterment. We found clear evidence that multiple burials were carefully removed. There are empty stone sarcophagi, and memorial plaques that have been relocated. Documentation has been carved into the walls recording the reinterment process.'

'So where did the remains go?' Ellie asked.

Dr Crawford consulted his tablet. 'According to the diocesan records, they were moved to a family plot in St Bartholomew's churchyard in Canterbury. All done properly, with full legal authority and appropriate religious ceremony.'

Mark Stevens was examining structural diagrams. 'From a building perspective, this is actually good news. The crypt is structurally sound and won't affect your renovation plans significantly. We'll need to make some modifications to ensure the floor is properly supported, but it's entirely manageable.'

'And from a heritage perspective,' Dr Whitfield added, 'this is a significant historical feature that adds considerable value to your property. We'll need to discuss access arrangements and conservation requirements, but it's certainly not a problem.'

Relief washed over Ellie. 'So, we can actually proceed with converting the chapel into a home?'

'Absolutely,' Mark confirmed. 'As I said, with some modifications to our original plans, and proper conservation measures for the crypt, but yes, you'll be able to live here.'

Dave was making notes. 'And there's no connection between the historical crypt and the remains we found in the garden?'

'None whatsoever,' Dr Whitfield said firmly. 'The crypt was a legitimate family burial place that was properly decommissioned twenty-three years ago. The garden burial was something entirely different – unauthorised, secretive, and almost certainly connected to the activity you're investigating.'

As the specialists packed up their equipment and departed, Ellie found herself standing in the chapel doorway, looking at her future home with new eyes.

The discovery of the crypt, rather than complicating their plans, had actually resolved one of their biggest uncertainties.

'So,' Dave said, joining her in the doorway, 'how do you feel about living above a former medieval burial chamber?'

'Honestly? Rather honoured,' Ellie said. 'It's part of the building's history; part of what makes it special. And knowing that the families who built this place took proper care of their dead, even when they moved them... it feels respectful.'

'Unlike whoever buried Violet Chapman in the garden.'

'Exactly. I'll feel much better when we've got her death resolved and her remains laid to rest somewhere appropriate. That was about hiding shame and avoiding justice.'

Dave nodded.

'This was about honouring ancestors and following proper procedures.' Ellie looked around the chapel, imagining it restored and inhabited. 'I think I'm actually looking forward to living here even more now.'

'Good,' Dave said, putting his arm around her. 'I'm getting rather attached to the place. Once the floor is put right, we can move back in if you want to...?' He planted a kiss on her forehead. 'Or we can find somewhere temporary to stay until the work's complete. It's your call.'

Chapter 37

The drive to Whitstable took Sylvia and Zoe through Rough Common, down Borstal Hill, past the old windmill and into the town. Sylvia turned off the high street into Yawl Lane.

'Elizabeth gave in and decided to get a door-cam,' Zoe told her.

'That's good. She'll be pleased to feel safe.'

Violet's great-niece had asked them to come over so she could update them on what the police and CSIs had to say about the threatening notes.

They pulled into Elizabeth's street and parked behind another car. The small, terraced house looked as it had during their previous visits – neat front garden, paintwork in need of a spot of attention.

Except – the shutters were closed at the windows. That wasn't like the last time.

They parked and walked up the short garden path.

'Good. She's got her door-cam set up.' Sylvia pointed at the silver box to the left of the door. She pressed the button, the tinkling chime echoing inside the house. No response. She tried again, holding the button down longer this time.

'Elizabeth?' Zoe called through the letterbox. 'It's Sylvia and Zoe. Are you alright?'

Still nothing. Perhaps she'd nipped to the loo.

Sylvia stepped back and looked up at the windows. 'Curtains are shut upstairs too,' she said.

An unsettling feeling had taken over Sylvia's stomach. Elizabeth had invited them over. Where was she? Surely she wouldn't have gone to bed.

'One of my mates lives in Whitstable,' said Zoe. 'There are alleys round the back of all these houses. Let's try that.'

They went back onto the pavement.

'There.' Sylvia pointed at a gap between two houses, six properties to their left.

They followed the narrow alley that ran behind the terrace, counting gates until they reached Elizabeth's back garden. The gate wasn't just unlocked – it was open, swinging slightly in the breeze.

'Oh, no,' said Sylvia.

The back door of the house was also unlocked when they reached it.

'Elizabeth?' Sylvia called as she pushed it open. 'We're coming in. Are you OK?'

The kitchen was immaculate as always, but there was an odd stillness to the house that made both women move more quietly as they made their way towards the sitting room.

Zoe saw her first.

'Oh no. Elizabeth.'

The young woman was lying on her back on the carpet beside the coffee table and an armchair. A pool of blood was around her head, and her eyes were flickering.

'Call an ambulance,' Sylvia ordered, already on her knees beside Elizabeth and gently checking her neck for a pulse.

Zoe fumbled for her mobile with shaking hands.

'Who's done this?' Sylvia muttered angrily.

Zoe was talking to the emergency services operator.

A rasping sound came from Elizabeth's mouth. 'U...'

Sylvia leaned closer, the hush of the room pressing against her ears. 'Say it again.'

Elizabeth's lips parted once more and with a brittle gasp, she uttered, 'U-N' in her final breath, her head then dropping to the side.

The sound clung to the air, fragile and finite.

She was dead.

'An ambulance is on its way,' said Zoe, hopelessly.

It was then that Sylvia noticed the piece of paper tucked under the edge of Elizabeth's armchair, deliberately placed where it would be found.

'Zo,' she said, pointing. 'Don't touch it but can you see what it says?'

Zoe leant over and read:

"Lizbeth,

Ye'd best ha kep thy snout from matters wot warn't thine. But no, nose pokin an tongue waggin, like a magpie wi summat shiny. Meddlin don't bring nowt but mischief, an now the mischief's come. Tongue's stilled now, ain't it? Silent as the grave, where it'll bide. A soul wot knows thy sins. Tap, tap."

'It's the same style as the other notes,' Zoe breathed. 'The archaic, Kent language.'

Sylvia nodded.

'I don't understand any of it,' said Zoe. 'What sins?'

The sound of sirens in the distance interrupted her, growing louder as they approached the house.

'I don't know,' Sylvia replied slowly. 'But whoever was threatening her is gloating here in this note. I just hope that her shiny new door-cam has the scumbag on video.'

Chapter 38

The next hour passed in a blur of paramedics, police officers, and CSIs.

Elizabeth's house was photographed and the note bagged as evidence. DS Carmichael questioned Sylvia and Zoe.

Just as she was finishing, Dave approached, his face like thunder.

'What were you doing here?' he asked, clearly trying to keep his voice calm.

'Elizabeth asked us to come over,' Zoe told him.

'Did you see anyone leaving?'

Sylvia shook her head. 'No-one.' Before she'd thought about it, she blurted, 'The dialect used is consistent across all three notes.' She knew Dave wouldn't be able to tell them much but hoped he'd let slip something useful.

'Someone's gone to considerable trouble to maintain the historical voice.'

'Exactly,' chimed Zoe. 'Why use that sort of language? Who actually speaks like that?'

'It's written as speech, but it's not speech though, is it?' said Dave. 'People use text differently. Someone's used this particular style for a reason.'

'On Netflix,' said Zoe, looking at her father, 'there was a killer who'd studied historical documents. He deliberately mimicked the style in letters he wrote to his victims.'

'For someone to go to such elaborate lengths,' said Dave, 'it's got to mean something.' He paused. 'Killers so often think they're being clever when really they're leaving clues.'

'It shows Elizabeth was getting close to something,' said Sylvia, an unpleasant feeling settling over her.

'What d'you make of "UN"?' Dave asked.

'I'm not sure,' Sylvia replied. 'Presumably it's the beginning of a word or something. Unforgotten? Unseen? Unforgiven?'

'I was wondering about: unfair.' He seemed to check himself. 'Anyway, whatever the motive and whoever the culprit, this is now a present-day murder investigation.'

Chapter 39
THURSDAY

Ellie and Dave spent another night at the Hop Picker's Rest and were both up early. Ellie hadn't slept well, waking several times in tears at the shocking loss of someone she had thought could be a friend.

Once Dave had left for the police station, Ellie rang Sylvia to discuss what "UN" could mean.

'Leonard and I were trying to come up with ideas last night,' Sylvia told her.

'You've got undone and unfair?'

'Yep. Along with several others.'

She walked Reeby, gave him his breakfast and settled him on the campervan bed in the sun. Then, she headed for the village to meet Zoe for some more local research. Given Elizabeth's murder, and her connection with

Violet, Ellie had promised Dave that the three sleuths would not go anywhere alone.

The morning sun cast a golden glow across Bramhurst's high street as the two women parked Zoe's van and made their way from shop to shop.

'Right then,' Ellie said to Zoe as they approached the bakery. 'Let's see if anyone can tell us anything new about the old days of the manor house.'

Ellie couldn't help smiling when she saw the name of the bakery: Pain au Bramhurst. The shop occupied a narrow Victorian building with a cheerful, red-painted frontage and windows displaying an impressive array of bread, pastries and cakes.

A bell jangled as they pushed open the door, and Ellie was immediately struck by the delicious smell of fresh bread and something distinctly French – perhaps brioche or croissants.

'*Bonjour*,' called a woman's friendly voice from behind the counter. The speaker was petite and elegant, probably in her forties, with black hair pulled up into a bun and flour dusting her navy apron. Her accent had a cheerful French lilt.

'Good morning,' Ellie replied with a smile, introducing Zoe and herself.

'Ah, *magnifique*.' The woman's face lit up. 'I'm Marie-Hélène. My husband, Paul, and I run the shop together.' She gestured towards a man of similar age who emerged from the kitchen area, wiping his hands on a tea towel.

'The chapel buyers,' Paul said warmly. 'We heard you'd had quite the excitement up there. Discovery of historical remains, wasn't it?'

'That's right,' Zoe said. 'We're trying to learn more about what things were like in the village in the late fifties. See if we can find out what happened and how the remains got there.'

Marie-Hélène's expression grew thoughtful as she arranged some fresh baguettes in a wicker basket. 'I didn't live here then. Paul and I met in France when he was working there.'

'That sounds romantic.'

Marie-Hélène smiled. '*Oui*. Paul had to return here to Bramhurst and I came with him.'

Paul laughed warmly. 'Yes, my family were expecting presents. Wine, cheese, chocolate. Instead, I brought a fiancée home with me.'

'So, your family is from the village?' Ellie said to Paul. 'How many generations back?'

'Oh, a good few.' His expression quickly changed. 'My grandmother worked as Mrs Hollinghurst's maid. She told me stories about the harvest workers when I was a boy.'

Ellie felt her excitement rise. This was exactly the sort of new information she'd been hoping for. 'You might be able to help with our investigation then.'

He nodded. 'Nan was very fond of her. Upset when she and the daughter left for a while...'

'When was this?' asked Ellie.

'After Violet Chapman disappeared.'

'Did they return?'

'After a week or so. The master was very relieved.'

'Did she know what prompted their departure?'

Paul nodded again. 'Yes. It was all the rumours about Violet's disappearance. Everyone saying the judge was responsible. She... she didn't want to be associated with any of it.'

Ellie accepted the warm baguette that Marie-Hélène offered her with a generous smile. 'My family's been in Kent for centuries too,' she said. 'Stories like these get passed down through the generations, don't they? And people *love* knowing about what goes on at manor houses and all the scandals...'

It was true.

Marie-Hélène was selecting some chocolate brioches from a display case, wrapping them carefully in paper. 'For you,' she said to Ellie. 'A "welcome to the village" gift. The chocolate is from Belgium – *c'est très bon*.'

'That's incredibly kind, thank you so much,' Ellie said, touched by the gesture.

Paul looked pensive. 'The thing is, from what Nan told me, the problems at the manor weren't the judge himself.'

'Gibson?'

'Yes. It was Gibson who employed the workers directly – he was the one with the bad reputation.'

Zoe looked up from her note-taking. '*Ernest* Gibson, right? He didn't have a brother or anything?'

'Yes,' said Paul, 'that's him. Nasty piece of work, according to the stories. The judge was often away on court business, and while he might've been harsh in court, Nan said all the workers were scared of this Gibson chap.' Paul's expression was regretful. 'He did what he wanted. It's perfectly possible he murdered Violet.'

'Really?' said Zoe.

'Actually,' he added, his expression growing more serious, 'given you're investigating, I probably should mention something. No idea whether it's related, but it struck me as odd.'

Ellie and Zoe listened, keen to hear what he was going to share.

'I overheard a conversation in the pub here the other night when we were playing darts.'

'When he says "we", he doesn't mean me.' Marie-Hélène smiled. 'I do indoor climbing on a Tuesday and Paul does darts. So, if you're looking for a new hobby and a bit of exercise...'

Ellie gave her an appreciative smile. So far, she'd had offers of pottery, rambling, a film club and now indoor climbing. She was going to be busy.

Paul gave Marie-Hélène an affectionate grin. 'As I was saying... the pub. Someone was asking about getting notes delivered and offering to pay for it.'

Ellie and Zoe exchanged sharp glances.

'What sort of notes?' Ellie asked carefully.

'I couldn't hear the details – I was collecting our pints, and the music was quite loud. But someone was talking about...' He frowned, as though trying to recall the words, '... paying a lad to deliver notes to a house in Whitstable.' Paul turned to them. 'Seemed a bit... well, dodgy, you know?'

'And they definitely said "Whitstable"?' asked Ellie.

'Yes.'

'Did you see who was having this conversation?' Zoe added urgently.

Paul shook his head apologetically. 'The pub was busy, and I wasn't really paying attention until I heard the bit about payment. By the time I looked around properly, I couldn't tell which group had been talking about it.'

'But you reported it to the police?' Ellie asked.

'Oh yes, although not immediately as it didn't occur to me that there was anything criminal about it. But as soon as I heard about poor Dr Merrin's death on the news last night, and that she lived in Whitstable, I thought about what I'd heard in the pub. I had no idea if it was connected, but decided I needed to tell the cops and let them decide.' Paul's eyes narrowed with growing concern. 'Don't they always say to tell them, no matter how incidental a piece of information might seem?'

Ellie nodded.

'Gosh,' said Paul, biting his lip. 'If whoever was in the pub that night was behind those threats, do you think they might've been behind Elizabeth's death too?'

'It's certainly suspicious timing,' said Ellie.

Marie-Hélène was looking increasingly worried. '*Mon Dieu*. What if this person is planning more murders?'

Ellie put her arm round Zoe and they stood in troubled silence for a few moments. The implications hung heavy in the warm, sweet-scented air of the bakery.

Ellie would need to check Dave had the information.

Outside on the pavement, as they walked towards their next destination, Zoe was quiet for a moment. 'This is the third time we've been told that Ernest Gibson was the real villain,' she said finally. 'Not Judge Hollinghurst.'

'I agree,' said Ellie. 'Which means we've been focusing on the wrong family entirely.'

'But if Gibson was the one mistreating the seasonal workers,' Zoe said thoughtfully, 'who's protecting his reputation now? He must have died a good decade ago, perhaps two.'

They paused outside the next shop, both lost in thought about the implications of what they'd learned.

'I've got to meet Kieran,' said Zoe. 'There's a bat in the woods that's having trouble flying. After it's seen the vet, I'll be monitoring it, and will do a "deep-dive" on the Gibson family. Find out who else in the village – apart from Andy, the builder – is descended from Ernest Gibson.'

'Or connected to him.'

'Yep.'

'Do it carefully, yes?' Ellie replied, looking back at the bakery where Marie-Hélène and Paul were visible through the window, serving another customer. 'Because whoever is behind these crimes, they're still here, still watching, and still dangerous.'

Chapter 40

While Ellie and Zoe went round some of the high street shops, Sylvia packed the sample cakes that she'd made for the bookshop into containers and a bag. She'd decided on a seasonal gingerbread traybake with cinnamon butter icing, a pear and almond tart, a lemon drizzle cake and biscuits in animal shapes for the children.

'That's the second one,' said Leonard, handing her a bag.

They were outside the bookshop.

'If there's any pear tart left,' he said, patting his tummy, 'bring me back a slice, would you?'

Sylvia smiled. She'd already told Leonard the cakes were for Rebecca to sell in the café.

'And don't forget – I'll collect you.'

Sylvia took the cakes into Bramhurst Books and left them with Rebecca, who began excitedly inspecting them.

Now it was the knit-and-natter group.

The wool shop was a cosy, corner building, a few doors down from the bookshop. Its window display was a riot of colourful skeins arranged in tempting rainbows that caught the morning light.

Sylvia pushed open the door and was immediately enveloped by the comforting smell of lanolin and the soft murmur of animated conversation.

The interior was larger than it appeared from outside, with wooden shelves lining the walls from floor to ceiling, each section organised by colour and weight of yarn. In the centre of the shop, a group of women of various ages sat in comfortable chairs arranged in a circle, their knitting needles clicking rhythmically as they chatted.

'Oh, how lovely,' exclaimed a woman with mousey hair and kind eyes, looking up from what appeared to be a complex Fair Isle pattern. 'A new face. Are you visiting or have you moved to the area?'

Sylvia introduced herself with a warm smile and told them about Ellie and Dave buying the old chapel.

A chorus of interested murmurs went around the circle, and several women shifted their chairs to make room for another.

'The chapel,' said a younger woman, probably in her thirties, who was working on what looked like a baby's cardigan in soft yellow wool. 'We heard about all the excitement there. Quite the archaeological discovery.'

'Indeed,' Sylvia said, settling into the offered chair. 'It's been rather overwhelming for Ellie and Dave, but fascinating from a historical perspective.'

'I'm Margaret Fleming,' said the woman who'd first spoken. 'I run the shop, and this motley crew and I are very happy to welcome you to Bramhurst Knit-and-Natter. It's as much about the nattering as the knitting, I'm afraid.'

'Thank you. Don't apologise,' Sylvia said genuinely. 'It sounds wonderful. I'd love to join if you'll have me. Used to love knitting when the children were young.' She smiled. 'And my daughter-in-law might be interested too, once she's settled in properly.'

'The more the merrier,' called out a woman in her forties who was wrestling with what appeared to be a complicated cable pattern. 'I'm Hannah, and trust me, we can always use fresh conversation. We've been nattering about the same village gossip for months.'

'Yes, new members are always welcome,' Margaret confirmed. 'What sort of projects do you like to work on?'

Sylvia had been eyeing the nearby shelves. 'I'll start a scarf today, something in a lovely autumn colour, but I'm thinking of doing a cardie too.' She stood up and selected a skein of burnt-orange wool, testing its weight and texture. 'This is beautiful. What weight is it?'

'That's a double knitting weight, perfect for cardigans *and* scarves,' Margaret said, getting up to help. 'Alpaca and wool blend, lovely to work with. Very forgiving if you need to unpick stitches.'

As Margaret rang up the wool on the till and provided Sylvia with pattern suggestions, the conversation around the circle continued to flow easily. The women discussed their current projects, shared tips about tricky techniques, and exchanged gentle gossip about village life.

'Actually,' Sylvia said, settling back into the circle and casting on enough stitches to start her scarf, 'I wonder if any of you know anything about Lark View care home in Canterbury? Leonard and I are looking into options for an elderly relative, and it's been recommended.'

'Oh, Lark View's lovely,' said the younger woman with the baby cardigan. 'My gran was there for her last two years. The staff are wonderful, very caring, and the facilities are excellent.'

An older woman, probably in her seventies, looked up from her intricate lace shawl. 'My friend lives there now. She's very happy. Says the food's good – proper homemade food – and they organise lots of activities.'

'That's reassuring,' Sylvia said. 'It's such a difficult decision, isn't it? Finding the right place for someone you care about.'

'Absolutely,' Margaret agreed. 'The important thing is that they maintain their dignity and have companionship.'

The older woman with the lace shawl hesitated for a moment, then said, 'Although, my friend did mention something rather unsettling that happened there a few years back...'

The knitting needles around the circle seemed to slow slightly as everyone's attention focused on her.

'What sort of thing?' asked Hannah, looking up from her cables.

'Apparently there were rumours about one of the residents being... well... murdered.'

There were gasps.

The woman lowered her voice. 'An elderly man called Chapman. Lived there with his wife. My friend said there was quite a to-do about it, though it was all hushed up eventually.'

Sylvia tried to keep her expression neutral, desperate to hear more. 'How awful. Do you know any further details?'

'Not really. My friend said the official story was that he died of a heart attack. Natural causes. But apparently some of the other residents thought something wasn't right. The wife was devastated, kept insisting that someone had... you know... hurt him.'

'Did your friend mention the man's first name?' Sylvia asked carefully.

The woman thought for a moment. 'Thomas, I think. Yes, that's right – Tommy Chapman. My friend remembered because her late husband was also called Tommy.'

Sylvia's hands stilled on her knitting needles. 'When did this happen?' she asked, trying to keep her voice casual.

'Oh, must be three years ago now. Maybe longer. Time does fly, doesn't it?' The woman resumed her lace pattern. 'My friend said the poor wife has never really got over it. Keeps saying her Tommy had been talking to too many people about old times, and that someone had wanted to silence him.'

'What sort of "old times"?' Margaret asked with interest.

'Something about what'd happened to his sister when they were young, working on the farm during harvest season.' She paused, as though trying to recall what her friend had said. 'Tommy and his wife settled here eventually. In the last few years, he'd apparently been talking to researchers and journalists, trying to tell them about things that happened back then.' The woman shook her head sadly. 'The wife thought someone killed him to stop him talking.'

The circle was quiet for a moment, the only sound the soft clicking of knitting needles.

'How terribly sad,' Hannah said finally. 'Whether he was murdered or died naturally, losing someone you love is devastating.'

'Especially when you feel like there are unanswered questions,' Sylvia added thoughtfully. 'How is the wife's health?' They'd been intending to visit Ida Chapman but Sylvia had got distracted, going to see Nellie Tuppen in Willow Haven instead.

'Still at Lark View, though my friend says she's become quite frail since Tommy died.'

Sylvia made a mental note to discuss this revelation with Ellie and Zoe as soon as possible. If Tommy Chapman had been murdered to prevent him from talking about what had happened in 1950, it was very possibly by the same person who'd killed Elizabeth.

'Well,' Margaret said, clearly wanting to move the conversation to lighter topics, 'shall we talk about something more cheerful? Hannah, how's that cable pattern coming along?'

As the conversation shifted to knitting techniques and yarn choices, Sylvia found herself only half-listening. Her mind was racing with the implications of what she'd learned.

When the knit-and-natter session began to wind down an hour later, Sylvia gathered her wool and said her goodbyes, promising to return the following week with her new cardigan project started.

'It was lovely meeting you all,' she said warmly. 'I'm so glad to have found such a welcoming group.'

'We're delighted to have you,' Margaret replied. 'And do bring your daughter-in-law next time. We'd love to meet her properly.'

As Sylvia went out to meet Leonard, her mind was spinning.

Tommy Chapman's widow deserved to know the truth about what had happened to her husband and his sister. And they owed it to Elizabeth to find out what had happened to her too.

Chapter 41

Behind the hedge, in the farmer's field in the sunlight, it was peaceful, and Ellie was keen to get stuck into some quiet research of her own in the campervan, where she could concentrate. But as she arrived, her mobile was beeping, and Rory Henderson was waiting for her.

The young podcaster looked eager. His thick-rimmed glasses were slightly askew, and he was clutching a leather messenger bag like a shield.

'Rory. If you're here to film–'

Her phone beeped again.

'No, nothing like that.' He pushed his glasses up nervously. 'I didn't get the chance to apologise at the coffee morning. I'm sorry about the TikTok live. It was intrusive and... well... a bit unprofessional.'

Ellie unlocked the campervan and before she could respond, Rebus came bounding out towards her, flanked by a wriggling Marple, who launched herself at Rory's legs with puppyish enthusiasm.

'Hello, sweetie,' Ellie exclaimed.

Rory crouched down to fuss over the bundle of brown fur.

'You weren't here an hour ago,' said Ellie, in her best baby voice. 'Has your mummy gone off to do something important?'

'She's Zoe's, isn't she?' Rory asked. 'I met her yesterday.'

'She is.' Ellie watched as Rebus ambled over more sedately, accepting ear scratches with dignified pleasure. 'So, if you're not here to film, what can I do for you?' She was keen to get on with her research.

Rory stood, brushing mud from his knees. 'I wanted to ask... I know this is presumptuous, but could I possibly look at the threatening notes that Elizabeth Merrin received?'

Ellie's expression hardened. 'How do you know about those?'

'I've been interviewing some of the shopkeepers. Paul from the bakery mentioned them. I have a postgraduate degree in forensic linguistics and–'

'I know. I looked you up. How do you know I've got copies of the notes?'

'Er...' He screwed up his nose and gestured to her phone. 'Someone's trying to get hold of you.'

'What? I know. I'll get it in a minute. How do you know I've got copies of the notes?' She slid her phone out of her pocket and glanced at the sender's name on the screen.

Zoe.

Ellie clicked on the message.

You're going to kill me. I'm really sorry. I told Rory about the–

She stuffed the phone back in her pocket, annoyed with her daughter.

'Thing is,' Rory continued, 'I'm qualified to analyse communications like these. Language patterns, dialectical markers, psychological linguistic profiles.'

Ellie studied him for a moment. He looked earnest, almost desperate to be taken seriously. She sighed. 'Will you give me your word you won't share them online or post them *anywhere*? Not show them in your TikTok lives? They're evidence in an active investigation.'

'Hundred per cent.' He met her eyes directly. 'I know you have no reason to trust me, especially after the TikTok live from behind the hedge.' He gestured to a spot a few yards away, presumably where he'd stood. 'But I genuinely want to help. Academic curiosity, if nothing else.'

Ellie made a decision. If he broke his word and shared the notes online, she'd know he couldn't be trusted. If he kept them private, he might prove useful.

'Alright. But we look at them together, and the photos stay on my phone.'

They settled at the tiny fold-out table in the campervan, Ellie pulling up the photos on her phone while Rory produced a notebook and expensive-looking pen from his bag.

'Right,' he said, slipping into what was clearly his academic mode. 'Let's see what we have.'

Ellie showed him the first note:

"*Dr Merrin,*

Violet Chapman met her end five-and-seventy summers past, and there's nowt to be gained from rooting through her shadow. Folk here have long memories. If you don't drop this meddlin o yours, you'll be joining her in the chalk. Barrel ash don't lie."

Rory leaned forward, his entire demeanour changing. 'Oh, this is trying very hard, isn't it?' He made rapid notes. 'And see this word choice? "Summers" instead of years – that's literary affectation, not authentic dialect.'

Ellie was trying to follow him.

'They're using "nowt"– that's Yorkshire or Lancashire, not Kentish. It's like someone's mixing dialects they've read about but never actually heard or used.'

Ellie showed him the second note.

"Told you afore, din't I? But you wouldn't do as you was told. I tell you agin; leave Violet Chapman be. Dig no more – or you'll be cold in the ground, cellar deep, same as she."

'Now this is interesting,' Rory muttered, completely absorbed. 'Look at the semicolon usage here – completely wrong. Someone who actually wrote in this dialect wouldn't use semicolons at all, but this person uses them incorrectly, like they're trying to appear more sophisticated than they are.'

'What does that tell you about the writer?'

'Educated enough to research but not immersed in actual dialect. They're performing rusticity rather than embodying it.'

Ellie kept her expression neutral, but her mind was racing.

'And the punctuation is particularly telling,' Rory continued. 'Using a semicolon where a colon would be more correct. No one writing authentic historical dialect would structure sentences this way.'

He pulled out his phone and showed her a linguistics database. 'I can compare these to actual twentieth century

Kentish documents. The differences are striking. Real historical writing from this area shows different vowel shifts, different grammatical structures entirely.'

'So, someone's deliberately faking it?'

'Absolutely. And not particularly well.' He looked up at her. 'This is someone who thinks they're cleverer than they are. They've done surface research but don't understand the deep structures of dialect and language. It's like... imagine someone trying to fake being French by just substituting every 'the' with 'ze'. That level of superficial.'

Rebus had settled at their feet, with Marple using him as a pillow. The pastoral peace of the field around them contrasted oddly with their dark discussion.

Rory studied the final note.

"Lizbeth,

Ye'd best ha kep thy snout from matters wot warn't thine. But no, nose pokin an tongue waggin, like a magpie wi summat shiny. Meddlin don't bring nowt but mischief, an now the mischief's come. Tongue's stilled now, ain't it? Silent as the grave, where it'll bide. A soul wot knows thy sins. Tap, tap."

'There's something else. The escalation pattern is textbook. First note is a warning. The second is a more specific threat. The third is direct and violent. And the language becomes angrier. See?'

'Meaning?'

'Meaning when they're emotional, their real voice comes through. And that voice is semi-educated, definitely someone who talks more than they read or listen.' He sat back. 'I'd profile this as someone between forty and sixty, who thinks of themselves as clever. Who has access to historical documents or books about local history, who's connected to the area, and someone who's written using this sort of language before.'

Ellie absorbed this analysis. 'That's quite useful. Not that it helps me know the writer's identity yet.' The first person she thought of was Gideon – and then quickly felt guilty. Next, the farmer's "Aye" came to mind. That wasn't traditional Kent dialect. He'd said it when she asked about using his field.

'Forensic linguistics is a real science, despite what my TikTok presence might suggest.' He closed his notebook. 'By the way, I hope you don't mind me asking. Zoe... is she seeing anyone?'

The change of subject was so abrupt Ellie almost laughed. 'She's nursing a broken heart, actually.'

'Oh.' His face fell slightly. 'The guy who's gone to Norway?'

'You know about Finn?'

'Gossip travels fast. My mum... er... mentioned it.'

'How does *she*...?' She stopped. There was no point.

Rory started packing up his things. 'Maybe when Zoe's feeling better... I could take her for a coffee? Help her with content creation for her wildlife rescue work? I see the centre is on TikTok.'

'That's up to Zoe,' Ellie said diplomatically. 'Give her time. I'm sure she'd be happy to be mates...'

As Rory stood to leave, he paused. 'There's something else you should know. I've been investigating the Morrison family. The solicitors?'

'Oh?'

'They have connections to half the local gentry going back generations. Marriage alliances, property deals, wagers, covered-up scandals.'

'What kind of scandals?'

'The kind that would be very damaging if they came to light. The Morrisons have been cleaning up messes for East Kent's elite for over a century. Making problems disappear, documents vanish, witnesses relocate.' He adjusted his messenger bag. 'If someone needed help covering up a murder, even a historical one, Hugh Morrison would be exactly who they'd turn to for help with documents.'

He paused and Ellie wasn't sure if he'd finished.

'His...er... Rottweiler brother does the more "hands on" side of the fixing,' he added with a knowing look. 'Drives a BMW.'

Chapter 42

Not long after Rory left, Zoe arrived, full of apologies.

'Sorry, Mum.' She stroked Rebus and bent down, scooping up a squealing Marple from the campervan doorway. 'I bumped into Rory in Deer Hollow. The rescue centre is monitoring the rutting there as some of the deer have been injured. He was taking some photos.'

'Uh-huh.'

'We got chatting and I let slip about the notes that had been left for Elizabeth. I mentioned the strange way they were phrased and he said he could use his linguistic skills to analyse them.'

Marple was licking Zoe's chin and wriggling.

'I was trying to watch the deer and wasn't concentrating properly on what I was telling him. Before I knew it, I'd mentioned that you have photos of the notes...'

She put the puppy back on the floor and climbed into the campervan.

'Sorry.' She pulled a regretful face.

'Well, we'll soon find out how reliable he is,' replied Ellie, not mentioning Rory's inquiry about Zoe's relationship status.

Zoe placed her laptop on the table.

Rebus claimed his usual spot on the narrow bench seat, while Marple seemed determined to investigate every corner of their temporary headquarters with boundless energy.

'Marple, leave,' Zoe said, extracting one of Dave's socks from the puppy's mouth.

'She's already chewed a hole in your dad's boxer shorts.'

Ellie shifted her position on the opposite bench, trying to find an angle where the light wouldn't create a glare on her laptop screen. 'I still can't believe we're doing serious historical research in what amounts to a garden shed on wheels.' She pulled off another tuft of Marie-Hélène's brioche and tucked it into her mouth.

'Could be worse,' Zoe replied, scrolling through search results. 'At least we've got WiFi now that Dad's set up the mobile hotspot. I didn't get much of a chance to get on the internet earlier. The bat was asleep and we got a call about a seal that'd got stranded at Pegwell Bay.'

'Shall we have a final blitz on the Hollinghursts and the Bramhurst estate? Then get stuck into the Gibsons?'

Zoe nodded. 'I'll go on the British Newspaper Archive. You go on Kent Newspaper Archives.'

After ten minutes, Zoe spoke. 'I've got several results for Judge Hollinghurst. Court appointments, social events, that sort of thing. Nothing particularly revealing though.' She clicked through several articles. 'Here's one about him opening a new courthouse in Canterbury. Another about him giving a speech to the local magistrates' association.'

'Anything about the family personally? His wife. Edmund?'

'Let me check.' Zoe scrolled down through the search results. 'There's a society page mention of Mrs Hollinghurst attending a charity garden party in July 1950. And... here's something about Edmund receiving a commendation from the local agricultural college for his essay on sustainable farming practices.'

'Well, that's rather ironic,' Ellie observed. 'Writing about sustainable farming while seasonal workers were being murdered on his family's estate.'

Marple was lapping at Rebus' water bowl, splattering drops all over the floor. Rebus opened one eye, assessed the situation, and went back to sleep with the philosophical resignation of an older dog dealing with puppy antics.

'Wait,' Ellie said. 'Let's try a different approach. Instead of looking up the Hollinghursts, let's search for Violet Chapman directly. See if her name appears in any contemporary records.'

'Good thinking.' Zoe opened a new search window and typed: *'Violet Chapman, 1950, Kent.'*

They worked in silence for several minutes, the only sounds the clicking of keyboard keys and Marple's continued shuffling exploration of the campervan's interior.

'Got something,' Zoe said suddenly. 'Article from *The Canterbury Herald*, August 29th 1950. *"Seasonal worker Accused of Theft'."*

Ellie looked up sharply. 'What's it say?'

Zoe read aloud: '*"Miss Violet Chapman, 20 of Flat 3, Block C, Wilmot Buildings, Wilmot Street, Bethnal Green, London, residing temporarily at Bramhurst Farm, has been accused of stealing personal items from her employer. The accusations were made by farm manager Ernest Gibson, who claims the girl took jewellery and money from the manor house. Miss Chapman has denied the allegations."*'

'That's interesting,' Ellie said grimly. 'Accusations made by Gibson.'

'It's dated the *day before* she and Edmund were reported as having eloped,' Zoe continued.

'So, Gibson was building a case against her character,' Ellie mused.

Zoe was already searching for more information. 'Let me check the parish database. Sometimes church records contain details that don't make it into the newspapers.'

She switched to a different website, one that specialised in digitised parish records from across Britain. After several minutes of scrolling, she let out a soft exclamation.

'Mum, look at this. St Mildred's parish register, August 1950. Baptism record for Violet Mary Chapman, age 20, August 20th, 1950.'

'You're kidding?' Ellie leaned over to look at Zoe's screen.

'No, and look at the witnesses listed: "*Thomas Chapman, brother; Bernadette Chapman, mother; Frank Chapman, father; and –.*"' Zoe paused dramatically. '"*Edmund Hollinghurst.*"'

'Edmund was there for her baptism,' said Ellie. 'That's not the behaviour of a casual summer romance.'

'And there's more,' Zoe said, clicking to another record. 'Marriage banns for Violet Mary Chapman and Edmund James Hollinghurst, read at St Mildred's on August 27th, 1950.'

'And two days later, Gibson accuses her of stealing.' Ellie felt pieces clicking into place in her mind. 'So, they were planning to marry locally, *not* elope. The baptism, the banns being read... this was serious. She was converting to Christianity, and they were going through proper Church of England procedures.'

'Perhaps Gibson needed a reason to discredit her before the wedding could take place,' Ellie suggested. 'Maybe he hoped it would be enough to stop them from marrying.'

Marple had tired of exploring and was now attempting to climb onto Rebus' bench seat. The older dog shifted slightly to make room, and the puppy settled down with a contented sigh.

'Let me search for Ernest Gibson's family,' Ellie said, returning to her own laptop. 'If his descendants are still protecting his reputation, we need to know who they are.'

They knew about the builder being a "Gibson" but Ellie had believed his story.

She spent the next ten minutes working through marriage records, birth certificates, and census data. Gradually, a picture of Gibson's family began to emerge.

'Here we are,' she said finally. 'Ernest Gibson married Dorothy Fleming in 1935. Three children: Valerie born 1936, Alan born 1937, and John born 1938. They'd all be in their late eighties or nineties now,' said Ellie.

Zoe ran her finger down the screen of an ancestry website. 'All three are dead. Valerie Gibson married a

Robert Morrison in 1956,' she continued, reading from the screen. 'One child, who had three children, Hugh, Evan and Bridget.'

'Aha. The solicitors who handled the sale of the chapel, the manor house and the farm.'

They sat in thoughtful silence for a moment.

'So, we have Gibson making accusations against Violet to discredit her,' Ellie summarised. 'Her baptism and marriage banns showing she was planning to marry Edmund and become part of the community...'

'Not just the community,' said Zoe. 'She was about to marry into the landed gentry. According to my research, that would've brought about huge changes for her – and potentially everyone at Bramhurst Manor. Especially when the judge died and Edmund took over.'

Ellie nodded. 'And we've got Gibson's daughter marrying into a family of solicitors who've – even now – been helping to suppress information about the estate.'

'It's all connected,' Zoe agreed. 'But it still doesn't tell us exactly what happened to Violet, or prove that Gibson killed her.'

They carried on with their research.

After a few more minutes, Zoe said, 'What d'you think about this? There are lots of reports in the newspaper archives of conflict between permanent staff and seasonal workers. There's this one: "14th September 1950. Disorder at Sillingwell Farm, Canterbury.'

She read aloud. '"*A minor fracas broke out when tensions between permanent domestic staff and seasonal hop-pickers came to a head. The disturbance occurred shortly after the midday meal, when a disagreement over laundry access escalated into a heated exchange in the rear courtyard. Witnesses described raised voices, overturned baskets, and one unfortunate incident involving a chamber pot. The estate's long-serving housekeeper, Mrs Edith Noble, is said to have confronted two of the seasonal workers over what she termed 'improper conduct.'*"'

'Maybe they weren't allowed to use the laundry?'

Zoe continued reading. '"*The workers, from Stepney and Limehouse respectively, were later seen departing the premises with their belongings in tow. Some injuries were reported, and laundry apprentice, Mr Lionel Peake, sustained a torn cuff and was thrown in the Stour. The local constable was not called, and the matter is understood to have been resolved internally.*"'

'That's interesting,' said Ellie.

'"*While the estate declined to comment, sources suggest the incident may reflect broader unease among permanent staff, many of whom have served the household for decades. With whispers of mechanisation and changes to estate management circulating in nearby villages, some fear that the influx of seasonal labour – once a temporary necessity – may signal a more permanent shift in staffing practices. This incident follows murmurs of unrest at other properties in the district, as the post-war economy continues to reshape traditional domestic arrangements and long-held expectations of rural employment."'*

'So, in addition to problems with unethical farm managers,' said Ellie, 'the seasonal workers got into conflict with the permanent staff. How awful for them.'

'Here's another one,' said Zoe. "'*Kitchen Row Ends in Dismissals in Whitstable. Two permanent staff were let go after a dispute over 'wage parity' with incoming oyster shuckers."'*

'So, they were treated differently.'

'Another report. "*Tyler Hill Hop-Pickers Clash with Housekeeper. Seasonal workers accused of 'overstepping' after requesting access to staff rations during harvest week.*" Another. "*Chartham Manor. Mr Reginald Fry, butler of thirty years, walked off duty after being asked to instruct seasonal staff in silver service 'without proper compensation'.*" Another. "*Tempers Fray in Fordwich. Permanent groundsmen at St Alfred's Lodge staged a brief work stoppage over fears that seasonal hires were being groomed for year-round roles.*"

Another. *"Bekesbourne Bust-Up: Laundry Staff Demand Reinstatement."* Another. *"Two maids were reinstated after villagers petitioned the estate, following their dismissal in favour of cheaper seasonal workers brought in from Dover."*'

'This isn't just about Gibson being a creep,' said Ellie. 'It shows very real conflict between the two different groups of workers. Do we need to consider that–'

Ellie's phone rang.

Sylvia.

'Hey.' Ellie put the call on loudspeaker. 'How did you get on at knit-and-natter?'

'That's why I'm ringing. A woman at the wool shop said Tommy's wife thinks someone killed Tommy to stop him talking.'

The campervan suddenly felt even smaller and more claustrophobic.

'If that's true, it's another contemporary murder,' said Ellie. 'What if that person also killed Elizabeth?'

'Are you sure about this, Gran?' Zoe shouted into Ellie's speaker.

'Tommy's widow is certain, apparently. There's one way to find out. We need to go to Lark View care home and ask Ida ourselves. Get it straight from the horse's mouth. We should have done it when we first talked about it.'

Zoe was watching her mum's face with growing alarm. 'If Tommy really was murdered for talking about what happened to Violet,' she said, 'then whoever killed him is extremely dangerous. We've got to tell Dad about this.' She began typing a text to Dave.

'Yes, and we've got to solve it. We can't leave it like this,' Ellie finished.

A growing sense of dread had replaced the excitement of their archival discoveries.

'What bothers me is,' Sylvia said solemnly, 'what if the killer has someone else in his or her sights?'

Chapter 43

Zoe took Rebus and Marple with her in the van.

Ellie and Sylvia drove to Lark View care home, which was in the St Dunstan's area of Canterbury. The yellow brick building occupied a converted Edwardian mansion. Crimson Virginia creeper brightened its facade.

Inside, the reception area had been modernised with light, airy decor that managed to avoid the institutional feel that Ellie loathed.

Sylvia introduced Ellie and herself to a plump and friendly young receptionist. 'We're here to visit Ida Chapman.'

The receptionist directed them to sign in while she fetched the matron.

They'd agreed they'd need to check whether Tommy's widow knew about her granddaughter's death. The police had presumably been in and notified her.

The matron appeared moments later, a brisk woman in her fifties with steel-grey hair and an efficient manner. 'Mrs Chapman's having quite the day for visitors,' she said cheerfully to Ellie. 'Your husband was here earlier.'

Ellie's eyebrows rose. 'Mine?'

'Yes, about an hour ago. Detective Chief Inspector Blix? I must say, that's a very flash car he drives.'

Ellie's mind raced. Dave's Audi was twelve years old and definitely not flash. 'What kind of car?'

'I'm not good with makes and models, but my hubbie would be green with envy. He's a big fan of BMW Motorsports. Always going on about them. This was one of those silver ones, very sleek.'

Ellie and Sylvia exchanged alarmed glances.

'I'm not sure that was my husband,' Ellie said carefully, trying to keep her voice calm. 'Could you describe him?'

'Fair hair, kept his sunglasses on, even inside, which I thought was rather odd. Quite pushy, actually. Insisted he needed to speak to Mrs Chapman urgently about a case.'

'Oh gosh.' Ellie grabbed Sylvia's arm. 'That's definitely not Dave. That's the man who's been following us. Sounds like he was impersonating a police officer.'

The matron's face went pale. 'But I… he seemed so official…'

'We need to check on Mrs Chapman,' Sylvia said sharply.

They charged down the corridor, the matron hurrying ahead of them. She fumbled with the doorhandle on room 27, and they burst in to find an elderly woman sitting peacefully in an armchair by the window, a young man in a blue uniform sitting beside her, taking her pulse.

'She seems to be alright now,' the young man told them. 'Pulse is back to normal, but she's had a nasty shock and went a bit peaky for a few minutes. I've been back to check on her every fifteen minutes since it happened.'

'Mrs Chapman?' Ellie said breathlessly. 'Are you okay?'

Ida Chapman looked up with bright, alert eyes that belied her ninety-plus years. 'I'm fine, dear. Though I can't say the same for that rude man who barged in here earlier. Fortunately, Scott came promptly when I rang my buzzer and sent him packing.'

Scott stood up, smiled and smoothed down his uniform. He was tall and broad-shouldered, with tattoos down both arms. 'Some bloke claiming to be police tried to interrogate Mrs Chapman about something that happened in the fifties. I asked to see his warrant card, and he got aggressive, so I told him to leave or I'd call security.'

'Thank goodness you were here,' Sylvia said with relief.

'I'm calling the real police,' the matron said, already pulling out her phone. 'You could've been in danger and impersonating an officer is a serious crime.'

While the matron made her call, Ellie and Sylvia settled into chairs near Ida, and Scott resumed his protective position.

'Mrs Chapman,' Ellie said gently, 'I'm Ellie Blix. My husband is the real Detective Chief Inspector Dave Blix of Kent Police, and we've bought Bramhurst Chapel.' She waited a few moments to allow Ida to get her bearings. 'We found human remains in the garden earlier in the week – you might've seen on the news – and these have been confirmed as belonging to Violet.'

Ida's weathered hands gripped the arms of her chair. 'Violet,' she whispered. 'After all these years.'

'I'm so sorry,' Sylvia said softly. 'We know she was your sister-in-law.'

'She was more than that,' Ida said, her voice stronger now. 'She was my best friend. We went to the same school and came down from Bethnal Green together that summer, along with my Tommy. I was already sweet on him.' She gestured towards a cupboard. 'Now, all I've got of them both is a few mementoes.'

The mention of family reminded Ellie to ask about Elizabeth once they'd discussed Violet.

'Can you tell us about that summer?' Ellie asked. 'About what really happened?'

Ida was quiet for a moment, gazing out of the window at the care home's gardens, nodding thoughtfully. 'That man who came earlier, he kept asking me to say that Tommy had problems with Judge Hollinghurst, and that the judge hurt Violet.'

'And did he? The judge, I mean.'

'No.' Ida's response was firm. 'That's what everyone got wrong. Tommy never had problems with the judge. The judge was strict, yes, but he was fair with the workers. Never mistreated them. Paid on time, didn't dock wages unnecessarily.'

'Did Violet have problems with him?' Sylvia prompted.

'Only about Edmund.' Ida's expression softened. 'The judge didn't want his son marrying a working-class girl. There were terrible rows about it.'

It was useful to have confirmation of this – in person – from someone who was actually there.

'Could he have killed Violet to stop her marrying Edmund?'

'Yes, but that's not what we thought happened.'

Ellie got closer, keen to hear what else they might learn.

Ida's jaw tightened and Scott squeezed her hand supportively.

'Tommy and Violet told me about a huge row one day. The judge and Gibson, going at it in one of the barns. The judge had found out how harshly Gibson had been treating the seasonal workers. Went to confront him over a young lad Gibson had beaten. Got into a proper scuffle, Gibson and the judge did. Staff watching and all.'

This must've been what Mabel was referring to when she wrote in her journal that Nellie had seen the judge leaving the barn after a dishevelled young man.

'Mrs Hollinghurst, the judge's wife, she looked after us girls. *Really* looked after us.'

'How do you mean?' Ellie asked.

'On the occasions when girls got into trouble – and in those days, that meant pregnant – Mrs H would pay for medical treatment. Quiet, discreet, no questions asked. She'd even accompany them to appointments with her daughter, sometimes all the way to London if needed.'

'Is that where they went when Violet vanished?'

Ida gave a small, sad nod. 'That was with a girl called Mary Tibbett. Kind to her, they were.'

Sylvia gasped. 'You mean Mrs H was helping them with prenatal care?'

'Yes. And with childbirth and adoption. Whatever they needed.' Ida's eyes glistened with tears. 'She saved a few of us from ruin, I don't mind saying. Used to take her daughter with her and say they were going to a medical appointment. As cover, like, you know.'

'What happened to Violet specifically?' she asked gently.

Ida's face crumpled slightly. 'She loved Edmund, truly loved him. And he loved her. They were planning to marry properly, had the banns read and everything. But Gibson... he couldn't stand a girl like Violet rising above her station and becoming lady of the manor. He knew she'd get rid of him.'

'Did Gibson kill her?'

'Tommy thought so. He was out strolling with Violet and Edmund one evening at the start of September. A few days after Gibson accused her of stealing. When they parted, Tommy saw Gibson in the distance, loitering with a sickle in his hand, his face full of hate. Tommy was uneasy, but was scared of the farm manager so he walked on past.'

'Was that the last time Tommy saw Violet?'

Ida gave a sniff. 'Yes. She didn't...' She stopped and blew her nose. 'She didn't return to our digs that night.'

'We're really sorry, Ida,' said Ellie.

'But Tommy knew better. Violet and Edmund would never have left without saying goodbye to Tommy and me. We were all friends. And Violet would never have left without her things. The shoes she'd bought for the wedding. The dress she'd made. And without the little money she'd saved and her diary.' She gestured again to a cupboard door.

Ellie had wondered what was in there when Ida had mentioned mementoes. 'Have you got her diary, Ida?'

Ida pursed her lips pensively. 'I have. Tommy told me to keep it safe.'

'I understand that.' Ellie gave her a reassuring smile. 'Would you mind if we had a look at it? Hearing from Violet herself could provide some key information.'

'As long as you promise to let me have it back...'

'The police will need to see it too. But I'm certain they'll keep it safe.'

'Scott, would you get it for the Blixes, please?' She pointed at the cupboard again. 'It's in a cream Freeman, Hardy & Willis box on the top shelf. It's got Violet's shoes in it.'

Scott had the box down quickly and handed it to Sylvia, who removed the lid carefully. White, closed-toe court shoes peeped out of thin, white tissue paper.

The shoes Violet never got to wear.

Ellie held her breath.

The diary was covered in green cloth. The edges were frayed, and the spine was soft from use. A moss green ribbon was tied round it in a bow.

Sylvia undid the ribbon. Ink writing sprawled across yellowed pages, dotted with mildew freckles. She glanced at Ida. 'We don't want to keep you while we look at this. Can we take it with us and give it to the police?'

She nodded. 'If it helps you to find out what happened to Violet, *she* wouldn't mind.'

'Thank you.'

Scott closed the shoebox and tucked it back in the cupboard.

Ellie paused a moment, allowing Ida to catch her breath, before saying, 'Can we check: did Edmund leave Bramhurst then?' She made sure to keep her voice soft.

'Tommy never thought so. He believed they were both killed there.'

'Did he report his suspicions?'

'Who to?' Despite the weakness in Ida's voice, the bitterness came through. 'Gibson controlled the local police through his connections. The judge was away in London that week. Mrs H was distraught but powerless. Tommy tried to tell people, but who listens to a young man from the East End?'

The matron reappeared in the doorway. 'The police are on their way. They're very interested in this impersonator.'

'Ida, love,' Scott said quietly, 'do you want to rest? This is a lot to take in. Upsetting for you.'

'No,' Ida said firmly. 'I've waited seventy-five years for someone to care about what happened to Violet. I'll rest when she and my Tommy have justice.'

She turned back to Ellie and Sylvia. 'That man who was here earlier, he wasn't interested in the truth. He just wanted me to say bad things about the judge. To say the judge was responsible for Violet's death... and he wasn't. When I told him about Gibson, he got angry, said I was confused.'

'Did he threaten you?' Ellie asked.

'Not in so many words but his intention was to intimidate me, I'm sure of that.' Ida shivered slightly. 'He insisted that no-one would believe me if I said Gibson had been involved with Violet's death. Scott arrived just in time.'

'We'll need to monitor you closely for a few days,' the matron told Ida.

'That's wise,' Sylvia agreed. She turned to Ida. 'The St Mildred's records from 1950 mention that Mabel and Arthur Brown moved into the manor as live-in housekeepers. Did that help with Gibson?'

'Oh yes. Things got better after that. Mabel was a force to be reckoned with. She wasn't going to have anyone causing trouble at the manor house.'

The police are on their way,' the matron said with satisfaction. 'I've given them the car's details from our CCTV.'

Ellie nodded. 'Before we go, can I ask you a couple more things?'

'Of course.'

'Someone buried Violet in the garden at the chapel. The anthropologist found additional remains, and said it's possible the soil has been disturbed there. Do you know anything about that?'

Ida took a long, deep breath. 'Tommy and I spent our whole lives scouting out places where they might have been buried.' She shook her head. 'We always wondered about the chapel as it was a favourite place of theirs, but by the time the plot was separated from the estate, we were too old to go digging. As for who might've put her there – I have no idea. It depends on who knew she'd been killed. Mrs Hollinghurst had a good heart. We also heard rumours that the judge regretted his harshness towards Edmund. It's possible he had the two of them buried in the chapel garden. Whatever he thought about his son's potential marriage, I can't imagine he'd have wanted Edmund dead.'

'Thank you.' Ellie checked the clock on the wall, aware Ida had been talking for a long time. 'Finally, could you tell us what you know about your husband's death?'

Ida placed her hand on her breastbone. 'They said it was a heart attack, but he had a visitor a few hours before he died. A woman with chestnut hair.'

Ellie caught Sylvia's eye. She looked as stunned as Ellie felt.

'He was fine before she got to him. He told me she made him a cup of tea, and an hour or so after that he began to experience chest pains.'

'You mean he thought she'd poisoned him?'

Ida nodded. 'Unfortunately, the police wouldn't do an autopsy.'

'We're really sorry.' Ellie wanted to say something about the security at the care home, but she'd speak to the matron later. 'Did he say what age the woman was? Young? Old?'

Ida pursed her lips. 'He said early thirties.'

Ellie and Sylvia thanked Ida for her help, reassured her that Violet's diary would be safe, and that they'd keep her abreast of developments.

As they prepared to leave, Ida caught Ellie's hand. 'Find out who killed our Violet,' she said urgently. 'And my Tommy.'

Ellie saw how frail Ida's fingers were. Bent and knobbly with arthritis, skin thin and veiny. Wedding ring loose but proudly in place.

'Tommy spent his whole life trying to get justice for Violet,' Ida continued. 'And that woman killed him to stop him talking, I know she did. Please don't let her get away with it.'

Ida's words sent a chill over Ellie. 'We won't,' she promised. 'We'll find the truth.' She paused, remembering that the police hadn't visited Ida yet. 'Before we go. I'm really sorry to tell you this, but did you know that your granddaughter, Elizabeth, is–'

'What granddaughter?' A deep frown creased her forehead. 'I don't have a granddaughter.'

Ellie met Sylvia's gaze.

'Hang on,' said Ellie. 'Do you not have a granddaughter called Elizabeth Merrin?'

Ida shook her head.

'She was an academic at Kent University,' Ellie continued. 'Sadly killed yesterday in her home in Whitstable. She told us she was Tommy's granddaughter.'

'I don't understand. We never had children...'

'I'll speak to my husband then,' said Ellie. 'I have no idea who she was.' Ellie hoped there would be no more nasty surprises for Ida and that Tommy hadn't got a girl pregnant and either not known about it, or not told his wife.

As they walked back through the care home corridors, Sylvia held Violet's diary tightly. She said under her breath, 'Crikey, this gets weirder by the moment.'

'Who the heck was Elizabeth then,' said Ellie. 'And if she wasn't related to Tommy, why has she been lying? And given it now seems clear the Hollinghursts weren't the villains after all, who is desperate to make them look like they were?'

'I want to know who's protecting Ernest Gibson's reputation after all these years,' Sylvia added, 'and why they're willing to impersonate police officers and possibly commit murder to do it.'

'I agree.' Ellie had Ida's plea ringing in her ears.

Don't let them get away with it.

'We won't, Ida,' Ellie said aloud. 'We won't.'

Chapter 44

Ellie and Sylvia left the care home, both eager to read Violet's diary.

'Let's go to the pub,' said Ellie.

They drove to the Hop Picker's Rest, where they got coffees and ordered a sandwich each.

It was the end of the lunchtime period. A walking group had just arrived late and there were rucksacks everywhere. They were chatting loudly, chugging water and removing their boots.

Ellie sat down opposite Sylvia at a table by the fire.

Sylvia opened the green book that had been stored for decades with Violet's unused wedding shoes. A few pages fanned in an arc, lying snug to the front cover. At the end, a white envelope had been tucked between the last page and the back cover.

'What's that?' said Ellie.

Sylvia lifted the envelope. It was addressed to: *"Mr and Mrs F Chapman, Flat 3, Block C, Wilmot Buildings, Wilmot Street, Bethnal Green, London"* and had a 2 ½ pence stamp on it. Unfranked. 'She didn't get round to posting it,' Sylvia whispered.

Ellie imagined Violet queuing up at the post office in Bramhurst to buy the stamp, eager for her parents to get her news. 'Come on,' she urged Sylvia, barely able to restrain herself from snatching the item up and doing it herself. 'Open it.'

Sylvia turned the envelope over. 'I was just wondering if it's already been opened but it has.' She slid out a piece of lined notepaper and saw Violet's round handwriting. The note was dated 29th August 1950 and said:

"Dear Mum and Dad. I can't wait for you to get to Bramhurst. Edmund says the thatched cottage on the farm will do nicely for you and the twins. Dad can lend a hand with the crops, and Mum, you'll help me in the big house."

'So, Violet and Edmund were going to shake things up on the Bramhurst estate.' Ellie's voice was quiet. 'That's Gibson's motive, right there. Stopping it from happening.'

'Gibson wouldn't have liked that at all,' agreed Sylvia.

They sat back in their seats.

'It might've meant he'd be out of a job, possibly without accommodation,' said Ellie. It was all falling into place. 'OK,' she said. 'Let's recap what we know and add in this new information. See if we can figure this out and make sure we haven't made any mistakes.'

She opened her notepad and took the top off her pen. 'Violet was killed in 1950.' She counted out the facts. 'Edmund might also have been killed. We don't know what happened to his remains, but Violet's were buried at some point in the chapel garden.

Sylvia sipped her coffee. 'At the time of Violet's disappearance, a lot of effort was put into making people believe Judge Hollinghurst was responsible for whatever happened to Violet. Whereas it seems likely Ernest Gibson was the person who was responsible.'

'In terms of perceptions,' Ellie continued, 'Tommy believed Gibson killed Violet. Plus, Gibson was seen with a sickle on the last evening that Tommy saw his sister.' She paused. 'Although this might be coincidental. It's hardly unusual for a farm manager to have a sickle.'

'Yes,' said Sylvia. 'And the judge's wife actively helped the women. She also got Mabel and her husband instated as live-in staff in order to improve conditions, which was successful, although it didn't prevent poor Violet's murder.'

Ellie drummed her fingers on the table. 'Who might want to silence Tommy and Elizabeth?'

'Wouldn't that depend on what they were saying and knew?' said Sylvia.

'True. We have a pretty clear idea what Tommy was telling people, but now that Ida has denied that Elizabeth was her granddaughter, we don't know who Elizabeth "was", why she was interested in Violet and what information she wanted to come out.'

'Exactly,' Sylvia agreed. 'What was Elizabeth fighting for and whose side was she on? Did she change sides at some point and that's why she was killed?'

Ellie nodded. 'Theoretically, anyone related to the Gibsons might want to shut down evidence that shifts guilt from the Hollinghursts and onto them.'

Something was niggling at the margins of Ellie's mind.

'There's a lot to unpick,' she said. 'The police will have to check the things we can't. We started out wanting to find out whose the remains are in the garden, and how they got there. It looks likely that Tommy was murdered a few years ago, possibly by a young woman. Are your suspicions the same as mine?'

'Probably.' Sylvia frowned. 'Given Elizabeth wasn't who she said she was, is it possible she might've been the chestnut-haired woman who made tea for Tommy?'

'Has to have been,' said Ellie. 'And speaking of Elizabeth, we have the added complication of not knowing why she told everyone she was Violet's great-niece.' She paused. 'I wonder if she only started saying that after Tommy died.'

Ellie recalled the solicitor, Hugh Morrison, had been involved with shady dealings with three properties that used to belong to the Hollinghursts: the manor house, the farm and the chapel. How Evan Morrison had been acting in a menacing way around the village in his BMW and had impersonated Dave to access Ida Chapman. Hopefully the police were dealing with him.

'We know that in the 1950s, Val Gibson, Ernest's sister, married into the Morrison family,' said Ellie. 'This will have created an alliance between the Gibsons and the Morrisons, but Val's family emigrated to Australia and have stayed there.'

'The only Gibson living locally now is Andy-the-Builder,' said Sylvia.

'There's something missing,' said Ellie, drumming the table again. 'Something that links Violet's death and the current ones. I'm sure of it.'

She reviewed the reasons Zoe had provided for why seasonal workers vanished.

Unrecorded illness or death.

Moving to a new workplace.

Elopement or marriage.

Returning home.

Running away.

Taking up a more permanent post.

They all involved changed circumstances.

She recalled Mabel's journals. The careful entries by someone who clearly cared. She reviewed the three notes that had been left for Elizabeth and considered what Rory had said about the language and punctuation. Why had Elizabeth said 'UN' as she was dying?

The journals. Something about the journals was niggling at her.

Ellie flicked through, on her phone, the snaps she'd taken of the black-and-white photos they'd seen in the pub and at Gideon's talk. The screenshots she'd made from online images.

Sylvia was looking at the dessert menu and Ellie's gaze fell there too for a few moments.

Next, she reviewed the news archive material they'd found. The family trees.

And then it clicked, and her frustration was replaced by a calm sense of knowing.

'Of course.' She turned to Sylvia, eyes shining, relief beginning to emerge. 'It's been staring us in the face all this time. It's the notes. Rory was right about the notes.' Ellie's thoughts were racing. 'And so was Dave.'

'What d'you mean?'

'They both said that however hard people try to include and exclude certain things when they communicate, they cannot prevent clues from coming through about their identity. The things that creep in without their conscious awareness.'

'Ells?'

'The killer's been under our noses the whole time. The misdirection's worked just the way they wanted it to.'

Ellie picked up her phone. 'With everything that's been going on, I completely forgot to ask Amanda if her son had managed to find out from his friend who'd paid him to deliver the notes to Elizabeth's house.'

The police would no doubt have followed this up, but they weren't going to share it with the Blixes.

She opened her contacts list and dialled.

Amanda answered the call quickly.

Ellie asked her question.

'Yes. He did. The person paying for the job was one of the guys in the Hop Picker's Rest. Ryan. Think he works behind the bar.'

He was the ponytailed chap Terry had introduced the first time they went into the pub. They'd seen him at the bike shop too.

Ellie scanned the bar but there was no sign of Ryan.

Ellie thanked Amanda, ended the call and turned to Sylvia. 'I know who killed Violet. And I know who killed Elizabeth.'

Sylvia gasped.

'It's time to put an end to all this.' Her mind was racing. 'There are a few things I want to clarify first, and I need to have a quick word with Daphne at the village shop and Paul at the bakery. See if they can help. Let's get moving – and meet back here in a couple of hours. Hopefully Ryan will be there.'

Chapter 45

A couple of hours later, the bar at the Hop Picker's Rest had thinned out when Ellie and Sylvia arrived back there with Zoe. It was late afternoon, and the lunchtime lingerers had finally left.

Gideon and Ellie's builder, Andy Gibson, were by the fire. Their dark pints of Guinness sat on the mantelpiece, reflecting the red and orange light from the flames.

Terry and Deb were behind the bar, serving, as usual.

Ellie raised her hand in a polite wave.

Terry was deep in conversation with Evan Morrison.

'Smuggler's Brew is smoother,' claimed Evan, talking about a local ale.

Terry shook his head, releasing the handpull and holding up a fresh pint glass full of amber liquid. 'But look at the colour of the Harvest Tilt. It's perfection.'

The three Blix women approached the bar, where Deb greeted them.

'Who knew men could get so passionate about which real ale is best,' she said with a smile. 'What can I get you?'

Sylvia ordered coffees and Zoe perched on a bar stool.

'Is Ryan about?' Ellie asked casually. 'I wanted to ask him if he could take a look at my old bicycle.' It was the only thing she could think of to check he was there, without arousing suspicion.

'He is. Terry's got him cleaning the pipes in the cellar. I'll shout down in a minute.'

Daphne from the village shop was picking her way round the bar, a book of raffle tickets in her hand. Her son was taking the money and fielding repeated questions about prizes.

'Yes, first prize is a pub lunch for two, courtesy of Terry and Deb,' Rory repeated patiently. 'Second prize is one of Gideon's history books...'

'No rush, Deb,' said Ellie. 'I'll just have a quick word with Daphne.'

She made her way over to the fruit machine, where Daphne was extolling the virtues of someone's damson chutney, another of the raffle prizes.

'Daphne,' said Ellie, loud enough for anyone interested to hear. 'You know we're investigating Violet Chapman's death?'

The older woman nodded.

'Could I ask you about your connections with Morrisons, the solicitors?'

Daphne cleared her throat. Hopefully she would remember what Ellie had asked her to do and say. 'Of course. It's not a secret, although people might've forgotten.' She spoke up. 'I married into the Morrison family. Shared a name with them but not blood. Many of them were – and are – decent, kind, hardworking people. Others are not.' She shot an accusatory glance at Evan. 'And I have nothing to do with them. Like my husband's cousin who runs the solicitors, or his brother here, as I've heard too many stories over the years about dodgy property practices.'

Evan snorted.

There was a lot Ellie wanted to ask Evan, but she was keen to confront their main suspect and not jeopardise that.

A face peered round the chimney breast – a local Ellie recognised from walking Rebus, presumably curious as to what was going on.

That was alright. It wasn't a bad thing for the locals to hear what had been going on and to find out who was behind the crimes in their community.

'Perhaps I should have made inquiries when I first heard the stories,' Daphne continued, 'or reported them, I don't know. But I didn't. My husband died ten years ago, and I separated myself from his family and made sure I lived in a very different way. I was keen to shed connections with the Morrison name and reverted straightaway to Henderson.'

'Thank you,' said Ellie.

The door opened and Reverend Jo arrived with Paul from the bakery. Dave followed them with DS Carmichael, who headed for the cellar entrance.

Ellie had pinged Dave a text, saying that's where Ryan was.

Two women used the interruption to join the group and listen in.

Ellie recognised one from Gideon's WI talk. She made her way back to the bar, pointing at the dessert menu. 'I'm really tempted to have some of your delicious chocolate torte,' she said to Terry.

'It's one of our best sellers,' he replied. 'Deb makes it.'

A handful of regulars moved closer, presumably curious or sensing something was about to happen.

Ellie waited for everyone to settle. 'I love the chalk boards,' she told Terry. 'Do you write the menus up yourself?'

'Yup.' He sniggered and cast a glance over his shoulder at his wife. 'Deb finds it hard to write in a straight line.'

'Cheeky so-and-so,' said Deb. 'He cheats and uses a ruler. At least I do it freehand.'

'So, you will have written that one then?' Ellie pointed at their dessert menu. 'The posset was delicious by the way.'

'Uh-huh,' said Terry.

'Sylvia got me thinking about it when we were here earlier. Likes her puddings even more than me, she does.'

A frown flickered on Terry's face.

The chalk board said:

"DESSERTS;

sticky toffee pudding with clotted cream:

blackberry and apple crumble with vanilla ice cream:

lavender and elderflower posset:

dark chocolate torte with salted caramel.

'It's an interesting way to use a colon and semicolon.' She turned to Gideon who wasn't far away at the fireplace. 'You're our academic. What's your view on these two punctuation forms?'

'Colons are used to introduce items in a list,' he explained, 'and semicolons are used to separate the items.

Most people would use the two the other way round from how they are on the menu.'

'Oh well.' Terry shrugged, blushing slightly. 'I blame my English teacher. That's what she taught us.'

'It's not important on a menu, is it?' Ellie fixed her gaze on him for a few moments then glanced at Sylvia. 'Nor is it important in a letter, or in an essay…' She paused. 'Or in a note, either…'

Terry's eyes narrowed.

'… unless something about *the note…* ' Ellie spoke slowly, 'links the writer with a woman who was murdered…'

Someone gasped and the bar went silent.

Ellie swiped her phone screen and showed Terry the third note that Elizabeth had received.

'Did you write this? It was left by Elizabeth's body.'

''Course not. What's going on?' He looked about, seeming to notice that everyone was staring at him.

The two women who'd joined them started whispering.

Dave stepped forward, ensuring Terry had seen him. He checked something on his phone.

'Are you sure?' Ellie asked Terry.

'Of course.' He glanced around the bar. 'What are you suggesting? Why are the cops here?'

'What about this one?' Ellie showed him the second note. 'The messages contain several references to pubs:

barrel ash in the first one. Cellar in the second. Tap in the last one.'

Terry was shaking his head. 'I haven't written any notes.'

'Sure? D'you want to see? Be absolutely certain?'

'No.' Terry grabbed up a cloth and began wiping the bar clean.

'What about this one?' said Ellie. 'It's got the same incorrect colon use.'

Terry rolled his eyes.

Ellie gave him a perfunctory smile and turned to the bakery owner. 'Paul, can you tell everyone what you overheard here in the pub recently?'

Paul narrated his story of hearing someone asking for a paid volunteer to deliver notes to a house in Whitstable. Like Daphne, Ellie had prompted him earlier on what to testify to.

'And who was that?'

'Terry's barman, Ryan,' said Paul. 'Someone mentioned accents, and I remembered that the person I'd heard had an Australian one.'

'I'm not responsible for my barman,' snapped Terry. 'You'll have to ask him about that.'

Dave spoke now. 'Oh, we will. However, Elizabeth's neighbour, Amanda, told us that her son's friend had confirmed he was paid by Ryan to deliver a note to Elizabeth's house.'

'So what?' said Terry, going pink.

'Well,' Dave continued. 'The friend has since given a statement in which he described Ryan's accent and ponytail. And I can confirm Ryan has just told DS Carmichael that it was you, Terry, who instructed him to get recruits to deliver the notes.'

'Rubbish,' the publican snarled.

'DS Carmichael has just collected him from the cellar,' Dave told him. 'He'll be going straight to the station for questioning.'

Things were coming together finally. It was time to push a few buttons.

'A couple of things got me wondering about you,' Ellie said, staring at Terry. 'Didn't click at the time, but you were very "helpful", weren't you?'

'That's me.' He flashed a fake smile. 'I like to be helpful.'

'No. This was different. It was the sort of "helpfulness" people engage in when they're guilty.'

'Nah.'

'You went to great efforts to paint Judge Hollinghurst as a baddie, didn't you? You offered your grandmother's journals. It was all to create a narrative which implicated him. You were carefully sharing insider knowledge and making yourself seem trustworthy.'

'Don't know what you're talking about.'

'I also wondered why Elizabeth didn't want to ask you for Mabel's journals. She'd asked Reverend Jo for Reverend Matthews' records.'

'She did,' said Jo.

'No idea,' he said dismissively.

'We'll come onto that shortly.' She changed the subject quickly to test Terry's reaction. 'Let's turn now to Wednesday. Elizabeth's door-cam will have captured you and your wife arriving at her house, won't it?'

'You what?' Terry flashed an angry look at Deb. 'We were here.'

Ellie gave Sylvia the signal to take over.

'Mr Hobbs,' said Sylvia, her voice unwavering. 'I want now to ask you about your grandmother's journals. We noticed that pages had been ripped out, and some entries seemed to have been doctored. The pen and handwriting are different in places. Did you do that?'

'I ain't touched them. They've been in the loft for decades. Just as Gran left them.'

'You see,' Sylvia continued, 'they paint a carefully-curated picture of ill-treatment of the seasonal workers by Judge Hollinghurst and his wife.'

'That's what Gran witnessed and wrote about.'

'Except it's not true, is it?'

'What d'you mean?'

'The judge and his wife did *not* mistreat the workers. The farm manager did, *Ernest Gibson*.'

Andy, the builder, wriggled uncomfortably in his seat.

'In fact,' said Sylvia, 'several reliable witnesses allege Gibson killed Violet.'

Terry shrugged. 'That's not what my gran told me. But even if Gibson did kill Violet Chapman – what's that got to do with me?'

'I'm coming to that. Obviously, the police can now explore everything further. Because we believe there's an alternative explanation.'

Surprise stretched over Terry's face.

'Isn't it true that your grandparents were worried about the way their jobs and financial security were being affected by the seasonal workers from London?'

'I'm sure they were. It's like some of the situations we have in the UK today. All sorts of concerns about job security.'

'Indeed,' said Sylvia.

They'd expected Terry to pretend he didn't know what she was talking about.

'Except it could've had a material effect on your grandparents' lives if Violet had married Edmund.'

'How's that?'

'Working class girl marrying into the landed gentry. Bet she'd have shaken things up a bit, no? Had a few ideas of her own about how she wanted to do things?'

While Sylvia was talking, Ellie watched Terry, whose breathing had deepened. His cheek twitched as he processed what she was saying.

'What if, for example, Violet had been planning to get rid of all the domestic staff. Move her own family in?'

Terry was silent for a few moments, then said: 'You've lost me, I'm afraid. What've my grandparents got to do with this?'

'Apologies. Let me explain. Firstly, we have a letter from Violet to her parents which she was about to post when she was killed. The police have it now but I've a photo of it here.'

She read the letter aloud. '"*Dear Mum and Dad. I can't wait for you to get to Bramhurst. Edmund says the thatched cottage on the farm will do nicely for you and the twins. Dad can lend a hand with the crops, and Mum, you'll help me in the big house.*"'

'So what?'

'The "big house" would've referred to the manor house, where your grandparents lived...'

'And?'

'I suspect your grandparents were just as anxious about *their* jobs as Gibson was about his. Perhaps even more so. They *lived* at the Bramhurst Manor.'

'And?' said Terry angrily.

'... and would've been homeless if they'd lost their job.' Sylvia waited for Terry to absorb the comment. 'Now, tell us, please, how they became the licensees of the Hop Picker's Rest...'

'What d'you mean?'

'Presumably you knew they became licensees? Because then your parents did, and now you.'

'I've no idea how it happened.' He attempted an innocent shrug.

Sylvia ploughed on. 'According to our research, it's not at all common for a housekeeper and her husband to be given the lease of a large pub. I wonder why they were?'

Terry shook his head.

'Let me read you this from the *Kent Courier*, 14th June 1955. I think things will become clearer.

"'In a quiet handover, Arthur and Mabel Brown, formerly in service at Bramhurst Manor, have taken over the licence of the Hop Picker's Rest in an agreement

negotiated by Ernest Gibson on behalf of the family. Locals note the Brown's sudden change in fortune, though none dare ask what the terms were and what was promised in return."'

Terry attempted a nonchalant expression. 'Everyone knows the pub belonged to the Hollinghursts. It changed hands. Happens all the time.'

'Does it? The last sentence of that article is interesting, isn't it?'

'Is this about semicolons again?'

'"*None dare ask what the terms were and what was promised in return*." What *was* promised in return?'

'No idea.'

'And the terms?'

'Same.'

'There are dozens of news articles online,' Sylvia continued, 'talking about the conflict between permanent and seasonal staff. I think your grandparents and Gibson did a deal. I think they'd both been getting rid of any seasonal workers who posed a threat to their livelihoods and–'

'Nonsense.'

'Your grandparents moved into the manor house, became live-in. It was all part of their plan for control of the domestic workforce. It wasn't about improving working conditions at all. That was just a story that was put about, along with gossip about the Hollinghursts, to provide cover for what your grandparents were doing. It was self-interest. Self-preservation, if you like.'

'You're wrong.'

'I suspect Gibson gave them the pub in exchange for their silence about what he – and they – had been doing. It was their pay-off.'

'Rubbish.'

'Yes, Mr Hobbs. You've seen, I take it, the print on your wall over there of the lease that was awarded to your grandparents?'

Ellie and Dave had examined it when they'd had supper earlier in the week.

'Clause 7b says: *"The licence shall be subject to immediate revocation should the licensee, or any subsequent licensee, engage in any conduct, whether by act or omission, which may bring the Hollinghurst estate into disrepute."*'

Terry grunted.

'What would Judge Hollinghurst have done if he'd known that his staff murdered Violet Chapman? Possibly Edmund too?'

'It was Gibson,' Terry muttered. 'You said it yourself.'

'Andy,' said Sylvia to Ellie's builder, 'would you mind having a look at this photo? Telling us, of these two men here, which one is your grandfather?' She showed him a copy of the image of the man they'd originally thought was Ernest Gibson, holding a sickle, and another tall man next to him.

'*This* one's my grandfather,' said Andy. 'I've seen other photos.' Then he pointed at the other man. '*This* one, with a birthmark on his cheek, holding the sickle, that's Mabel's husband, Arthur. He helped out on the farm and was a similar build to Gibson.'

'They do look similar, don't they?' Sylvia asked.

'Oh, yes. People confused them regularly, I gather.'

Sylvia thanked Andy. 'So, Mr Hobbs. We know from Ida Chapman that Tommy saw someone following Violet and Edmund one evening, a few days after Gibson accused Violet of stealing.'

'And?'

'Tommy *thought* that person was Gibson. However, it was dark and Gibson was at a distance. And *Andy* has identified the person as Arthur Brown.'

'Nah.'

'Is it possible that the person Tommy saw following them was your grandfather?' Sylvia was spelling it out for Terry, making it impossible to deny. 'Not Ernest Gibson at all.'

'No.'

'Yes,' said Sylvia. 'The photographs don't lie.' She paused. 'Violet deserves justice. And so does Edmund.'

Terry was silent. He deposited the cloth on the bar and stared at the bar floor.

'Both those young people had their lives stolen from them,' said Sylvia, her voice sombre.

'It was Elizabeth,' blurted Terry. 'She killed Tommy... Poisoned him.'

'Go on.'

'She wasn't related to the Chapmans. That was a story she made up to get information. She was *my niece*. Tommy Chapman was telling lies about our family and she wanted to stop him. So, she killed him. Went to the care home and poisoned his tea.'

'But then she went soft,' Deb added, 'and lost her bottle. Decided she wasn't going to help anymore.'

Sylvia glanced at Dave, checking, as they'd agreed, that he'd heard. 'Mr Hobbs, we know you killed Elizabeth,' said Sylvia.

'No.'

'Before she took her final breath, Elizabeth said something which I heard. It was one word or part of a word. It was "UN". Initially, I had no idea what this meant.' She glanced at Ellie. 'Ellie went along the lines of unfair and undone. I thought of those too, plus unfinished, unmarked, unforgotten, unseen, unforgiven..." It wasn't until we realised you'd killed Elizabeth that it became clear. She was your niece and was trying to say "uncle", wasn't she?'

'No.'

'She was.'

'Oh, tell them, Terry,' came Deb's anguished voice from behind the bar. 'Or I will.'

'Shut up, Deb,' Terry shouted.

'Mrs Hobbs?' Sylvia stared at her.

'We were desperate,' said Deb. 'Elizabeth threatened to tell the press that Terry's grandparents had worked with Ernest Gibson for years, getting rid of troublesome seasonal workers, to maintain their own financial and social security. We couldn't have her doing that.'

'Deb, stop. You don't know what you're saying.'

Deb glanced at Terry, tears in her eyes. 'We knew that if she did, we would lose the pub, and it would bring everything crashing down. We went over to her house to try and talk sense into her. Told her that the police would find out she'd killed Tommy, and she'd go to prison. But – she claimed she would say *we* killed him.'

Deb shook her head in apparent disbelief at the events that had unfolded.

'We got into a terrible row,' she continued. 'Elizabeth was furious and lunged at us. Terry pushed her away and she fell back. Hit her head on the corner of the coffee table.'

A gasp went round the bar.

'We panicked.' Deb covered her face for a moment. 'We didn't mean to kill her, just scare her into staying silent. She was still alive when we left the house.'

Terry had his head in his hands.

'Isn't the truth, Mr Hobbs,' said Sylvia, 'that you didn't just inherit the pub? You inherited your ancestors' secrets?'

Mutters went round the bar.

Terry shook his head.

'It's over, Terry.' Deb turned back to Sylvia. 'Because of that clause in the licence, we knew we'd lose the pub if it came to light that Arthur and Mabel had been involved with Violet's death.' She swallowed. 'I went with Terry to Elizabeth's house, to help him reason with her, frighten her if we needed to.'

'We've worked hard to make a success of this place,' said Terry, now sad rather than angry. 'It's always been our dream to run a village pub. We couldn't have Elizabeth ruining everything.'

'What brought about her change of heart?' asked Sylvia.

'It was after she killed Tommy. She'd met Ida at the care home. Seen how frail she was. Said she felt guilty.'

Everyone was paying close attention.

'Initially, she just stopped helping us.' He let his gaze drift to Deb. 'And that was OK. But after a few weeks, it was clear she'd shifted further and actively wanted justice for Violet.'

'One final question,' said Sylvia. 'Did you move the soil in the chapel flowerbed?'

Terry shook his head.

'That's OK, said Dave, stepping forward. 'The CSIs will have the results soon from the footwear prints. Terry Hobbs, I'm arresting you on suspicion of the manslaughter of Elizabeth Merrin. You do not have to say anything. But it may harm your defence if you do not mention, when questioned, something which you later rely on in court.'

He signalled to DS Carmichael, who'd handed Ryan over to a uniformed officer and approached Deb.

'Deborah Hobbs. I'm arresting you on the suspicion of the manslaughter of Elizabeth Merrin. You do not have to say anything...' DS Carmichael finished the caution.

A second uniformed officer approached Evan. 'Evan Russell Morrison, I'm arresting you in accordance with Section 90 of the Police Act on the suspicion of impersonating a police officer...'

Ellie released a deep sigh.

Finally, the truth had been revealed. The pub lease had secured everyone's silence. First Mabel and her husband, then Terry's parents, and most recently Terry and Deb. But now Violet and Edmund's story would be known, and they could rest in peace.

Chapter 46
SATURDAY

'It's wonderful to see the chapel grounds peaceful again,' Reverend Jo said as she and Ellie strolled in the mid-morning sun along the old stone wall that bordered three sides of the property.

Lily, the red setter, bounded energetically ahead, while Rebus trotted more sedately beside them, already knowing every inch of the ground.

'I wasn't sure how I'd feel about the place,' Ellie admitted, 'after everything that was found here. But somehow it feels... cleansed, I suppose. Like the truth being told has lifted something heavy.'

It was true: the garden felt different now that the archaeological grids had been removed and the tents packed away. The carefully marked excavation sites had been filled in and seeded with grass. What remained was a space that felt both strangely familiar and entirely new. The beginnings of Ellie and Dave's garden, finally, with all its secrets laid bare.

The old wall itself was a thing of beauty. Old Kentish stone mellowed by centuries of weather into warm honey and grey tones. Moss and small ferns had found purchase in the mortar joints, and the top was crowned with a mixture of ivy and campanula, which would no doubt attract butterflies in summer.

'Look at this,' Jo said, running her hand along the stonework. 'This must be medieval. The craftsmanship is extraordinary.'

They paused at the corner where the wall met the orchard. There was a small grove of ancient apple and pear trees whose gnarled branches spoke of decades of faithful fruiting.

'Dave's planning to restore this area into a proper orchard,' Ellie said, touching the bark of an old apple tree. 'Apparently, these are heritage varieties that are quite rare now. Someone clearly cared for them at some point.'

'It's like a secret garden,' Jo observed, watching Lily follow a scent at the base of a pear tree. 'Hidden away behind these walls, with all this history.'

Beyond the orchard, the garden opened into what must once have been a more formal space, now softened by time and neglect into something approaching a wild meadow. Ancient oak and beech trees provided shade and structure, their massive trunks and spreading canopies giving the garden an ethereal quality.

The marquee wasn't far away, and locals were scuttling in and out with decorations, food and drink, crockery, cutlery and glasses. It was all-hands-on-deck to get it ready for the evening.

Ellie waved at Belle, who was up a ladder, hanging bunting and balloons.

Earlier in the morning, after a few discussions, Daphne Henderson had persuaded the rest of the barn dance organisers to relocate the tent from Bramhurst Farm. Ellie and Dave had been happy to offer the chapel garden for the event. Violet and Edmund had adored it there, and everyone agreed it seemed a fitting way to honour their memory, and begin the healing process. Giles Finch had instructed his farm workers to dismantle the marquee, to take it over to the chapel and set it back up. Andy-the-Builder and his apprentice, Wayne, were relaying the hard floor.

Behind the marquee, the branches of an enormous yew tree stretched up to the sky – an ancient specimen that must have been old when the chapel was built. It created a natural shelter, and its thick trunk bore the scars and records of centuries.

'That tree must be seven hundred years old,' Jo said wonderingly. 'Maybe older. Yews can live for millennia.'

Hanging from one of its lower branches was an old rope swing. Two thick pieces of hemp rope supported a weathered wooden seat that moved gently in the breeze. It looked like it had been there for decades, a reminder that children had played here.

Ellie showed Jo the photo that Zoe had found of Violet on the swing.

'It's a bit rickety now but I love that someone kept it,' Jo said. 'It makes me believe that joy was had here. Not just burials.'

They wandered further, Ellie sharing her and Dave's plans with growing enthusiasm. 'We're thinking of putting the vegetable garden over there, where it'll get the best sun. And maybe some raised beds for herbs near the kitchen door. Dave wants to plant more fruit trees. Quinces, maybe, and some modern apple varieties to complement the heritage ones.'

'It sounds wonderful,' Jo said. 'Very much in keeping with the tradition of the place.'

'And we're planning some garden rooms,' Ellie continued, gesturing towards different areas. 'An archway through there, leading to a pond. Nothing too formal, just somewhere for wildlife. Some benches positioned to catch the evening sun. Dave's keen on a greenhouse, though I'm not sure where that'll go yet.'

Jo smiled at Ellie's obvious excitement.

'I'm beginning to wonder if he's thinking about retiring.' Ellie sniggered. It was something they'd only ever discussed as being in the future. After all, Dave had just been promoted.

'It's lovely to hear you talking about the future of the place. After all the darkness we've uncovered, it's important to remember that this is going to be a home.'

They had wandered back towards the ancient yew, and Ellie found herself drawn to examine its trunk more closely. The bark was deeply furrowed with age, and she could see where generations of visitors had carved initials and dates into the living wood.

'Look at all these,' she said, tracing some of the older carvings with her finger. 'Some of these must've been here for decades.'

Most of the initials were worn almost smooth by time and weather, but as she moved around the trunk, one carving caught her eye. It was deeper than the others, cut with obvious care and deliberation.

'Jo,' she called, her voice suddenly sharp with excitement. 'Come and look at this.'

The vicar hurried over, followed by both dogs who seemed to sense the change in atmosphere.

There, cut into the bark at about shoulder height, were the words: *'Edmund and Violet forever, September 1st, 1950.'*

Ellie studied the carving more closely. The letters were deep and carefully formed, cut with love and attention. This wasn't a memorial carved by a third party. This was personal, intimate.

'Look at the way it's been carved,' she said. 'The spacing, the style. This was done by someone who wanted to commemorate a specific day that was important to them both.'

Ellie pulled out her phone and took several photographs of the carving from different angles.

As they walked back towards the chapel, both women were quiet, lost in thought. The garden felt peaceful and full of future promise.

'You know,' Jo said as they reached the chapel door, 'I'm beginning to wonder if this place will ever be finished revealing its secrets.'

In the evening, the barn dance began.

The marquee rose like a pale sail, its canvas sides gently billowing in the crisp October breeze. Straw bales lined the edges of the marquee, while lanterns glimmered gently. Corn sheaves caught the warm glow from strings of fairy lights that crisscrossed the ceiling of the tent. Belle's multicoloured bunting stretched along the walls, and mason jars filled with chrysanthemums and rosehips dotted the trestle tables that lined one side of the space.

Inside, the air was rich with the scent of damp earth, mulled cider, fresh bread and woodsmoke drifting from a brazier near the entrance, mingling with the earthy scent of the autumn leaves that decorated the doorways. Strings of warm fairy lights crisscrossed the marquee poles, casting a golden glow over multicoloured bunting. Feet clattered on the hard floor, adding a percussive rhythm to the fiddles tuning up in the far corner.

At one end, trestle tables groaned under the weight of harvest pies, Kentish apple cakes, and sausage rolls wrapped in flaky pastry. Jam jars filled with marigolds and late dahlias stood among platters of local cheeses and pickled walnuts. The smell was heady: sweet, savoury, and faintly herbal.

Ellie stood in the doorway for a moment, taking it all in. The band was already tuning up on the small stage: a fiddle player, an accordionist, a flautist, and a guitarist who looked as though they'd played together for decades. But once the scrape of rosin on strings began, and the wheeze of the accordion's bellows, the evening jumped into life and notions of age became irrelevant.

'Quite something, isn't it?' Dave said beside her, his hand finding hers. 'Hard to believe it's only been under a week since we found the remains.'

It felt like a lifetime.

Violet Chapman's murder solved after seventy-five years. Terry and Deb Hobbs arrested. Their elaborate deception exposed; even doctoring Mabel's diaries to throw suspicion on the Hollinghursts. Four lives lost unnecessarily – Violet and Edmund all those years ago, Tommy Chapman in the care home, and Elizabeth Merrin, who'd also got caught up in historical family secrets.

'Penny's got the results back on the second set of remains at the chapel. It's Edmund.'

'So, they *were* buried together,' said Ellie.

Dave nodded. 'Edmund's remains were more scattered, perhaps by an animal.'

'Ah.'

'The CSIs have confirmed the footwear prints in the chapel flowerbed belong to Terry. Exactly what he was doing, we've yet to find out. It's a criminal offence to disturb human remains without lawful authority, so if that was what he was doing, that'll add to his charges.'

'Crikey,' said Ellie. 'The lengths people go to. Arthur and Mabel were protecting their positions and Terry was doing the same.'

'I know,' said Dave. 'We've spoken to Ida Chapman. Once both sets of remains are released, she's asked if Violet and Edmund can be cremated together. She's going to think about where they'd like their ashes scattered.'

Finally, laid to rest in peace.

'Evan denies pretending he was me, but several people heard him say it, so we're hopeful we'll be able to charge him. We've had some information come in about him. He's been issuing threats to a number of people locally, so we'll be getting him on that too.'

'Good. Odious man.'

'He's Hugh Morrison's "fixer". On the payroll at the firm and involved with keeping family secrets buried.'

'Ugh.'

'We also found out who was going to buy the chapel a while back,' Dave continued.

'Oh?'

'Terry and Deb.'

'Good grief,' said Ellie. 'They had big plans, didn't they?'

'Yes. Very ambitious. But their finances didn't work out.'

Ellie saw that Sylvia and Leonard had arrived. They were over at the food table, where Sylvia was helping arrange plates of sandwiches and sausage rolls. Leonard was deep in conversation with Reverend Jo, probably discussing the memorial service they were planning for Violet and Edmund.

The marquee was filling up now. The pottery sisters Mel and Dee were chatting with Marie-Hélène from the bakery, while Margaret from the wool shop was admiring someone's hand-knitted shawl. Even Gideon Marsh had come, looking rather dapper in a golden corduroy jacket and cream neck scarf, and copper corduroy trousers. Ellie felt a twinge of guilt for having had suspicions about him.

Notably absent were Terry and Deb, whose pub, Ellie learned, would normally have provided the bar for such events. In their own ways, the villagers were all processing the news that their friendly publican had been a killer, protecting his family's dark secrets with violence.

'Ladies and gentlemen.' The caller, a cheerful woman in a floral dress and sensible shoes, took the microphone.

'Let's start the evening with something simple to warm up – Strip the Willow.'

There was a general shuffling as people formed sets of eight, and Ellie found herself pulled into line by Dave. Across from them, Sylvia had dragged a protesting Leonard into position, while further down, Zoe stood with Rory Henderson, the true crime podcaster, who'd somehow become part of their extended circle during the investigation.

Ellie watched her daughter's face carefully. Zoe was smiling, but it didn't reach her eyes. She was going through the motions, polite but distant with Rory, who seemed eager to engage her in conversation whenever he could. Finn's absence clearly hung over Zoe like a shadow.

The music started – a jaunty reel that immediately got feet tapping – and suddenly they were moving. Down the line, turn, back again, swing your partner, and on to the next. The repetitive patterns were soothing somehow, requiring just enough concentration to push darker thoughts aside but not so much that you couldn't enjoy the simple pleasure of movement.

Ellie caught glimpses of the village whirling past – Daphne from the shop executing a surprisingly nimble *do-si-do* with Gideon. Rory attempting to master the steps to impress Zoe. Even Rebus had been allowed in, sitting by the door with Reverend Jo's red setter, both dogs watching the human antics with patient bewilderment. Marple was at Dave's flat, where Zoe was living.

'Having fun?' Dave asked as they came together for a swing.

'More than I expected,' Ellie admitted, breathless from the dancing.

The caller moved them through Gay Gordons, the Dashing White Sergeant, and a simplified version of the Eightsome Reel. Sweat beaded on foreheads, jackets were discarded, and the initial politeness of the evening gave way to genuine laughter and cheerful chaos when someone went the wrong way.

After a break, the ceilidh band struck up a reel, and the marquee came alive again. Boots thudded, skirts twirled, and laughter spilled out into the evening air. Children darted between dancers, clutching toffee apples and paper lanterns, while older villagers leaned against the side of the marquee, watching with misty eyes and mugs of cider in hand.

The evening shimmered with promise. It was a place stitched together by memory and music, where the past had been unearthed and honoured, and the future danced again.

The drinks table was a sight to behold, wedged between two straw bales and draped in a white cloth which looked like it could've come straight off the altar at St Mildred's. Behind it stood Reverend Jo, in a 'dog collar' and tunic, jeans and Doc Martens. Her sleeves were rolled up, and she was wielding a ladle like a medieval innkeeper, dunking it at intervals in a bowl of punch. Beside her, Leonard was also in his dog collar, but with more conventional suit trousers and shoes. He was attempting to tap a barrel of cider.

The table itself was a patchwork of Kentish indulgence. Two oak barrels of cloudy apple cider, one sweet, one dry, were both labelled in Leonard's looping script. A vat of ginger wine. Bottles of home-brewed ale, their labels featuring hand-drawn hops and a badger. A small crate of mead, donated by a beekeeper from Harbledown.

Ellie and Dave approached, hands still warm from dancing, cheeks flushed with cider and laughter.

Jo spotted them and beamed. 'Ah, the hosts of the hour,' she cried, brandishing a ladle. 'What can I get you? Sweet cider or some of Leonard's ale?'

Leonard tittered. 'I call it Original Sin. Goes down well but may lead to questionable decisions.'

Ellie laughed and reached for a mug. 'I'll have a bit more cider, please. Though I'm tempted by the mead.'

Jo poured generously, the golden liquid sloshing into the mug with a satisfying glug. 'To Violet and Edmund,' she said softly, 'and to new beginnings.'

Dave raised his drink. 'To Bramhurst. And to finding a village where the vicars are more entertaining than the pub regulars.'

Leonard winked. 'We aim to serve. Spiritually and otherwise.'

As Ellie sipped, the taste hit her: sharp, golden, and strong. Around them, the marquee pulsed with music and laughter. The drinks table – half-altar, half-tavern – couldn't have been a more perfect image.

The band struck up the Virginia Reel with a flourish of the fiddle, and the marquee seemed to lift an inch off the ground with the collective energy of stomping boots and swirling skirts.

Dave swept Ellie into the line, grinning like a man born to the rhythm. His hand was warm and confident in hers, and before she could protest, they were off, stepping, clapping, and spinning through the figures. He moved with the easy precision of someone who'd spent three years dodging sticks and jingling bells in village greens across the country. Ellie, on the other hand, was doing her best not to collide with the elderly couple beside her or trip over the hem of her skirt.

'Left hand star,' shouted the caller, and Dave twirled her into the centre with such enthusiasm that someone applauded.

'You've been holding out on me,' Ellie gasped, breathless and laughing.

'I shouldn't have had that extra coffee this morning,' Dave said, executing a perfect *do-si-do.*

As they reeled and turned, Ellie caught sight of Reverend Jo, still at the drinks table, nudging Leonard and pointing. Leonard raised his mug and called out, 'Look at him go, the dancing detective.'

The nickname rippled through the marquee. Someone shouted, 'Give him a bell and a hanky,' and another added, 'He'll be solving crimes with a jig next.'

Ellie nearly missed her next step, laughing so hard she had to clutch Dave's arm to stay upright.

By the time the reel ended, Ellie's cheeks were flushed and her feet sore.

As they stepped off the dance floor, Ellie leaned towards Dave and said, 'You know, I think Bramhurst is going to be fun. I'll look forward to more of these dances.'

Dave raised an eyebrow. 'Only if you promise to keep stepping on my toes. It's the most fun I've had in weeks.'

During a break for refreshments, Ellie went to the drinks table with Sylvia and Zoe.

'Rory seems nice,' Sylvia ventured carefully, watching as the young man showed Gideon something on his phone.

'He is,' Zoe said flatly, taking a long drink of cider. 'But I'm not interested, Gran. In anyone. It's too soon.'

'Of course, darling,' Sylvia said quickly. 'No one's suggesting–'

'He keeps trying to impress me with his TikTok follower count and his theories about historical linguistics,' Zoe continued. 'As if I care about his social media fame. None of that matters when–' She broke off, blinking rapidly.

Ellie put an arm around her daughter. 'When Finn's in Norway...' Living his dream without you, she thought, but tactfully didn't say out loud. There was nothing else Ellie could say. Sometimes hearts just needed to hurt, until they didn't anymore.

Dave joined them. 'So, we can finally get on with the renovations.'

'Yes,' Ellie agreed. 'Though I'm half expecting to find another body somewhere. In the vaulted ceiling perhaps.'

'Don't even joke about it.' But he was smiling. 'We just got the structural engineer's revised report through. Once we get the damp sorted and the floor properly supported, we can actually start living there.'

'Our home,' Ellie said, testing the words. 'Our beautiful chapel home.'

'With a medieval crypt in the basement and a garden we're going to turn into a haven,' Dave added wryly. 'I'm looking forward to retiring.'

'*Retiring?* Since when?'

This was news to her.

'Oh, I don't know. The idea's been growing on me.'

This was a conversation for another day.

'At least Violet will have a proper resting place now,' Ellie said. 'Her family can finally mourn her.'

Ellie looked around. These people had welcomed Dave and her into their community, shared their stories and helped solve a mystery that had haunted the village for generations. Yes, two of their own had been killers – Terry and Arthur Brown – but the rest had shown remarkable resilience and kindness. And then there was Elizabeth, who wasn't quite part of the village, but had been caught up in its history.

'I'm glad we moved here,' she said eventually.

Dave pulled her closer. 'Even with everything that's happened?'

'Maybe *because* of it. We've seen this village at its worst and its best already. We know our neighbours' secrets now, and they know ours. That's ... that's real community, isn't it?'

The waltz ended and the caller announced the last dance of the evening – a Circassian Circle. Everyone joined in, even those who'd been sitting out, forming a huge circle around the marquee.

As they moved through the patterns – in, out, swing, progress – Ellie danced with person after person from the village. The locksmith, the pottery sisters, Belle, Marie-Hélène, Gideon and Rory.

The final chord rang out, and everyone applauded the band, themselves, the evening, the village, the very fact of being together after such dark revelations.

People began gathering coats and children, making plans for meeting up.

'I'll help with the clearing up,' Sylvia said, already stacking plates.

'We'll walk Zoe to the bus stop,' Dave offered, seeing their daughter standing alone by the door, looking lost.

As they prepared to leave, Reverend Jo appeared at Ellie's side. 'Thank you,' she said tenderly. 'For not giving up. For finding the truth about Violet.'

'It was the right thing to do.'

'By the way, I haven't mentioned it before, but I've got form on the heartbreak front. Jilted my fiancé at the altar and joined the church. I'll happily have a chat with Zoe if it'd help.'

'Thank you,' said Ellie, hiding her surprise.

'Shall I call for you in the morning? Dog walk before church?'

'Lovely. Seven-ish? I'll look forward to hearing about that fiancé.'

Outside, the October night was crisp and clear, stars visible despite the village streetlights. Ellie could smell wood smoke from someone's fire, and somewhere an owl called from the churchyard. Their new village, settling into sleep.

'Come on then, Zo,' Dave said, linking arms with his daughter. 'Let's get you on the bus.'

'And you two back to the campervan,' Zoe said with a weak smile.

'Not for much longer,' Ellie promised. 'Soon we'll be in the chapel properly. You can have your own slab of stone and an inflatable mattress when you visit.'

They walked slowly through the quiet streets, Rebus padding alongside, past the shuttered shops, past St Millie's, past all the houses full of people who were part of their lives now.

'Do you think it's over?' Zoe asked suddenly. 'All the drama, the mysteries, the murders?'

‘I hope so,’ said Dave firmly. ‘I don’t think my career could stand another one of your investigations. They’ll start regretting promoting me to chief inspector.’

Ellie thought about how trouble seemed to follow them wherever they went. ‘I’m relieved this case is over,’ she said carefully, ‘and justice will be achieved.’

‘But?’ Zoe prompted.

Ellie looked at her daughter, at her husband. At the village around them that was now home. She thought about the renovation work ahead, the community they were joining, the stories yet to be discovered in this ancient place.

‘Well, life has a way of surprising us, doesn’t it?’ She smiled, despite everything. ‘But we’ll convert the chapel, make it beautiful and settle into village life.’

She paused, looking up at the stars, thinking of all the possibilities that lay ahead. For some reason, Evan Morrison's words came into her mind.

This village has more secrets than just the one in your garden.

‘And...' she said, drawing them closer, 'we'll have to see what happens next.’

The End

If you enjoyed Ellie, Dave, Sylvia and Zoe's story in this book, you can follow their adventures in the next one, *Murder at the Christmas Panto*, which is available on Amazon here.

This is the blurb...

MURDER AT THE CHRISTMAS PANTO.

The curtain's down... but who's hiding a deadly secret?

It's two weeks before Christmas, and Bramhurst's festive spirit has taken a tumble: the village panto has been cancelled.

Ellie Blix, who's only recently returned to amateur dramatics, is reluctant to dismantle the set. But when she and her friend, Belle, meet the new director, Neville Snipe, at the village hall to give him back his property, a scream and a sickening thud interrupt their plans.

Neville is found at the foot of the loft ladder — and it wasn't a slip.

With more suspects than disappointed cast members (including Belle and herself), Ellie and her co-sleuths must untangle backstage rivalries, old grudges, and some very curious casting decisions.

When a witness reports seeing the former panto director sneaking into the hall, suspicions fly. And then there's the thorny question of what happened to Neville's original "Cinderella"?

Can Ellie solve the case, find a new director and save the panto — all before Christmas?

Order *Murder at the Christmas Panto* here.

A note from the author

Dear reader,

Thank you so much for reading this book. It has been a pleasure to write. Without you, however, it would simply be words in a document on my hard drive.

If you'd like to receive news on my writing, the best way to keep in touch is to join my newsletter. This is where I share news first, including exclusive offers, early reads, 'behind the scenes' & giveaways. You can join here.

Supporting the series

You can do this in three ways:

a) telling your friends, family, book clubs, and online groups. Word of mouth is one of the best forms of marketing.

b) leaving a quick, written review on Amazon. A few lines saying what you liked about the story helps other readers to know what the book is like.

c) pre-ordering the next book in the series, which you can do here.

Please note: I am a British writer and I write using British English. This story is set in an English village and the manuscript has been edited and proofread by British professionals. A few spellings, terms and words may, therefore, be different for some readers. I've tried to ensure, however, that the meaning is clear for everyone. In addition, the stories are intended to be lighthearted reads. They aren't police procedurals and genre norms mean that the sleuths do things detectives aren't allowed to do. This is intentional and is meant to be part of the fun of a cosy mystery.

Bramhurst isn't a real place. Sorry. It is a fictional village which I've created by borrowing elements of many of the villages outside Canterbury, mixing them up and fictionalising them. If you try to plot places, you may find I've moved them, changed them and given them different names!

Finally, writing a novel is a team effort. I come up with the plot and characters, and write the words, and other people contribute at various stages. Without their input and magic, this story would not have made it into print.

I owe massive thanks to the following people for their help. In no particular order: Scott Pack, Louise Grieves, Lynne Nazareth, Amy Sinclair and Doug Collins. Lucy Lawrie, Matthew J Evans, Pete Jones, Trudy Cairns. Thanks, too, to Ian Rankin, whose crime novels I've devoured for years. The name of Ellie's dog is a tribute to Ian's detective. I must, also, mention Agatha Christie, as I've used the name of her sleuth for Zoe's puppy. Finally, to all my early and beta readers – thank you.

Sincere apologies to anyone I've forgotten.

About the author

Izzie Harper is the pen name of British writer, teacher & story coach, Vicky Newham. Vicky lives on the south coast of England.

As Izzie Harper, she writes cozy mysteries.

Vicky's first crime fiction series was published by HQ/Harper Collins. Her debut in this police procedural series, *Turn a Blind Eye*, was optioned for TV and was shortlisted for the CWA John Creasey Debut Dagger in 2019. She has MAs in Creative Writing and Effective Learning.

To keep up to date with Vicky's releases, special offers and promotions, please join her newsletter here.

If you like pictures of dogs, the sea, the Kent countryside and behind-the-scenes of Vicky's writing, you can follow her on Instagram at @vickynewhamwriter.

If you have enjoyed this story, Vicky would be hugely grateful if you could leave a quick review on Amazon and if you could tell your family and friends about it. Reviews and word-of-mouth recommendations are the best way to help authors.

And, please pre-order the next book in the series, *Murder at the Christmas Panto,* here.

Printed in Dunstable, United Kingdom

72122642R00241